CYPHER

Loretta Scott Miller

For my sons, Ted (nee Terry) and Chris, whose wide and varied knowledge of computers and other things that go *BUMP* in the night is an unparalleled resource.

"'But is this really the poet?" I asked. "There are two brothers, I know; and both have attained reputation in letters. The Minister I believe has written learnedly on Differential Calculus. He is a mathematician, and no poet.'

'You are mistaken; I know him well; he is both.. As poet and mathematician, he would reason well; as mere mathematician, he could not have reasoned at all, and thus would have been at the mercy of the Prefect.'"

The Purloined Letter, E. A. Poe

PREFACE

SINCE THIS BOOK was written technology has leapfrogged. So when I decided to publish a second edition, through my own independent press, I had to make a choice whether to update it to current standards or leave it as a kind of period piece. I chose the latter, since updating the computer and internet related aspects would have required extensive changes in the story, and, in my view, the story is everything. I settled for a fierce editing job which has corrected mainly spelling errors (now thoughtfully underlined in red squiggles by the word processing software). I am chagrined to report that I was (originally) right only about half the time; I thought I was a much better speller than that.

What follows, minus spelling errors, is as it was when first printed. Though it has only been six or seven years, please view this work as a product of the late Nineties and roll with the characters and storyline. I think, and very much hope, you will enjoy it.

Loretta Scott Miller
September, 2006

AUTHOR'S NOTE

FOR MORE THAN a decade the commercial encryption software industry in the US has been at odds with the Federal Government over restrictive export licensing policies which put them at a significant disadvantage with respect to their international counterparts. These prohibitions against exporting all but the weakest encryption algorithms were based —misguidedly according to most in the commercial marketplace—on concerns over national security. In January, 2000, the government finally decided to relax their restrictions, allowing US companies a more solid footing in global marketing of strong cryptographic products. For those who might be interested, more on the *encryption wars* may be found in the web pages of the International Association of Professional Security Consultants (www.iapsc.org) and the Electronic Privacy Information Center (www2.epic.org).

Among the liberties taken in this novel it should be noted that Santa Cruz University is a small, fictional institution of higher learning. It has no connection whatever with the University of California at Santa Cruz, which does exist (although it has been considered by some to be fairly far removed from reality in its own right).

It should also be stated that at the time of publication, all Internet addresses used in this book were fictitious; i.e., had no real counterpart in the InterNIC database. That could change at any time, of course.

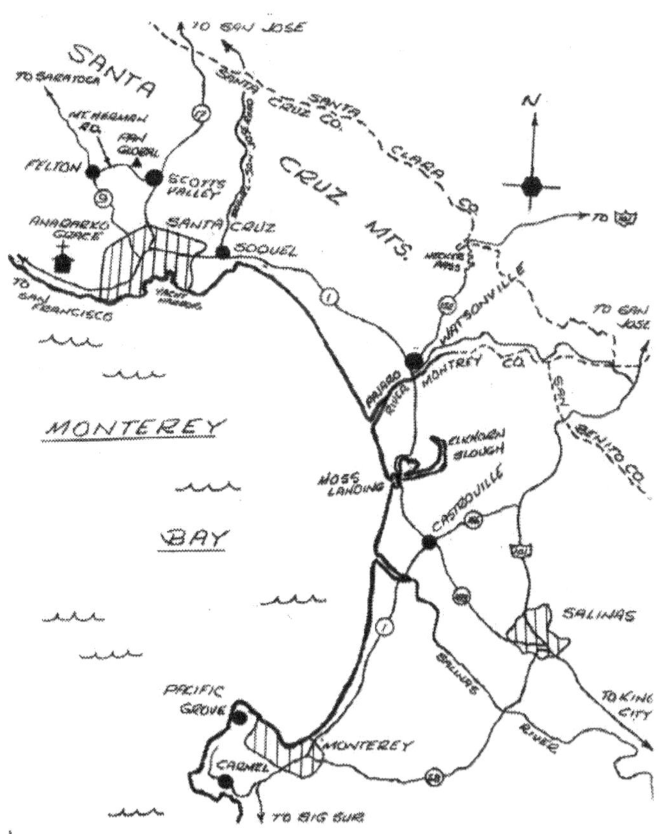

Monterey Bay Area

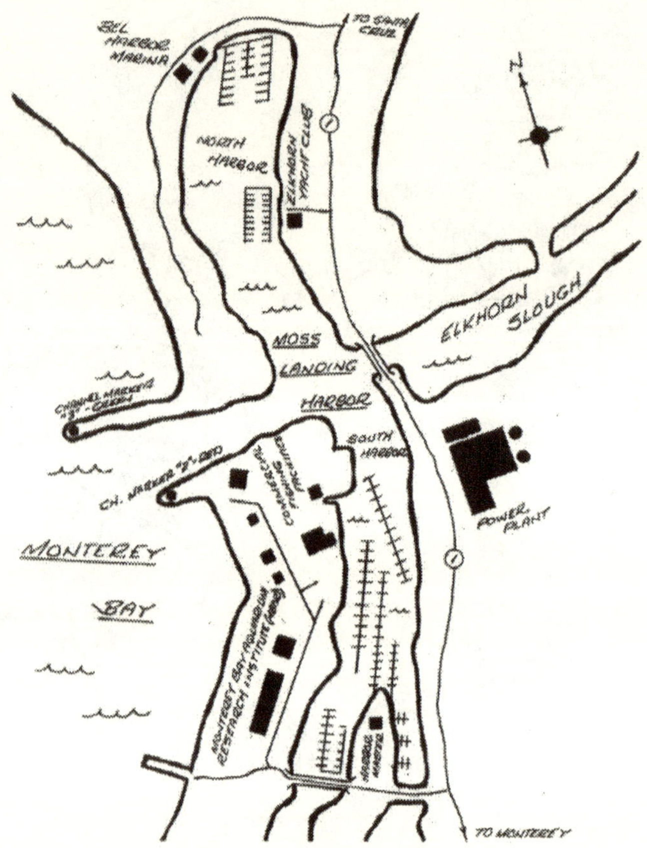

Moss Landing Harbor

ONE

HARLEY'S SKIN WAS stretched tight over his bones. It would make a sound if you touched it, like a drumhead. His sandy hair was gone—all of it. Blue veins stood out in relief on his forehead. He tried to smile when TJ Billings entered, holding out a skeletal hand, which the younger man took between his own.

"Harley, I'm so damn sorry," TJ said. "I should have come before this."

The old man shook his head.

"No, you shouldn't. It's a pain in the ass to watch somebody die." He stopped to catch his breath.

"I wouldn't have asked you now, except for Chipper."

TJ nodded.

"He's missing. Been three days now since he was here—used to come every day."

"Have you reported it?"

"Yeah, but you know those fucking cops. They're going to screw it up like they did with Jim Locksley."

"They didn't fuck it up any more than I did," TJ said quietly.

Harley's eyes were closed. TJ thought maybe he had fallen asleep.

"No," he finally said. "At least you didn't give up on it. Still haven't, have you?"

After more than twenty-five years anybody in his right mind would have given up, TJ thought. But he didn't say that to Harley. He said what the old man wanted to hear.

"I guess I'll never give up, Harley. I'm a lot more stubborn than I ever was bright."

Harley smiled.

"That's what I thought. Now listen.
I've got a feeling Chipper's on the boat. It's where he always goes when he doesn't want to be found. I've had my man at the marina, Cortez, check it out, but Chipper could stay out of his way pretty easy if he wanted to. He knows Bel Harbor better than anyone—it's going to be his soon."

"What about his mother? Would Chipper have . . ."

"No! She's not a part of his life anymore. Hasn't been, really, since he was born and she dumped him on me. She goes her way, we go ours."

"Okay, take it easy, Harley."

The agitation had thrown him into a fit of coughing and TJ cursed himself for unwittingly triggering it.

"I'll check it out and get back to you. He's probably just gone off partying or something. Which boat is it?"

Harley lay back, breathing heavily. He pointed toward the oak chest of drawers.

"The *Emmy T.* . . . key's there on the chest."

A persistent vision of the one fatal slip that would catapult him off the edge of the continent plagued TJ as he moved cautiously along the wooden dock, lethally slick in the cloying fog. Fuzzy circles of light shimmered from the lampposts at every other slip stretching out from the backbone of the dock, but one had burned out near the end and an unruly current was making itself felt even this far into the north harbor, causing the boards beneath his feet to ripple and creak with the motion. The dark leather jacket over sweater and jeans didn't quite keep the bone chill at bay, but at least he'd had sense enough to wear boots with rubber lug soles. TJ shivered, balling both fists deep into the sheepskin-lined pockets of his coat.

All the slips were occupied, but most of the boats were dark. Only one, in the next dock over, showed a gauzy yellow glow through a round window shadowed with some kind of filmy curtain. Through the fog he could hear the frantic beat of a commercial on TV, followed at length by crowd roar and the crisp bark of the play-by-play announcer. Saturday night college football.

"LSU," he said aloud into the darkness, recalling it from the morning's paper, though he couldn't remember who they were playing. Some small school without much chance of winning, but grateful for the TV coverage and the money it would bring their athletic program. It was barely two weeks into the season, and the Oklahoma Sooners at least had one win under their belts with the new coach. Not a pretty win—but a win. Too early to tell if they were on their way up from the dismal slump they'd been in for the best part of a decade.

Ahead, the trawler *Emmy T.* looked dark and deserted. She was beefy and sturdy, but with that slim-ankled delicacy of a well bred draft horse, her bow arcing gracefully forward over the rough wood of the dock. Teak railings dripped moisture on the Fiberglas hull, and the thickly woven nylon lines that tethered her were flemished neatly at their cleats like sleeping snakes. The only sound besides the drone of the neighboring television as TJ approached the boarding steps was the creaking of the wooden planks beneath his feet and the slap and slosh of the incoming tide. He conjectured creaking docks were probably part of the normal background noise in a marina, but as he mounted the steps and grasped the boat's railing lightly, the vessel dipped gently in its slip. You weren't going to board a boat this size without its occupants knowing about it. There wasn't any reason for stealth in this instance, but TJ's mind tucked the information away for future use — after more than twenty-five years in the private investigation business, the need for caution had become a habit.

It was the eerie quiet of an unfamiliar place that had preached caution to him, TJ decided. He shook it off and called out as he stepped up through the open rail gate, "Hello the *Emmy_T.,* anyone aboard?"

He'd heard that phrase in some long forgotten movie and it sounded pretty melodramatic in his ears, but there wasn't any doorbell to push.

Silence.

TJ peered through darkened windows, then passed along the deck's narrow walkway to the stern, noting the only indication of possible habitation; a window open just a crack on the aft deck. It looked like a skylight, flush with the deck, about two and a half feet square—what did they call the damned things on a boat? A hatch? He moved on, and when he had circled the vessel from the outside, he tried the sliding door beside the lower helm. It was not locked, and slid open with only the minor protest of the doorframe's aged, damp wood.

The wheel was right out of the same old movie that had brought to mind the few things nautical TJ knew; a wooden circle with six ornately carved spokes, their rounded ends protruding from the circumference to fit snugly in the grip of curled fists. The spokes emanated from a brass hub whose shaft disappeared into the smooth teak beneath the helm. Above it was a bank of instruments. TJ recognized a compass, tachometer, fuel and pressure gauges, but the rest were foreign to him. Letting his eyes become accustomed to the dimness, he turned from the wheel to survey the main cabin. It reminded him of a studio apartment, compact and efficient. Behind the helm seat was the galley, comprised of a double sink, four-burner stove and apartment-sized refrigerator. On the other side of the salon was an L-shaped couch and a hardwood table with leaves that folded out. And just to the rear of the settee, another sliding door to the outer deck. On all four walls—bulkheads he corrected himself, the term jumping to mind from that well of hidden Hollywood memories—were vast wood-framed windows. Three hundred sixty degree visibility from anywhere in the cabin. A necessity when you were trying to avoid running into something, like a dock or another boat. No side mirrors here. The cabin was a masterpiece of functional design; and it was totally empty.

To the rear, two wooden steps led to a closed door, and just left of the helm seat three steps led to another. The sleeping quarters, according to the hastily sketched plan Harley had made of the boat; spidery pencil scrawls on a piece of lined tablet left with the keys on the chest in that tastefully decorated cell where he would spend his last hours. Aft, a large stateroom—the Captain's quarters. And forward, two vee-bunks and access to the engine room below. The well leading down to the closed door was a close fit for a man his size, but TJ descended the two steps to the aft cabin, one hand on a teak grab rail, and knocked. When there was no answer, he opened the door.

There were windows on either side as well as the glass hatch overhead, so the room was not much dimmer than the cabin had been. In the center was a queen-sized bed, complete with down comforter and square tapestry pillows depicting nautical scenes; lighthouses, a harbor of fishing boats. It was smooth and neat—no one had slept there recently. Teak shelves and cupboards lined both walls of the stateroom below the windows, and a door to his left was half-open to reveal a bathroom with toilet, sink, and half-size sit down tub. A few toilet articles on a small shelf, but nothing there that didn't belong as far as he could see. The sink and its surrounding countertop were dry. TJ turned and started for the forward cabin.

There was another teak grab rail along the wall where three steps descended at a much steeper angle than the two at the rear. TJ held it with his left hand and in an uncomfortable half crouch, with his shoulders touching the polished wooden walls, knocked before grasping the brass handle of the door and pushing it inward. It glided smoothly for about six inches, then jammed. He pushed a little harder, feeling bile rise in his throat when the door gave slightly, then sprang back. Whatever was blocking it wasn't completely solid; and the cloying odor that was drifting up through the partially open door, engulfing him, made his stomach lurch involuntarily. He forced himself to look down and examine the swatch of carpeting leading from the bottom step into the stateroom. The toe of a very scuffed dark leather deck shoe jutted toward the ceiling, its light colored rawhide laces trailing onto the deck. The door was lodged against the ankle of the bare foot that was in the shoe.

TWO

Harley Sullivan had a fleet of four fishing boats when TJ Billings first met him on his arrival in California. That was back when fishing was still a viable and usually profitable occupation along that stretch of the Northern California coast. Before the major swell of population engulfed what were for the most part small cities and country towns; before the high tech revolution's irresistible call reached out to ambitious souls from damn near everywhere, spawning the urban sprawl that would become known as Silicon Valley.

The waters of the perennially bone chilling Pacific Ocean had been relatively clean and teeming with fish and other underwater delicacies. One of the first meals TJ could recall eating in a restaurant in Santa Cruz had consisted of three items, only one of which he had ever heard of in his life—a baked potato. The other two were deep fried abalone steak so tender you could cut it with a butter knife and steamed artichokes with creamy lemon mayonnaise for dipping the thorn-pointed leaves. Amelia had shown him how to eat it—he wouldn't have had the faintest idea the spiny vegetable was even edible, let alone the best means of attacking its forbidding exterior. The dinner had cost just under $7.00, a steep price then, and he'd thought at the time it was damned near worth it. Today, if you could even find abalone on the menu, you'd have to take out a small loan to pay for it, though artichokes were still plentiful and relatively cheap.

The fishing fleets from San Francisco to Monterey were made up in great part by independents like Harley, though most were family operations which had been established by Italian and Portuguese immigrants, passed from father to son for generations. Harley, with native shrewdness and only a daughter who hated boats to offer any objection, divined the demise of this source of income in time to parlay three of his four boats into ownership of a shabby little marina at the entrance to Elk Horn Slough, just north of the Elk Horn Yacht Club and the municipal harbor at Moss Landing. The fourth boat he retained for trading stock. Harley invested all of his time and most of his limited funds in sprucing up the neglected docks, dredging the channel to provide access for both fishing and recreational boats of reasonable size, and general upkeep and maintenance of the rest of the facilities—restrooms, showers, marina office—until such time as he could afford to renovate them completely. He optimistically christened his long shot investment Bel Harbor Marina.

The little marina's tenancy steadily rose, catering to a small segment of the commercial fishing fleet spilling over from the municipal harbor, which had a growing waiting list; but the slip rentals from pleasure boaters and sports fishermen provided the bulk of Harley's income by the time Bel Harbor started turning a profit.

The newly successful businessman, however, still loved the sea, and the one boat he retained was traded up several times, its last descendant being the well-appointed motor yacht *Emmy_T.*, whose top speed barely pushed eight knots, but whose cruising range approached 1,500 miles of steady reliability.

Harley had used her strictly for pleasure in the last ten years, taking his grandson off the coast fishing for salmon, as he had taken his long-time friend, Jim Locksley, years before. They had been his life—the boy and the boat.

TJ crouched in the stairwell and gently lifted the protruding foot while pushing the door back enough to allow entry. This cabin was darker than the salon; only two small windows above the vee-shaped bunks which followed the line of the hull admitted what little light the night provided. TJ directed his pocket penlight on the scene below.

The man lay wedged between the side of the right hand bunk and the door to the forward bath. One arm was flung outward, as though he had tried to pull himself up onto the high narrow bed but not been able to manage it. His head, with its profusion of light brown curls, fell forward onto his chest, and one jeans clad knee was flexed so that it nearly touched his forehead. The stench of sweet rum and vomit was overpowering. A nearly empty fifth of Ron Rico dark rum lay on the carpet beside the body in a damp pool of its former contents.

"Probably pills somewhere, too," TJ said to himself. "If the poor little bastard didn't down 'em all." He started to reach for Chipper's pockets, then stood up, running a hand along his lower back to relieve the pressure of stooping. "Screw it. Let somebody else find them."

After stretching his complaining muscles, he bent again, feeling the neck beneath the once handsome face, now bloated and puffy, to assure himself of what he already knew. The boy was dead. Had been for a while.

He needed to find a phone. The call to the Sheriff's office to report the death would be relatively easy; the visit to Harley Sullivan to report that he had found his missing grandson would not.

It wasn't all that much later when the forest green cruiser of the Santa Cruz County Sheriff's Department, with it's gold star emblazoned on white doors, pulled into the marina parking lot; 10:30 TJ guessed, maybe 11:00 PM. The deputy who alighted from the vehicle was tall, blond, and familiar. His square, handsome face looked a bit older than the last time TJ had seen him, but the laugh lines were still more predominant than the frown creases.

"Evening, Justin," TJ said, "You working Monterey County now too?"

Justin Highstreet didn't smile. "I was just up the way and Monterey's got an all hands pileup over on Highway 101; I said I'd drop by until someone could break loose. What about you? You expanding the business of discovering dead bodies to cover both counties now? When are you going to retire and leave this stuff to the pros?"

"To tell you the honest truth, Deputy, it was just a slow day at the office so I figured, 'what the hell,' I'll just take a run over to Bel Harbor and see if there aren't any dead bodies lying around."

Highstreet knew TJ Billings and, against his better judgment, liked him. They had even gotten drunk together once a few months back. And more than that, the deputy liked TJ's daughter.

"Jesus, I can sure see where she gets it. Okay, no more bullshit. Let's have what you found."

"I'm getting too old for this shit. But this one wasn't supposed to be dead, just doing a disappearing act."

"Who is it? Do you know?"

"Yeah." TJ rubbed his eyes, deathly tired. "Yeah, it's a kid named Chipper Sullivan——grandson of the guy who owns the marina. The old man's dying, and this is going to help him along. I'd appreciate it if you'd ask them to put off notifying him until morning. I've got to go see him anyway."

Highstreet nodded and gestured for TJ to lead the way. "Let's go see what you've got here, and then I want you to do something for *me*——get on home and explain to your daughter why I'm not going to be able to keep our appointment tonight."

TJ stopped. "What?"

"Tell Elizabeth I won't be able to make it tonight because you called me out at the end of my shift to baby-sit a corpse. Tell her I'll call her tomorrow."

When Elizabeth Jane Billings, opened the door of her apartment, the brilliant welcoming smile faded only slightly. Her resemblance to her mother was increasing with time, and TJ found a lump in his throat more and more often these days when he looked at her. The deep brown wings of hair framing the fox-like face, wide-set eyes, dusty blue and faintly exotic looking, fringed with thick black lashes. It was difficult to believe Amelia Jane had been dead fifteen years; had never seen Lisbee a grown woman. TJ thought she would have been proud of her daughter.

"Hi," she said brightly. "I wasn't expecting you."

"I know. I'm afraid the guy you were expecting isn't going to make it, and it's my fault."

"You'd better come in and explain that," Lisbee said, holding the door wide.

TJ sat on the too soft sofa and stretched his legs to the scarred coffee table littered with books, a half empty wine glass, and the cat, Hester. Giving his feet a baleful blue glance at their uncalled for intrusion into her territory, Hester jumped lightly down and followed Lisbee into the kitchen.

"Want a drink?" Lisbee called over her shoulder.

"God, yes."

When she returned from the kitchen she held an open wine bottle under one arm, TJ's glass filled to within an inch of the rim with scotch and water in that hand, and a basket of popcorn in the other. TJ saw the wine bottle slipping as she neared the couch and leaped to retrieve his glass before she dropped the whole damned thing. Recovering quickly, Lisbee filled her glass from the wine bottle, setting it among the rest of the debris on the coffee table. Sitting at the other end of the sofa, her back against its arm, long legs crossed under her, she faced her father.

"Okay, let's have it," she said. "What new ploy have you come up with to ruin my social life and relegate me to the Spinster's Hall of Fame?"

"Now wait a minute. I didn't even know you were seeing the deputy socially. Are you telling me you're going to marry him?"

"Hasn't gone that far yet. In fact, this would have been our first date."

"Isn't he a little old for you?" TJ said, knowing he was making a mistake but not being able to control this parental imperative. He'd learned long ago that objection to Lisbee's questionable goals only served to increase her commitment to their fulfillment.

"He's thirty-two; I'm twenty-five. Not exactly a generation gap. Are you going to tell me what happened tonight or are you just going to continue being a dutifully interfering parent?"

TJ closed his eyes and leaned back against the couch. He wished there were some way they could just talk for a while. About nothing. They did that; though not as often these days as he would have liked. But tonight wasn't one of those nights. She'd been expecting Highstreet and he wasn't going to make it. And only TJ had the answer to the reason why.

"I found old Harley Sullivan's grandson. On Harley's boat. He's dead."

THREE

On A FRIDAY afternoon, the 28th, Dorsey Pettigrew "Beau" Billings stood reflecting on the golden shapes of late October sunshine making patterns on the thick amber carpet where once had been an altar. The wall of glass, which spanned the width of the old church and extended to its peaked roof, looked out on a stand of second growth redwoods which filtered the sunlight into shafts of brilliance as the afternoon wore on. Deep red leather chairs, antique lawyer's bookcases, their tiered shelves covered by sliding glass doors, and a free-standing fireplace gave the expanse the feel of its current function; that of a library for use by the owners and operators of Anadarko Grace Investigations.

Uncle Beau had been behind the acquisition of the church at the northern edge of Santa Cruz, on a long-term lease from the harried church elders who were reluctant to sell the property to developers that would raze the handsome old building and replace it with something more economically viable, albeit aesthetically bereft. As the aging occupants of that old residential area had been replaced by younger families with fast-paced lives, its congregation had dwindled to the point where the church was a financial burden, not even approaching paying its own way. The agreement had proved mutually beneficial to all concerned for the first ten years of the fifty year term of the lease. Only Elizabeth was likely to be alive when the lease ran out, and Beau cherished the hope that his lovely, if somewhat independent, grandniece would be a happily married retired grandmother by the time it did. Meanwhile, the renovated building served its new and rather arcane purpose with grace and dignity.

Beau turned at the gentle harrumphing from the throat of the sad-eyed brindle hound sitting at his feet and stroked the drooping ears.

"Why, Smiley, I believe you're right," Beau said, as his only brother's only son entered through the great oak double doors. "Come on up, TJ, I've just made a fresh pot of coffee."

TJ moved up the aisle past the paneled, doorless rooms, which now served as offices, framed in where the congregation had once knelt in prayer. His athlete's body, the broad shoulders still impressive above the narrow though slightly thickening waist, bore an uncharacteristic slump. He looked tired, Beau thought, searching the lean tanned face. It was rare to see him with no hint of a smile, not even at the corners of the wide-spaced blue eyes. TJ sank into one of the leather chairs and stretched his feet onto its matching, claw-footed ottoman. He flopped the manila envelope he had been carrying onto the small side table next to the chair.

"I'd rather have a beer, Uncle Beau, if there is any," TJ said as the hound, Smiley, greeted him by snorting in his outstretched hand.

"I believe there is, now that you mention it," Beau said and departed for the vestry—remodeled to serve as a small kitchen in its new incarnation—returning with a frosted glass.

Since his younger brother, Jefferson Davis Billings, had been killed in the early action in Korea, Beau had assumed a mantle of responsibility for TJ, who was only three at the time. Like many parents before him, Beau was surprised to learn that TJ's attaining adulthood would not necessarily lessen that feeling. Beau had come to California from Oklahoma for the funeral of TJ's wife, Amelia, more than fifteen years ago. TJ had been fighting a desperate battle with an all-encompassing depression, and ten year old Elizabeth was a frightened and lonely child. Finding that he was still needed from time to time, Beau stayed on, secure in the knowledge that Wandell Montgomery, his erstwhile partner in the land lease business back in the Oklahoma oil fields, would be able to manage just fine without him.

Handing over the icy glass of beer, Beau seated himself across from his nephew. Smiley assumed his normal position at Beau's feet, head resting on his size 12 boot, and Beau cast a meaningful look at the manila envelope.

"That from the lawyer?" he said.

"Yeah."

"Now I don't mean to pry, son, you know that's not my style, but you appear to lack a little of being alive, and I've got to figure it's got something to do with that envelope. Want to tell me what's in it?"

The ghost of a smile hovered around TJ's eyes at the example of what he'd come to call Uncle Beau's 'mother hen' syndrome; with a bit of plain old nosiness thrown in.

"No reason not to. It's the title to a boat."

"A boat," Beau said, nodding as if this revelation were an everyday occurrence.

"And a letter from Harley Sullivan."

Beau leaned back into the smooth leather of his chair, hands folded across his neatly buttoned vest. His eyelids drooped until it appeared he was about to take a nap, but it was only his listening posture.

"Harley left me his boat as payment for my services." TJ ran a hand over his eyes, swallowed a draught of beer and rested his head on the soft padding of the chair back.

"I tried to tell him after I found the boy it was most likely suicide. So did the authorities. Suicide or an accidental overdose. That lethal a combination of booze and drugs might have been either one. There wasn't any note, but that doesn't mean a damn thing. I told him that at the hospice, before he died, but I guess he didn't believe me. Or just didn't want to."

"So he left you his boat and a little posthumous assignment, is that it?"

"That about sums it up. He's convinced . . . or he was before he died, that someone killed Chipper."

Beau sighed. "Well, son, you have my sympathy," he said, rising with coffee cup in hand. He stood gazing once more at the fading autumn sunlight sifting through the redwood branches, then turned toward the kitchen.

"There is positively nothing worse than owing a debt to a dead man," he said softly as he moved down the steps. TJ made no response. He might not have heard, Beau thought; and maybe it was just as well if he hadn't.

At 4:15 Elizabeth Billings slammed the door to her apartment with the sole of her left shoe, but still managed to drop one armload of books and her canvas briefcase before she could make it to the couch. Hester, wise to her mistress's ways, waited for the avalanche to subside before stationing herself between the two loafer-clad feet, weaving and purring, as Lisbee made her way to the small kitchen. After pouring a glass of nonfat milk for herself and a bowl of same for the cat, Lisbee retrieved the briefcase and headed for the bedroom. She booted up the Macintosh, propped the briefcase on the floor beside it, and stretched out on her bed.

"Silly asses," she said aloud, apparently to the cat, for it leapt up beside her and stuck a sympathetic nose next to the cloud of dark hair that had fallen across her cheek.

"Hester, don't ever get into this business. It sucks. You try to help people and all they do is smile and pay you and ignore what you've told them so you just have to go back and do it all over again. Makes for a nice bank account, but I'm not sure the aggravation is worth it."

It wasn't so much that Lisbee had formally joined her father and Uncle Beau in the investigation agency as that she'd always been there. Underfoot at first, then later making herself useful. And finally, after college, modernizing the business with her infernal computers which, though often cranky, streamlined the bookkeeping as well as the lowly skip trace. Her expertise in computer security fell naturally into the arsenal of Anadarko Grace Investigations and she had developed a solid clientele of her own in a relatively short time. The real crime at her end of the operation, Lisbee believed, was the prices charged by those thieves who ran computer security seminars and sold 30-minute video tapes for $500.00 and up; but they were beyond the law, and unfortunately there were always crowds of the uninformed who stood in line to pay up.

She sighed and pulled herself off the bed. Might as well get on with it. Seated at her own machine, she began the telnet session that would repair the holes left gaping in her latest client's network because they had neglected to take her advice. She had been working only about ten minutes when the phone rang. Separate lines for computer and voice were a necessity in her line of work and a legitimate expense until DSL or cable were available in the area, but she decided to let the answering machine get this call and finish what she was doing. Until she heard the deep voice, complete with faint southwestern drawl, begin a message on the tape.

". . . didn't think I'd find you in, being the last minute, but I thought I'd try anyway."

She hurriedly left the keyboard and stabbed the button on the answering machine.

"Justin? I'm here. I was working."

"Working or hiding?"

"Both. Aren't you working?"

"No, that's why I called. Got the evening off. I know it's kinda late, but if you don't have plans I thought we might have dinner. I still owe you one."

"That's not very flattering. You don't owe me anything."

"You know what I mean. How does scampi sound? Even if you're planning to work all night, you still have to eat."

"It sounds great. What time?"

"I'll pick you up in . . . say two hours? About 6:30?"

"Make it 7:00. I can finish what I'm doing and take the rest of the evening off."

Lisbee replaced the cordless phone in its stand and grinned. Scooping Hester up she laughed aloud and turned, flinging open the double closet doors to stare at the eclectic assortment of garments, in which she normally took a small measure of pride. Under present circumstances, nothing in there would be exactly right, she was sure.

It was a new and bittersweet experience for Lisbee, this need for complex strategic planning. She had known Justin Highstreet for nearly six months now, and had yet to attain her objective; an objective whose precise definition was still hazy in her mind. Unwilling to characterize it as a purely carnal interest, she had to admit that was, nevertheless, a large part of it. And in her previous experience, it had always been she who set the pace, handing out gentle rebuffs until the level of excitement reached the proper pitch. But not with the quiet, slow-talking deputy.

It was not a case, she had decided, of him playing her own game against her. He had been trying to extricate himself from a messy affair with a married woman when she met him. It had turned violent and tragic, and she understood it would take him some time to get over that. But although they had developed a rather tentative friendship, he continued to treat her more like a little sister than a potential lover, pushing her frustration level to its peak.

More than a month ago, when she believed she had finally made significant progress, TJ had arrived at her door instead of Justin, bearing a tale of a last minute duty call that wasn't even his responsibility. Since then, double shifts and a week-long class in investigative procedures had kept him from keeping his promise—to buy her dinner as repayment for the help she had given him in a night class he was taking on computer applications for law enforcement. 'I owe you one,' he'd said and it confounded her; stuck there between them like a rock wall was the unspoken 'I wouldn't be asking you, but I feel obligated.' Well, she'd take it. It wasn't what she wanted, but it was a start.

The scampi was thick and spicy. Through the glass at their window table, lights from the wharf shops winked playfully in the rise and fall of the gently rolling surf. When their plates and bowls had been cleared Highsteet smiled across at her. It would have been the perfect time for a whispered confidence, except that Lisbee could not have heard herself shout for the din in the restaurant, let alone whisper. So she smiled in return, drained the last of her wine and made a hand gesture toward the door, her fine dark brows arching the query. He nodded his agreement, and when the harried waiter skimmed by, asked for the check.

It was cool on the beach. Lisbee had removed her low-heeled pumps and was walking barefoot on the sand, enjoying the childhood feel of it through her toes, successfully keeping at bay the adult foresight that told her it would be uncomfortably gritty when she had to put them back on again. Justin rested a long arm companionably around her shoulders as they walked, and she leaned into him, her feet sinking luxuriously into the powdered beach with each step.

When he had arrived at her apartment, she'd been impressed with the handsome lamb suede sports jacket he wore over tan twills; his blue oxford cloth shirt open at the throat. Now she could smell the leather of his sleeve, and in the rising breeze detected an old-fashioned scent of shaving lotion. Nothing trendy; Old Spice, maybe? It was heady stuff, whatever it was. Pure male, in its combination with the leather and the scent of his skin.

Cool air off the sea insinuated itself through the bulky cable knit of the silk sweater she had finally chosen from her cluttered closet, and she shivered. He turned to look down at her.

"Cold?"

"No."

He smiled, pulling her a bit closer to him anyway.

"You ever ride on that thing?" he said, nodding toward the towering wooden structure that supported the roller coaster track. The Boardwalk was well-lighted, even though all the attractions were closed. It was eerie to view the amusement park without sound or motion; silent empty tracks, Ferris wheel frozen in flight. Lisbee found her brain filling in the crowds of people, the cacophony of hawkers and noisy children, from memory.

"Sure. I grew up here. It's obligatory. Haven't you?"

"No, I was too old for that kind of thing when I came here," Justin said, smiling.

"You're never too old for that roller coaster. It's the biggest one on the West Coast, or it used to be," Lisbee said. "I'll take you next time they open. Came here from where?"

The deputy gave her a dubious glance, and she wasn't sure if her question had prompted it or the promised ride on the biggest roller coaster on the West Coast.

"A little town in West Texas you've never heard of; about thirty-five miles west of Odessa. Monahans."

"You don't sound much like a Texan."

He smiled again.

"It's not obligatory."

They walked on in silence. As they neared the end of the boardwalk, approaching the mouth of the San Lorenzo River, they could see across the wide sandy expanse the glow of lights from the elegant restaurant perched in regal solitude at the end of its own pier—Orlando's. Lisbee looked up covertly and saw what she had feared; a stony expression had overtaken the smooth planes of his face. She hadn't been paying attention and let it go too long; let them walk right into it.

The restaurant's owner, Orlando Cruz, had come very close to killing Deputy Highstreet six months earlier, when he was trying to end a messy affair with the man's wife. Cruz *had* shot his wife, Sandra, and she had nearly bled to death in Justin's arms. Lisbee thought of bringing the subject up, examining it objectively with him, but decided she had too much to lose to try playing shrink.

"Let's go back," she said brightly, and in an attempt to restore their prior mood, she began to chatter. She knew she was doing it; knew a lot of men didn't like that particularly feminine trait and would automatically tune the non-stop talker out, but she hurried on, riding the cresting wave of words, hoping he would catch it as it went by.

". . . so when I checked my email there were two hundred and seventeen messages. I get a lot of mail, but not that much. It was a mail bomb."

"What?" Justin said.

"A mail bomb. It's a nasty little trick to clog up the works; clinically known as a *loss of use* attack. The miscreant gets a list of email addresses off an Internet provider's mail server—legally or illegally—and sends some diatribe to hundreds of people he doesn't know; then when people receive it and don't know any better they write back asking to be taken off his 'list'. Only they use the 'Reply' function in the mail reader, so their response goes back to everyone on the original letter. Even if only a few people make that mistake, it can crash the mail server."

"Electronic vandalism. Or is it more sinister than that?"

"It's hard to tell," Lisbee said. "Mostly vandalism I'd guess; bored kids on a power kick. But concerted attacks on specific targets are getting more commonplace."

"Isn't it pretty obvious who starts sending the things? Don't they have return addresses?"

"None that mean anything if they use an anonymous remailer, which they would unless they're complete amateurs."

They were nearing the wharf, and the lot where Justin's jeep was parked. Leaving the sand, they stood on the sidewalk while Lisbee brushed at one bare foot, then the other, preparatory to slipping on her shoes. She lost her balance momentarily, and a strong arm circled her waist. Taking her time she leaned into it, gauging how long she could enjoy the contact without being obvious. Finally standing on shod feet, she moved off toward the car.

"Mind going by my place on the way home?" Justin asked as he held the door for her.

"Okay by me," Lisbee said carelessly, glad the sudden rise in her blood pressure wasn't visible.

"It won't take a minute. There's something I want you to see."

My Lord, not very original, Lisbee thought, but remained silent.

"I probably shouldn't have done it without asking you first," Justin said as he backed the jeep expertly out of its space.

"Done what?"

"I bought a second-hand computer from one of the guys at City Hall," he said. "It's a Macintosh."

FOUR

At 8:32 SATURDAY morning, TJ wheeled the elderly Jaguar XKE into the lot and parked it a carefully measured distance from the other two vehicles—Uncle Beau's Oldsmobile wagon and Lisbee's burgundy Mustang. The skin of the Jag gleamed in its brand new metallic blue paint, a recent renovation sponsored in part by Uncle Beau since Elizabeth, as Chief Financial Officer for the firm, flatly refused to sanction it as a business expense. He closed the door and locked it after extracting a manila envelope from the passenger seat, then walked briskly through the morning fog toward the portico of the old church which now housed the offices of Anadarko Grace Investigations.

The neat lawn was freshly trimmed, and he noted some different kind of flowers, primroses maybe, had replaced those that had bloomed from spring through summer and early fall in the carved stone fishpond now situated where the church's plain, wooden announcement board had once stood, listing times of services and appropriate quotations from the scripture. Lisbee did the gardening. They could have afforded a professional gardener according to her—a *legitimate* business expense—but she enjoyed the outdoor work. There was none to do at her apartment, and it was a break from sitting in front of those damned machines. By which she meant her computers.

TJ was never quite sure why she had chosen to become involved with them in the first place. Though admittedly expert at what she did as far as he could tell, she seemed to have a 'love-hate' relationship with them and had often commented that she loathed programming. She went out of her way to avoid the remotest resemblance to the image of the hacker—a modern version of the *hair* generation of the sixties; flowing locks and studied sloppiness as external indicators of the iconoclast—though she had often to deal with them for professional reasons, and seemed adept at doing so. When asked point blank why she had chosen Computer Science as her major at college, she could not explain. He supposed it was the challenge of a complex puzzle that held her; or maybe it was just her practical nature since that was obviously the way the world was heading.

TJ walked into Uncle Beau's office and found the old man stretched out in his disreputable recliner, a steaming mug of coffee at his elbow. Though usually easy going, Beau continued to hold out against Lisbee's pleas to let her replace the faded, gangrenous-hued chair with something more suitable to the rest of the decor. It was the only personal item he had seen fit to ship out to California from his home in Oklahoma more than fifteen years before, after he realized he was not going back.

His thick white hair neatly combed, Beau was in his *Saturday* uniform. This concession to California casual dress took the form of freshly pressed twill slacks, suede vest over an open-necked tattersall shirt, topped by a light-weight, impeccably tailored Harris tweed sports jacket. TJ had learned the basics of what constituted a gentleman's attire from Uncle Beau when he was a child, but he recognized he would never have the old man's flair for it. In his jeans, white shirt and deep blue cotton cable-knit sweater, he was overdressed for <u>any</u> day of the week in Santa Cruz, but still evoked a mildly jaundiced eye from his uncle.

"Morning Uncle Beau," TJ said, smiling.

"TJ."

"Want some more coffee?" he added, laying the manila envelope on the scarred refectory table that served as Beau's desk.

"Thank you, son, but I don't believe I do. Seems like two cups about do me in the morning these days. Must be getting old. Used to be able to drink a potfull before lunch and start on a fresh one after."

TJ nodded his agreement with the vagaries of aging and had started for the vestry-kitchen when a voice piped over the wall.

"I'll have some if you're going." As he passed the doorway to her office, TJ saw a hand raised in salute, but Lisbee's eyes remained fixed on the screen in front of her.

"And a gracious good morning to you, Elizabeth," he said and walked on.

When he had dropped off Lisbee's coffee and received a mumbled "Thanks," TJ took his own mug and sat behind Uncle Beau's desk.

"Doesn't seem too bright-eyed this morning, does she?" he said softly as he began removing the contents of the manila envelope and spreading them on the polished wood of the refectory table.

"So I noticed," Beau said.   "What all have you got there?"

TJ, who had decided the previous afternoon to postpone the initial evaluation of the unwanted case left to him by Harley Sullivan until morning when he might be in a better mood to view it, placed the papers in a neat row in front of him and began to enumerate.

"Let's see. Coroner's report and death certificate for Steven 'Chipper' Sullivan. Registration, keys, and title to the Motor Vessel *Emmy T*. A copy of Harley's will. Some snapshots of the kid and the boat. A business card for some outfit in Scotts Valley. And his letter to me—handwritten." TJ winced, looking at the spidery scrawl of this last, remembering the old man's feebleness, though it hadn't succeeded in damping the fire in his eyes the last time he'd seen him.

"What's in the letter besides him asking you to find out if the boy was murdered?"

"There's no 'if;' he was convinced it was murder. My job is to find out *who* and see justice done. The rest is background information, mostly. Everything he could think of that might be helpful, I guess. His daughter's name and address. Megan Sullivan; that's Chipper's mother. The kid's real name was Steven Harley Sullivan. Father, one Steven Andrew Prentice. His mother was only married to Prentice briefly, according to this, and she took her own name back for both herself and the boy. Current whereabouts of the father unknown."

"She inherits everything, does she?"

"Yeah, except the boat. I imagine she'll try to sell the marina. She doesn't care much for boats, Harley said. Lives in Soquel and works at the University, I think."

"What about the business card?"

"Some company in Scotts Valley. The kid apparently had a part time job there before he died. Some kind of gofer work where he could learn the trade, according to his grandfather. It's not the boy's card, it's one of those generic things you pick up on the counter in reception. Pan Global, Inc. 'Freedom and Integrity in the Shrinking Digital World.' That could mean anything. A computer chip manufacturer, maybe? It sounds kind of familiar—does it to you?"

"Wasn't Elizabeth doing something for them a few months back?" Beau said.

FIVE

Eʟɪᴢᴀʙᴇᴛʜ ѕᴀᴛ ѕᴛᴀʀɪɴɢ blankly at her monitor. Her efforts to concentrate were waning as images of the previous evening flitted indiscriminately before her, snatches of conversation running through her mind like a poorly dubbed tape. The temptation to read volumes into isolated words and gestures, offhand comments lightly made, was nearly insurmountable. She swore under her breath.

In the shadowy hours between midnight and three AM, when she had finally fallen into an exhausted but restless sleep, Lisbee had reached the conclusion that self-examination might be enlightening, but it wasn't very flattering. She was spoiled. For the first time in her life, she was suffering from the effects of a physical attraction that was not reciprocated. Most women must be familiar with this feeling of frustration, this gathering of niggling doubts, biting at their metaphorical heels.

"Welcome to the club, Lisbee, you arrogant bitch," she muttered to herself, turning from the computer screen to see her father standing in front of the desk, watching her.

"Tough night?" he said lightly.

She forced a dazzling smile to her lips.

"Not at all. It was fun. Justin sends his regards."

TJ returned the smile and took a chair.

"You look pretty today. That a new sweater?"

So much for wearing the mask, at least with TJ.

"Yeah, it is. Thanks."

"You in the middle of something, or can you spare a few minutes?"

"I'm all yours. What's up?"

Her father leaned back in the chair and related the pertinent facts concerning Harley Sullivan, his grandson, and the unwelcome assignment the old man had left around TJ's neck like a great squawking albatross. When he had finished, Lisbee stared at him in astonishment.

"You've got a boat?"

"That's a fact."

"How big?"

"It's pretty big."

"Can I see it? When can we go out in it?"

"Sure, you can see it. I don't know about going out. I've got to get somebody to check me out in it. I don't know a damn thing about boats that don't have oars."

Lisbee grinned.

"I get the feeling you didn't come in here just to expound on your lack of qualifications as a mariner."

"No, as a matter of fact, I didn't." He placed a small white card on the desk in front of her. "I wanted to see what you know about this. The boy worked there part time. Beau thought it was a company you'd had some dealings with."

Lisbee looked at the glossy card, slightly dog-eared and a bit stained.

"Pan Global. Sure. I did some work for them in August." She smiled, recalling Mick Deering's cynical interpretation of the firm's name. Mick, her friend and informant on the fringes of the digital underground.   And without realizing she'd done it, she repeated the name aloud.

"*Planned Gabble.*"

"What?"

"*Planned Gabble.* It's what they're called in the geek culture.

"Would you care to enlighten me? What the hell does that have to do with a chip manufacturer?"

"They don't make chips; they're a software house. Pan Global develops and licenses encryption algorithms. File encryption, digital signatures that can't be forged; that kind of stuff. A lot of the big names use their encryption in applications software and operating systems so they can't be pirated. But that's become a small piece of the pie these days. Global marketing on the Web is where it's at; cyberdollars, on-line banking, stock trading, you know."

TJ looked at her blankly. "No, I really don't, but I don't have to as long as you do. What's their background? They been around a while?"

"For this business they've got long gray beards. A couple of math wizards from Cornell started it up in the late eighties. They were brilliant when it came to encryption, but you could've stored their pooled knowledge about running their own business in a teacup. They almost folded until they brought in a third guy; an MBA from Stanford. They seem to be doing okay now—there hasn't been much competition until recently. Just two other good-sized outfits that I know of in the private sector; one up the peninsula and one in Canada. But the atmosphere is ripe for startups—at least until the Internet crashes and burns from the overload."

"Private sector? Who else is there?"

"The spooks, of course, or rather their industrial contractors. Lucent Technologies, *nee* Bell Labs, those guys, but they're not marketing the stuff. Just the reverse. All that government-sponsored Clipper Chip kind of hoo hah. They want to force computer manufacturers to include a back door in all their products that the Justice Department has the key to. 'Don't handcuff the FBI, the terrorists will overrun us.' They're still back in the seventies where they think all they need is a phone tap to catch the bad guys."

TJ smiled slightly.

"Is that a policy statement? I didn't think you were political."

"I'm not and it isn't. But even someone as level-headed and lovable as myself can get irritated by blatant stupidity once in a while."

"Amen. Think you could check out what Chipper Sullivan did for this *Planned Babel?* Talk to some of the folks he worked with? I doubt it's got anything to do with what happened to him, but I've got to start somewhere."

"*Gabble.* Sure. I'll go over there this afternoon, if I can reach Cory Floyd. He's the Stanford MBA, now CEO. I worked with him last summer. Nice guy, but a little on the Yuppie side. Horny, too, apparently. He was working up to making a serious hit on me, but I blocked it with the picture of his wife and kids on his desk."

TJ raised an eyebrow.

"Well, do what you can short of compromising your principles. I'm going to talk to the boy's mother, over in Soquel, then go down and meet Beau and Clyde at Moss Landing. Come on down when you've seen this guy, and I'll show you the *Emmy T.*"

"*Emmy T*? Is that it's name? That's kind of old-fashioned, isn't it? Why not something like the *Zephyr*?"

TJ looked mildly alarmed.

"Just kidding," Lisbee said. "What time will you be there?"

"Oh, I don't know. Three or thereabouts?"

"Sounds good. How do I find it?"

"Turn right off the highway about a half mile before you get to the Moss Landing bridge. There's a sign there that says Bel Harbor Marina."

"Okay, but if I'm not there in time, go ahead. I'll find you." She grinned mischievously. "Unless my principles suffer an assault they're not up to repelling."

Clyde Allbright, retired after nearly thirty years spread somewhat unequally among three of the four city police departments in Santa Cruz County, sprawled in the sturdy kitchen chair, one meaty hand curled protectively around a chipped mug of coffee while the other patted his pockets in a vain search for his ever present pack of cigarettes. Nodding wisely at his wife Ellen, in animated if unappreciated conversation as was her custom in the morning, he recalled with a dismal onslaught of depression that he was out. He had thrown his last pack in the garbage the night before in a fit of repentance after reading an article on middle-aged men and heart disease.

It wasn't something he himself would have chosen for light reading. Ellen had left it out for him, on the table next to his favorite chair, turned apocryphally to the proper page. His attempts to ignore it had succumbed to the rationalization that he would merely skim the article, but with the staring fascination of a rabbit pinned in the oncoming headlights of a speeding truck, he had read the entire thing while a film of sweat slowly engulfed his slightly pudgy body.

Now, in the gray morning light, the nightmares having vanished with the darkness, he was considering whether the cigarettes might be salvageable—not broken or soggy with coffee grounds—and if by chance they were, how he could extract them from the trash can and still retain some shred of dignity.

". . . so it's a chance for me to start really working on something I've always wanted to do. It doesn't cost that much, Clyde. What do you think?"

"What?"

"About me taking the class in Creative Writing at the University. Can we afford it?"

"Oh, sure. Go ahead. What did you say it costs?"

"I didn't say. I *said* it doesn't cost *that much*. You haven't been listening, have you?" A look of long-suffering irritation crossed Ellen's still pretty round face.

"Sure I have. You want to take some writing course. How much is 'not that much' in dollars and cents?"

"Three-hundred and fifty dollars for the first course, Introduction to Professional Writing."

"*First* course? How many are there?"

"After the introductory course—it's a prerequisite to the others—there are courses in specific kinds of writing; non-fiction, short story fiction, novels, that kind of thing."

"How many do you think you're going to take?" Clyde asked warily, the vision of broken cigarettes being replaced by one of his dwindling bank balance.

"I won't know that until I take the first one, will I?" his wife answered with mild asperity. "That's what I've been trying to explain to you, if you'd only listen."

The pink phone on the brightly papered kitchen wall rang once and Clyde leaped from his chair to answer it.

"I've got it—hello?" He listened for a moment while Ellen removed their empty coffee cups from the table and set them in the sink.

"Yeah, I can make it. Nothing going on here I can't take care of later. What time?"

Clyde ran a hand over his unshaven jaw, nodded twice, said "Right, see you there," and replaced the receiver.

Ellen's back was straight and stiff as she stood rinsing the cups and placing them in the dish drainer beside the sink.

"I'm going to meet Beau for lunch at Moss Landing. They've got some kind of case he wants to talk to me about."

"I thought you were going to clean out the back yard for the Fall Pickup next week," she said without turning.

"It's not until Thursday, for Christ's sake. There's plenty of time. When do you have to decide about that class thing?"

"Registration doesn't start for a month, but I told Meg I'd let her know next week. Those classes fill up quickly, and she can get me the registration materials ahead of time so I get first jump at it."

The minor pang of guilt Clyde had been suffering was dissipating rapidly.

"Well, go ahead, then. You don't need the money 'til registration do you?"

Ellen turned, her face wreathed in smiles.

"No, and I've got a little saved back from the household money. Oh, Clyde, I'm so excited!" She flung her arms around his neck and he patted her clumsily on her firm, though inexorably widening, backside.

"Okay, okay. I'm going to take a shower. I'll be back later this afternoon."

"Was Elizabeth at the office when you talked to Beau?"

"I guess so. He didn't say. Why?"

"Well, I'll have to have some sort of word processor for the class, and she can probably find me something used that doesn't cost too much," Ellen said, beaming.

SIX

MEGAN SULLIVAN'S HOUSE in Soquel had once served the small community as a one room school, accommodating twenty-five students from first through fourth grade. It was situated three and a half miles inland on the Soquel-San Jose Road, a narrow two lane highway which winds through the Santa Cruz mountains toward Silicon Valley.

The house sat well back from the road. What had been a playground, and still contained an ancient but well preserved wooden teeter-totter, was now a wide expanse of lawn leading to the covered porch, which extended the full width of the building. On the peaked, shingled roof perched a bell tower, complete with bell, its rope clearly visible descending into what had probably been the cloak room.

TJ Billings surveyed the house with a growing sense of nostalgia. He guessed there were few people in this area who remembered when it had last served its original purpose, or what it had looked like inside—but he did. Not this particular one, of course, but one so similar as to make no difference. He had started school in just such a simple structure back in Oklahoma.

It had had hardwood flooring throughout; an antechamber immediately inside the double doors, cloakroom to the right—small, rather dark, with rows of brass hooks lining the walls above a rough hewn shelf for muddy galoshes. To the left the bathroom door, primly closed; just the one for boys and girls alike, not to mention the teacher. And straight ahead, opening wide into a large, light, high-ceilinged space, the school room.

Commanding an uninterrupted view, the square wooden teacher's desk faced the room, flanked by a large blackboard whose top border was a perfect alphabet alternately in upper and lower case letters, both printed and cursive. In one corner of the room a black, round-bellied wood stove would provide heat on cold winter days, its cylindrical chimney rising to the high ceiling. Recess was not only a break for the fidgeting students; it had allowed the teacher to replenish the fire.

The student's desks, in neat rows, were the kind now found only in antique stores; solid wood with wrought iron filigree sides, the desk top slanted from a four inch wide level shelf, abutted to the seat back of the desk in front. In the right-hand corner of this level surface a round hole was cut, originally intended to contain a removable glass inkwell, though in TJ's time the holes were usually empty, or if the well was there it was dried up. He suspected the advent of the ballpoint pen had had less to do with the inkwell's demise than the removal of temptation from small boys rarely able to curb a desire to dip some pretty ponytail in the well and see the black arc it made on the back of a white blouse.

The slanted writing surface of each desk was hinged to the level base and lifted to reveal a storage area for books, pencils, and whatever small contraband a boy or girl might successfully hide there. Carved initials would be found on some of the desktops and would inevitably get in the way when writing compositions, causing the pencil to punch a hole in the paper. The seats were benches, also hinged so they could be pushed up out of the way for cleaning the floor beneath them. Connected in rows, the desks, like small boxcars, rested on wooden rails to which their wrought iron sides were bolted.

Lost in thoughts of garter snakes, dirty pieces of string, and lunches packed in paper sacks, TJ parked the Jaguar in the long drive which led around to the back of the house, and started for the porch. To make a place like this comfortably livable there must have been additions as well as renovation, but if so they were in the rear, preserving the look and silhouette of the original. It was a lovely job.

There had been no answer when he called Harley Sullivan's daughter; not even an answering machine, which was unusual these days. But he had decided to stop by anyway, and if she wasn't home, to leave a note.

When there was no response to his knock, TJ turned and surveyed the sloping lawn playground from the railed porch, considering what he should say in the note. He wasn't sure if Harley had told his daughter what he intended to do. From his reaction the last time TJ had seen Harley and mentioned contacting her, he wasn't sure if she and the old man had even been on speaking terms. Not a pretty situation, to be dying and still refuse to see your only child, no matter what might have gone on between you in the past. Though he tried, TJ couldn't imagine anything that could come between him and Elizabeth that would make him react that way.

Megan Sullivan must know her father had left TJ the boat from reading his will, but she would be suffering the double shock of her son's death followed in less than a month by her father's. Estranged from her father or not, she would be vulnerable and most probably not too pleased with some joker by the name of TJ Billings. He decided to keep it simple. Pulling a business card from his wallet, he scrawled on the back, *"Harley asked me to see you. Please call at your convenience."*

After all, there was no rush. Just that uncomfortable feeling of something hanging over his head. It wasn't unusual to receive an advance on a case; in fact TJ insisted on it most of the time. But not payment in full. And not for a job he wouldn't have accepted given the choice; a job he wasn't even sure he could finish.

He stuck the card between the door and its frame and turned toward the Jag. It was time to take a look at his new boat.

Lincoln "Sunfish" Cortez sat in his usual window booth in the rear of the shabby cafe sipping a not very cold beer, and keeping a discreet eye on the two old men at the corner table. The scruffy, balding one wasn't really old, he decided. More like middle-aged. But the other, well-dressed one was, though he'd moved like a younger man when they entered, tall and elegant, not really needing the gnarled cane he carried. They were conversing quietly between themselves. Cortez wouldn't have paid them much attention except the white-haired old guy was also being affable with Louise, the sour-faced, footsore waitress who'd worked at the Gull's Nest so long and offended so many customers, that the cafe's owner,

Sam Osborne, had decided he'd either have to fire her or marry her. He'd done the latter.

Sunny Cortez sipped his beer and pushed away the red plastic basket that held the congealing remains of his lunch of deep fried calamari and french fries. Osborne had recently added one or two limp and uninspired salads to the menu under the banner *Heart Healthy*, in deference to the cholesterol-phobic crowd, but they weren't very good sellers. Apparently even the tourists that made up a large portion of his trade allowed themselves a break from their routines of jogging and juice bars when they encountered the genuine greasy spoon cafe just on the northern edge of Moss Landing. And the employees at the Monterey Bay Aquarium Research Institute, which had opened a year or so ago after replacing most of the sleazy waterfront fish packing houses with a sleek modern facility, either brought their lunches or ate in the cafeteria provided for the MBARI workforce. Or being mostly scientists and therefore dedicated, maybe forgot to eat at all. Cortez didn't worry about what he ate. The life he had been born to, with its immediacy of legitimate injury or even death, had pushed any concern about the long term effects of diet to a small dark corner of his consciousness.

Born and reared in the bosom of a Salinas rodeo family, Sunny had grown up among cowboys crippled by the whims of half wild mustangs, wall-eyed steers, and foul-tempered Brahma bulls. His father, who walked with the limping gait of an old man at forty-two, still managed to manipulate a lariat in his big-knuckled hands like a master, but Sunny, after earning his nickname by being lucky enough to survive two consecutive *sunfishing* broncs in a row, had had enough. At twenty-two, he'd decided only a fool would live the life of a rodeo rider unless he was too stupid to find something else to do. And Sunny wasn't stupid.

With a battered duffel bag and the clothes on his back, he left Salinas for Monterey, where he caught on doing backbreaking, but slightly less dangerous labor with the fishing fleet. He discovered a previously unknown talent with diesel engines, and after meeting Harley Sullivan by chance in a waterfront delicatessen, secured a job at Bel Harbor as a dockside dogsbody. Harley had explained to him that when he gained enough experience to accept some real responsibility, his pay would be increased in proportion to the loads he was shouldering. By the time the old man began to slow down, as his illness gained a grip it would never relinquish, Sunny Cortez had become indispensable; literally running the operation when Harley no longer could. And he'd continued to run Bel Harbor after Harley's death with the ease of an old-timer, having uncovered yet another hidden talent; a cool head for business combined with a disarming affability. He was liked and respected by both the boat owners who were his customers and by his associates in the Moss Landing Harbor District, the fishing fleet, and more recently the seafaring members of the Research Institute. Admittedly his future was uncertain, the marina being now in the hands of the old man's daughter, Megan, but that didn't bother Sunny. At twenty-seven, he was whole and healthy with skills that commanded respect on the waterfronts. If he'd stayed with the rodeo, he'd probably be well on his way to being a permanent cripple.

Louise, the surly waitress, was standing at the two stranger's table nodding solemnly when Sunny looked up from his check. The older, white-haired one was talking in a low voice. Then a strange thing happened. She smiled. He said something else and she leaned closer to the table and actually laughed, resting the hand which held their bill on the table's edge. Cortez was now staring boldly, forgetting his former discretion. These were definitely not casual tourists, stopping for lunch on their way to Monterey or Carmel. In the nearly five years he'd spent in Moss Landing, Sunny had learned to recognize tourists, and not just from their predictable mode of dress. They would smile if you smiled first, but they remained locked within a cocoon of their own devising, as if to protect them and their insular lives from intrusion by foreign influences. Until they were ready, he supposed, to open some small door and accept the canned experiences prepared for them at their final destination. The Aquarium, the lavish restaurants serving rum punch drinks garnished with fruit, flowers and paper umbrellas, and the endless gift shops.

Sunny Cortez finished his beer and was about to rise when he saw Louise nod in his direction. The two men got up from their booth and followed her as she sauntered over to his table.

"Hey, Sunny, these two gentlemen would like to talk to you," she said in her nasal twang.

"Sorry to bother you, Mr. Cortez," the old man said in a mellow voice, slowed by a Southwestern accent. "I'm Beau Billings and this is my associate, Clyde Allbright."

The balding man nodded.

"We're kinda new to this, and Mrs. Osborne here was kind enough to say if we had questions about boats or the marina, you were the man to ask."

"Could be I am, depending on the questions. You looking for a boat?"

"Well, not exactly. We've sorta got one—that is my nephew does."

"Where?"

"At the marina."

"Bel Harbor?"

"If that's the one back down the road there, I guess that's it," the old man said and smiled.

Cortez answered with a slow smile of his own while he gathered his thoughts. He hoped his shock didn't show. Just as he'd known they weren't tourists, he also knew they sure as hell weren't boaters. He knew every boat in the marina, and every owner. No recent sales had taken place. The only vessel it could possibly be had been left to Meg Sullivan by her father, along with the marina itself, as far as he knew.

"It wouldn't be the *Emmy T.* would it?" he finally said.

"Why yes, I believe that *is* what TJ said it was called," the man Billings said. "You know the boat?"

"You might say that," Sunny Cortez said. The smile remained on his sharp-featured face, but it had left his eyes.

SEVEN

THE JUNCTION OF Highway 17 and Mt. Hermon Road, which meanders through the mountains to end in the town of Felton on Highway 9, had once been a bus stop known as Camp Evers for the Peerless Stages line that ran between Los Gatos and Santa Cruz. In the fine print of the bus schedules that were folded neatly to fit inside a pocket or purse, it was precisely sixteen minutes between departure from Camp Evers and arrival at the station in downtown Santa Cruz; in reality it had often been a good bit more, depending on the weather and the amount of sleep the overworked drivers had had since their last shift. The junction lay at the southernmost tip of Scotts Valley, a pleasant two-mile meadow split down the middle by SR 17, the pulsing artery connecting Santa Clara Valley and Santa Cruz through the heavily wooded section of the Coast Range. At the time of the Peerless Stages a hamlet sporting a few gas stations, cafes, and motels with small rental cabins inhabited the flats on the western side of the highway, while the minor fantasy that was Santa's Village Amusement Park insinuated itself throughout the hilly forest at the valley's northern entrance.

When the technology boom in neighboring Santa Clara County began, Scotts Valley became its dubious beneficiary in the form of a swollen real estate market for housing and, later, high tech manufacturing facilities, the land being an order of magnitude less expensive than anything available some thirty miles distant in the South Bay, which had by then become known as Silicon Valley.

There is little reminder today of that decades old Scotts Valley and Camp Evers, with the exception of a commanding view of the surrounding mountains that bounded them. Shopping malls with mammoth parking lots flank banks of split-level condominiums. Santa's Village succumbed to the onslaught, and in its wake huge cinderblock buildings housing software and manufacturing facilities dot the landscape. Across the highway the Scotts Valley Lumber Yard, the only remnant of the original lumber mill that once spanned the valley floor, sits just north of the sprawling facilities that are home to Seagate, manufacturers of high end hard disk drives.

Lisbee had chosen to bypass all the traffic and congestion at Camp Evers by taking Highway 9 through Felton to the home of Pan Global, Inc., which lay five miles east on Mt. Hermon Road, just outside the city limits of Scotts Valley. When she had phoned Cory Floyd at his home and explained briefly what she needed, he assured her he would be delighted to be of assistance. He hadn't remembered Harley Sullivan's grandson himself, but there was no reason he would. Even in a relatively small company such as *Planned Gabble*, which like most of its counterparts boasted an intimate extended-family culture, it was unlikely the CEO would recall a young man who had worked part time in the stock room or its euphemistic equivalent.

There were half a dozen cars and two motorcycles in the parking lot on the south side of the single story stucco building. The asphalt drive curved around the rear of the structure in a horseshoe, where the loading dock and the northern leg of the drive, which exited back onto Mt. Hermon Road, were bordered by an undulating, 9-hole golf course. Lisbee was about to park near the front entrance when she noticed some sort of commotion at the rear, and recognized the short, stocky form of Cory Floyd in jeans and sweatshirt, gesticulating at something or someone hidden from view behind the corner of the building. She eased the Mustang down several slots closer to the rear and parked.

Cory Floyd was in his early thirties; his square, heavy-jawed and somewhat florid face beneath a shock of thick black hair played counterpoint to startlingly blue eyes under heavy straight brows. At five foot nine, he was only marginally taller than Lisbee, but his wedge-shaped body was thick and muscular, the result of regular workouts in one of the health clubs that had sprung up like mushrooms after a rain to serve the needs of busy young professionals whose working lives were spent behind a desk. He was, she thought, a very attractive man until he opened his mouth. Then it was pure *empty-speak*—everything he said had been said before by multitudes like him, copied from MBA classrooms and fast track seminars aimed at molding a paint-by-the-numbers corporate identity. His after hours persona was undoubtedly the flip side of the same coin; the Starbuck's latte, local brew pub, and health club side.

As she approached she was struck by the silence. Something big must have happened to render Cory Floyd speechless. When she'd gone far enough to see around the corner of the building she began to understand.

The forest green cruiser with the gold star on its white door had parked discreetly out of sight of the main road, behind the loading dock. A door beside the concrete steps leading to the dock stood ajar, and kneeling on one knee beside it, examining the doorframe where the heavy brass lock had been wrenched open, was Deputy Sheriff Justin Highstreet.

The deputy stood regarding Elizabeth Billings gravely. Her long dark hair, swept carelessly back and tied at the nape of her neck, hung softly against the lemon yellow of her sweater. A black leather shoulder bag with tan trim rested against the swell of her denim clad hip. A fleeting image from the night before assailed him. Lisbee sitting in total concentration at the small screen of the second-hand computer he had bought on an impulse, tongue protruding slightly between her teeth. She had looked about seventeen—eighteen tops—but wise in her knowledge of that lump of silicon and plastic and supremely confident in her ability to make it dance and sing. Today she looked different. Older. A woman in all the most provocative aspects of the word. How the hell had he missed that? She gazed solemnly at the twisted brass that had been the lock plate of the door, arms folded under the soft rise of her breasts.

"Pry bar?" she said, raising finely arched brows.

"Looks that way," Highstreet nodded. "Did you ever think your family might be in the wrong business?"

"What business do you think we should be in?"

"Well, you and TJ seem to have some kind of genetic timing when it comes to crime scenes. You'd have made a hell of a newshound." His voice was cool and professional, but he couldn't stop the smile that tilted the corner of his mouth.

Lisbee grinned.

"True as far as it goes, but I don't think either one of us has enough of the killer instinct to make it profitable. Aren't pry bars a little old fashioned?"

"Not in the circles I run in."

"What about the alarms? Wouldn't ripping open a door like that have set up a howl?"

"Should have. Maybe the computers were down," Highstreet said with a straight face, then smiled again. "This was phoned in by an early golfer; saw some figures slinking around the side of the building and thought it didn't look right. He didn't see enough to be of any real help though."

The Pan Global CEO, temporarily forgotten, had watched this exchange with his mouth half open. Now he found his tongue.

"You two know each other?" he said to Lisbee, laying a square, short-fingered hand on her arm as though ready to do the gentlemanly thing and introduce them in the event that it was not clearly unnecessary.

"You could say that," she said. "How bad is it, Cory? What did they take?"

"That's just it, I don't know," Floyd said, spreading his arms wide in a theatrical gesture. "It's a disaster in there. Shelves turned over, packaging thrown everywhere. It'll take hours to sort through it all. I'll have to call the Facilities Manager, get his team in here to clean it up, before we can even begin to evaluate the extent of the loss."

Floyd's ruddy face suddenly turned pale, his eyes widening slightly.

"Listen, this doesn't have to be reported to the newspapers, does it? I mean, this kind of publicity can affect public confidence, influence teaming agreements, you know?"

Highstreet looked at him.

"The Sheriff's Office doesn't report to the press, but there's always somebody hanging around checking on the calls we take. If they want to pursue it, there's not much we can do. And that golfer probably won't be too disappointed if he gets his name in the paper."

"Shit," Floyd said softly, almost to himself. Then, smiling his stockholder's meeting smile he straightened his shoulders.

"Well boys and girls, damage control time. I'll get Cavanaugh and his Ops wizards in here right on the ass of the facilities team; do the numbers, come up with the recovery plan. It can't be so bad that the PR team won't be able to make it look like those creeps actually did us a favor. I've got some calls to make," he said, starting to move off toward his car.

"Just hold on a minute, Mr. Floyd," Highstreet said quietly.

"Before you go calling in a raft of people you should know the crime scene officers will take a couple of hours once they get here, and the Sergeant will want to go over your statement. Nobody's going to have access to this part of your building until then."

"What about the front offices? They're not off limits are they? We can get the strategy meetings going at least."

"As long as you make yourself available," Highstreet said noncommittally.

"Listen, Cory, I'll get back to you on that other thing," Lisbee said. "You've got enough to worry about right now."

Floyd turned to smile at her, smoothly covering the obvious fact that until the moment she spoke he had forgotten she was there.

"Hey, no problem; I can still do that. Once the recovery teams are in place, I'll get that information you were looking for. This won't take all day." He reached out and grasped Lisbee's hand, trapping it in his own. "I know. We'll have dinner. I can have everything you need by then. The Trout Farm? Say, 7:00 o'clock?"

"Tonight?" she said, removing her captive hand to brush back a lock of hair that really didn't need it. "Well . . ."

Knowing it was a gamble, but believing from her hesitation that the odds were favorable, Justin Highstreet interposed in his most solemn, official voice.

"Miss Billings has a previous engagement," he said. "She's having dinner with me tonight."

Lisbee flashed a brief, stony gaze at the deputy, then smiled at Floyd.

"I'm afraid that's right, Cory—I'd nearly forgotten. The deputy and I have some unfinished business to discuss. I'll phone you in the morning. We'll set up another time that's convenient." She turned a mischievous grin on Highstreet. "Your place, wasn't it? About eight?"

"Eight . . . right," Highstreet said, wondering where in the hell he was going to come up with something to give her for dinner.

EIGHT

THE TRAFFIC WAS heavy on the two lane stretch of Highway 1 between Watsonville and Castroville. It always was on a sunny Saturday, no matter what time of year. A fertile island of rural agriculture holding steady against the otherwise burgeoning development, it was the bottleneck through which travelers coming south from either Highway 101, via Hecker Pass, or directly south on coastal Highway 1, must pass to reach Monterey and Carmel. TJ braked sharply as the endless line in front of the Jaguar became a sea of red taillights. Someone turning off to browse one of the numerous vegetable stands, probably. He had to come to a full stop before the line of traffic began to move sluggishly forward once again.

The twin stacks of the Pacific Gas & Electric Power Plant rose starkly into a cloudless sky, their plumes of white steam canted south by the brisk wind off the sea. A landmark visible for miles when it wasn't foggy, they towered over the boat clogged harbor, dwarfing the village of Moss Landing. Beyond the plant, which marked the half-way point of the two lane section of road, stretched seemingly endless fields of artichokes. Row upon row of glistening green, the lacy plants covered the flats surrounding Castroville, self-proclaimed **Artichoke Center of the World**. Dusty dirt drives with hand-lettered signs advertising ARTICHOKES FOR SALE led off to white wooden farmhouses in the distance. TJ recalled his first view of those alien fields; spiky stems rising from each bush, topped by blooms that were the strange vegetable whose delicate meat lay hidden beneath coarse, thorn-tipped leaves. He wondered who had first had the idea that those overgrown thistles harbored something good to eat.

"Had to have been somebody who was goddamned hungry," he mused.

Passing the turnoffs to Bel Harbor Marina and the Elkhorn Yacht Club, TJ signaled for a right turn and pulled into the rutted dirt and gravel expanse that was a parking area bordering the harbor at the mouth of Elkhorn Slough, where he had agreed to meet Beau and Clyde. It was here that a group of homely seaside eateries lay gathered at the water's edge, their only asset the stunning view of boats gently swaying in their wooden berths, and the diamond blue sea on the horizon. Uncle Beau's station wagon sat sedately at the entrance to one of the restaurants—the Gull's Nest—at the end of the lot. Standing outside, leaning on a wooden railing, he could see Beau's broad back next to Clyde Allbright's stocky silhouette; and beside them a third, younger man, tall and lean. He parked the Jaguar some distance away where only Clyde's fading Cougar was within two spaces of it and got out.

As he approached, a tawny tan missile launched itself from its position at Uncle Beau's feet. Smiley leaped on TJ, tongue lolling and tail wagging. Small groans and yelps of unrestrained joy issued forth as TJ grasped the hound's large head and fondled his ears. Uncle Beau turned a stern glance on the pair of youths.

"Now Smiley, calm yourself and remember your manners," he said gently as he clipped a lead on the dog's collar.

"TJ, this is Mr. Cortez, from the marina. My nephew, TJ Billings."

"Sunny," the tall man said, extending his hand. TJ studied the stranger as he shook hands. Smooth olive skin over fine, high cheek bones. A shadow of heavy beard on the narrow chin. Dark, delicately arched brows under a mat of thick, straight black hair. Lean but muscular frame and exceptionally large, long-fingered hands on finely veined forearms so well developed they made him think of Popeye the Sailor Man. Slightly hooded black eyes you could easily mistake for lazy——but if you did it might just be your last mistake.

"Your Uncle tells me you bought the *Emmy T.* I didn't know Meg Sullivan had her up for sale yet," Cortez said, smiling to reveal slightly uneven but very white teeth.

"She didn't," TJ said. "I got the boat from Harley. You know her?"

"Meg or the *Emmy T.*?"

"Both."

"Yeah."

"Good. I'm going to need some expert advice on how to handle her."

"Meg or . . . ?"

"Both."

The docks were awash in earnest boat owners cleaning, polishing, and generally puttering in the early afternoon sunshine. TJ found it difficult to reconcile this scene of bustling industry with the eerie desolation he had felt six weeks before when he found Chipper Sullivan's body wedged in the darkened forward cabin of the *Emmy T.* Sunny Cortez waved and spoke to nearly everyone they passed, receiving smiles and salutes in return. One boat owner, enormously tall and bent like a bird of prey hovered on the decks of an old wooden Chris Craft. He smiled absently when Sunny hailed him as *Professor*, then receded back into the bowels of his vessel as they approached. TJ walked beside Cortez, while Clyde hung back a bit studying the boats they passed. Uncle Beau brought up the rear, tugging gently on the lead as Smiley stopped every few feet to investigate some new olfactory treasure.

TJ had no trouble recognizing the squat but comely lines of the *Emmy T.*'s bow, it's dangerous looking plow anchor extended nearly to the edge of the dock. The white fiberglass of her hull and the navy blue canvas tonneau that covered the flying bridge looked dingy under a thick layer of windborne dirt and excrement from the endlessly circling gulls. It occurred to him that if he kept the boat, he'd have to put in some time cleaning her up; and the thought of spending weekends in the sun and salt air, or even the billowing fog, washing and polishing, suddenly had an almost irresistible appeal.

As they reached the trawler's berth, the wooden door to the salon slid open to reveal a grim-faced woman with trailing strands of auburn hair escaping from a blue bandanna tied severely back on her head above large gold hoop earrings dangling from her ears. Lacking only a dagger clenched between her teeth to complete the image of a pirate, she stepped onto the deck and glared down at the group.

"Sunny, I need to talk to you. Who the hell is this?"

"The new owner," Cortez said with a crooked grin. "TJ Billings, meet Meg Sullivan."

The atmosphere had progressed from strained to merely stiff, primarily due to the calming effect Smiley seemed to have on Harley Sullivan's daughter. While Sunny Cortez busied himself on some mysterious mission in the engine room beneath the main salon, Megan Sullivan sat on the curving settee stroking the hound's silky head. TJ stood at the helm seat watching Clyde and Uncle Beau through the windows, conversing as they examined the forward deck and inspected the neighboring vessels.

"I'm really sorry to intrude on you at a time like this," TJ said. "But it's what your father wanted. I had no idea he was doing this. Leaving me this boat. I'd be happy to sign it over to you right now—I don't have any use for it."

Megan looked at him briefly, then resumed staring into the distance through the window over the galley sink.

"I don't want it. I hate boats. I just didn't know, is all."

"He didn't tell you?"

"No. He didn't talk to me much. He and Chipper lived in a world all their own. They didn't waste their time talking to me."

TJ searched for a note of bitterness in the monotone voice, but couldn't find it. Couldn't find any sign of emotion at all.

"I didn't look at his will until yesterday; there was no reason to. I assumed he'd left everything to me. There was no one else with Chipper dead."

"I'm sorry," TJ said again, struck by the painful inadequacy of that overused word.

"I came down here to talk to Sunny about selling the marina, and I thought I'd better check to be sure everything was off the *Emmy T.* Personal things, I mean. I haven't been here since Chipper died, and Harley was already bedridden, so he wouldn't have been able to . . ."

Meg Sullivan's shoulders, broad for a woman and accentuated by her narrow waist, refused to slump under the strain. She sat rigidly straight, wide eyes dry and staring while her left hand stroked the dog's head. It was like a rehearsal gone bad, with an actress who just couldn't get into the part, TJ thought.

"There's nothing here I want," she continued in that strange, inflectionless voice. "It's all yours; enjoy it."

Ready to be sympathetic, TJ found himself only irritated at this woman who refused to fall into a decent charade of grief before strangers, even it she didn't feel it. Consequently, his next words came out sharper than he intended.

"I'm not going to enjoy this boat—not until I've earned it. Your father left me with a job I wouldn't have taken if he were still alive and I'm not sure I can do any more than I've already done. But I'm going to try. And I'll sure as hell need your help."

Megan Sullivan looked at him. He might have imagined it, but he thought he detected a slight softening around her eyes.

"I doubt that I can be much help to you," she said quietly.

"My son Steven and I were never close even when he was a boy. It was always his grandfather he loved, and it was mutual, because Harley Sullivan finally had the son he'd always wanted. Dad was the one who started calling him *Chipper* when he was seven or eight—Jesus what a loathsome nickname. Like some presidential pet. They never told me why, where it came from. It was something they shared that was none of my business.

"When he got older, in his teens, his indifference toward me turned into an active dislike. We avoided each other as much as possible. I didn't know what to do about it, so I didn't do anything.

"He still had his room in the house, but he was never there. I can't even tell you who his best friends were. Harley could have."

She was staring through the window again, recounting the story of a lonely woman, excluded by both son and father, bereft of husband, as if it had happened to someone else, some stranger.

"I used to think maybe it was something I did without realizing it . . . something that made him hate me for the rest of his life. But I gave up trying to figure out what it might have been. If it was my fault, so be it. To tell you the truth, I can't summon enough energy to give a damn."

TJ looked at the woman, wondering how she would appear with a smile on her face, or even an angry frown that would etch lines in her pale freckled skin. Pretty, he thought, if she were animated by any kind of emotion. He walked to the rear of the salon and gazed out at the horizon where sailboats scurried off shore in the stiffening wind.

"Then we'll just have to start with what you *do* know," he finally said, a burr in his voice that made it come out gruff.

"Will you be home tomorrow? I'd like to see his room, even if you never saw him in it, and you can tell me what he was like before he decided to write you off. Who his friends were then. It's not likely he'd drop all of *them* just because you'd become a pain in the ass to him."

TJ turned at the low, coughing sound splitting the silence behind him. He thought she might be choking, or maybe even starting to cry, but it wasn't that. Meg Sullivan was laughing. And she wasn't pretty, she was beautiful.

NINE

Professor DEAN DEUTCH withdrew into the polished wooden warmth of the cabin cruiser *Prime Number* like a startled turtle withdrawing into its shell. Standing in his normal stoop-shouldered posture, he watched through the salon windows the progress of the three men and the dog, led by Sunny Cortez. The old man with the dog hung back while it sniffed at coiled hoses and flemished lines; the others proceeded at a leisurely pace until they reached the slip of the *Emmy T.*, where they stopped. He might have known. Meg Sullivan was not a woman to let things slide. She was bound to sell the boat as quickly as she was able, although he had seen no 'FOR SALE' sign on it these past weeks.

Still, they were probably weekenders—partners perhaps who had pooled their resources to have their own fishing vessel. He would have time during the week. They wouldn't think of changing the lock; he doubted it was feasible anyway. There must not be much of a locksmith trade in Taiwan where those lovely trawler yachts were built. Even the newer ones had the same old locks on the sliding salon doors; locks that could be opened by almost any skeleton key. And he still had his to the *Emmy T.* He fingered the gap-toothed piece of metal in the pocket of his sagging khakis as if it were a talisman, then turned and descended into the small but efficient galley. He would have another cup of tea.

With the steaming mug in hand, Professor Deutch returned to the salon, drawing the curtains once again and seating himself in front of his laptop, where it rested on the gleaming wooden table. While the PC booted up and established the connection for the telnet session to the Supercomputer Facility at the University of California at San Diego, he reviewed his notes. Nothing at Urbana-Champagne. Nor at Carnegie Mellon. The University of Glasgow had given him a mild fright the week before, but it had turned out to be a fluke; some bright graduate student taking a shot in the dark. His results—or perhaps hers he chided himself—weren't even up to the current standard. Still, the approach was unique and it had been close enough to bear watching.

The PC hummed and chirped, gathering its data and saving it to the new external drive, an Iomega JAZ with its one Gigabyte removable disks, recently provided by the University to senior staff now that their cost had dropped again. Probably in lieu of a salary increase according to his more cynical colleagues, for although tuitions were comparable to its more well known contemporary private seats of higher learning, the Santa Cruz University budget was guarded zealously by the financial oversight committee. He chuckled to himself and said aloud what he hadn't said to the other professors at the time.

"Fine with me, I'd rather have it. What do I need more money for? If you wanted wealth, you chose the wrong profession."

While the PC worked, he considered his schedule for the following week. Gloria Chen, his graduate teaching assistant, could handle most of his classes. His paper's publication date was fast approaching; no one would question his need to devote nearly all his time to its completion. There was only the faculty meeting on Wednesday which would require his attendance.

The first beep from the machine indicating it had finished its current task escaped his attention; after a few seconds of inactivity, it beeped again, louder this time, like a nagging wife. Knowing himself as he did, Professor Deutch had programmed the PC to continue beeping until he acknowledged it. Sometimes it took three or four sharp squawks to bring him back from his thoughts, but this time two were enough. He touched the keyboard, disconnecting the current session and redirecting the modem to log onto a local Bulletin Board System.

Immediately upon signing in, a message flashed across the screen declaring the BBS would be shutting down in two minutes. Damn the boy! What in the world was he up to now?

"Well, hello, stranger. Don't I know you?" the young woman behind the bar of the Troon Saloon smiled broadly. "Who's your friend?"

"Hi, Bren," Justin Highstreet said. "Meet Jack Delaney, Scotts Valley PD." The thin, wiry man with him sketched a salute and slid onto a barstool next to Highstreet.

"So that's why we haven't had the pleasure of your company lately," Brenda said, drawing two draft beers and setting them on the bar. "Got you on the hill beats, huh?"

"That's this week," the deputy said. "It was South County for the last couple of months."

Santa Cruz County was divided by the Sheriff's Office into six patrol areas. The three beats covering the mountain communities from Felton to Boulder Creek, and the area from Soquel to Summit Road, were known colloquially as *hill beats* because they covered the not inconsiderable population centers of that segment of the Santa Cruz Mountains, with the exception of Scotts Valley which had its own police department. The south county outside the city limits of Aptos and Watsonville, which townships also had their own police forces, made up two more beats, and the north county which encompassed the village of Troon, about half a mile off Highway 1 near the San Mateo County line, constituted the last, known as the north coast beat.

Named by a wealthy but homesick Scotsman in honor of his Ayrshire birthplace, Troon was one block long. First Street—a name apparently chosen by the founding fathers as an alternative to the ubiquitous *Main* street though there was no Second or Third—intersected on the south with the county road which ran from Highway 1 inland. At its northern end stood the comely bulwark of St. Lucy's, rather grand for its surroundings, serving the faithful of several north county hamlets besides Troon. A grocery-cum-bait shop, a bakery, and a coin laundry were the mercantile neighbors of the only other successful enterprise on First Street—the Troon Saloon—owned and operated by Sam Onnaker and staffed primarily by his twenty year old daughter, Brenda. Sam's wife, Olivia, ran the bakery; the quick-stop bait shop proprietor was his brother-in-law, Leo Cortelli, and the laundry was owned by some nameless conglomerate with operations as far south as Monterey and north as Half Moon Bay. A dark blue van stopped once a week to empty the coin machines; that was all Sam knew, though his wife could probably have provided the van driver's name, age, and number of children by his current spouse if asked. Sam didn't care. They weren't locals.

Highstreet, who lived in a cottage just south of Troon, had worked that beat primarily until six months before when he had requested and received a transfer. But the bad taste of the events that had prompted his request was beginning to fade; maybe it was time to come back home, where he knew everyone and they knew him. He wouldn't be patrolling the beats for much longer, anyway, if things worked out.

Jack Delaney kept an appreciative eye on the fulsome figure of Brenda Onnaker as she moved down the bar to serve some regulars talking quietly at the other end.

"Very nice," he said to Highstreet. "She married?"

"No."

"Even nicer."

The deputy smiled and sipped his beer.

"I didn't ask you over here to court the barmaid, Jack. Do that on your own time. I need to pick your brain about high tech heists."

"What for? You trying to solve a case out from under the Detective Sergeant?"

"I might be."

"I thought you liked the status quo. Driving the beats, nobody bugging you, no desk work to speak of."

"Things change."

"Not without a reason. What's yours?"

Highstreet gazed into his beer glass for a moment. "I'm not sure; naked ambition is the obvious one. Will you buy that?" he asked, half joking.

Delaney gave him a long look, then smiled and shook his head.

"No, not in your case. Mine, maybe. What do you want to know that you don't already?"

"I know the incidence of burglaries and armed robberies is up, especially in Silicon Valley, but what's the market? Wholesale houses? Selling memory chips?"

"Yeah, that's where most of the action is. There are more independent warehouses selling those goddamned things than you can count, and a lot of them aren't too particular where the stuff comes from if the price is right and they can make a few bucks."

"Don't the manufacturers know which vendors are straight and which ones aren't?"

"Probably; but when you're trying to grab a piece of the market share in the biggest boom in recent history, you tend to look the other way a lot. Especially if you've got a hot seller where the demand is outstripping the supply." Delaney sipped his beer and wiped a lean, long-fingered hand across his mouth in satisfaction.

"Then there's the black market action, for lots of stuff besides chips."

"Where do they unload it? Flea markets?"

"Yeah, some of it. Used to be you'd check the flea market for stolen stereos and TVs; still do for that matter. But they've expanded into the computer business now too.

Although I'd guess the conventional flea markets just handle a small fraction of it—most of that kind of take is unloaded through the Internet."

Highstreet shook his head.

"That'd be kind of hard to stake out."

"Tell me," Delaney grimaced.

"There's no shortage of buyers, either—one-horse BBSs set up with used equipment. And kids, of course, the ones whose parents aren't around much, or would be too stoned to notice a computer suddenly appearing if they were. Or even give a shit, for that matter."

"But how would a kid get on line? Don't you have to have some kind of service provider?"

"Not for the BBSs; only a phone and a modem. But if they wanted to hit the big time, there are so many giveaways it wouldn't be hard. They pack those America On Line disks with fifty free hours in cereal boxes these days. Some guy told me the other day he got one with the fucking peanuts on an airline! Take the freebies, quit the service, and plug in the next one. They collect those damned things like baseball cards.

"You know how resourceful a kid is. In fact, a lot of the strong-arm stuff is like *gun for hire*, right out of the movies. Teenagers doing the job for a fee, and adding a little cream to the top by filling their pockets with merchandise they don't hand over. But those are all pretty small fish."

"And the big fish?"

"Organized distributors. Porn, pirated software. They can tap into some legitimate mainframe to store the goodies, but it takes some horsepower just to transfer the stuff to the holding pen, especially imagery. *Dirty peekchures.*" He grinned. "You heard about that one at Livermore Labs some time back, didn't you?"

"A couple years ago? Yeah, I think so. But I didn't pay much attention."

"Porn ring. Had a buncha gigs of very prime pictures stored right there on the home machines of the computer attack gurus of the country. CIAC—*Computer Incident Advisory Committee*—run by the Department of Energy. Those clowns must have laughed their asses off, pulling that one, and the govvies were not amused. There was someone on the inside, of course. There nearly always is."

"Did they catch them?"

"Not at the time. Perps got suspicious and moved out in a hurry—just left the goods. Don't know if they ever caught up with them; probably not."

"What about the heists themselves? Is there usually someone inside on those?"

"Not necessarily. Are you talking about that thing at Pan_Global?" Highstreet nodded. "That's gotta be something else again. They're a software house—they don't manufacture chips or hardware. Might have a few in stock and their own machines could have been stripped, but it wouldn't be enough to make it worthwhile for any of the big boys. They do encryption, digital signatures, security stuff. Whole different ball game."

Highstreet was looking into his empty beer glass as if it were a crystal ball when Brenda reached for it with a delicate hand and let one finger linger on his before removing it.

"Do it again, gentlemen?" she said.

"Sure," Delaney smiled. "This one's on me."

She returned the smile and drew beer into fresh glasses from the freezer.

"Bren, does your mother still make her own lasagna to take out?" Highstreet asked when she had set the refills in front of them.

"Not much any more, but for you I'm sure she'd make an exception."

"How long would it take?"

"About two more beers," she replied. "She's just finishing up a week's worth to put in the freezer."

"Done," Highstreet said.

TEN

RUDY TANG SAT rigid in the scuffed wooden chair, watching messages scroll by on the screen of the 14" monitor whose dreary colors seemed to be hidden behind a dark smoky filter.

"Fucking monitor's about to go now," he said quietly to himself, his eyes glazing as the words passed swiftly, unread, before him. His head ached, and he passed a hand through the thick, spiky black hair on top of his head before reaching back to massage the tightened muscles in his neck and shoulders, beneath the ponytail that flowed down his back. Then he bent forward again, tapping a few keys to launch the shutdown macro; setting in motion the programmed commands which would send warnings at two minute intervals that the BBS would be shutting down in ten minutes. He turned off the monitor. Might as well save what little time the piece of shit had left. It could be a while before he'd be able to replace it.

It wasn't all that easy lifting stuff at *Planned Gabble* anymore. They were such a bunch of dorks. It had been a joke at first, picking up the goodies and slipping them out to his van. Bunch of pudding-faced math drones who couldn't say what day it was, never mind what time. They didn't know what the hell they really had there, let alone if any of it was missing. He could have snagged the Dockers right off their fat asses and they wouldn't have missed them until they had to take a leak. It was a candy store.

But in the last few months things started changing; some of them got a little nosy. Not the *numberheads*—they still walked around in a dream world. The others.

There were looks from some of the twits on the dock, and then they'd brought in that broad a couple of months ago. 'A consultant,' they said. Consultant my ass, Rudy thought. Nosy bitch. No consultant asked that many questions. He'd told Chipper about her; he'd been off when she came. 'Not a problem,' he'd said in that lazy way of his. 'She didn't find anything, did she?' he'd asked, already knowing the answer.

No, she didn't find anything. Rudy had seen to that. Now Chipper was gone. God, that had blown him away. Chipper. Big and bad and dead. Just like that.

Rudy continued to sit there, staring at the blank screen. He felt like jumping up and running outside; through the sagging back gate, choked with blackberry vines, and into the trees that stretched so high the forest floor remained in continuous twilight, even at high noon. Running so far and so long that he would reach a place where nobody could find him.

With an effort, he pushed the fantasy of flight from his mind and rose from the chair. No flight for this bird. Camellia would be waking from her nap soon, and he'd have to supervise while she executed the simple tasks required for the preparation of their evening meal. She had managed without a hitch for more than two weeks now, but that didn't mean anything. He knew from painful experience she could regress at any time, maybe spill something hot and burn herself. Or even set the place on fire.

Not that that would be any great loss, he thought, reviewing the shabby room with its uneven floor and cracks in the plasterboard walls. Camellia tried to brighten it up with colored scarves draped over the sagging couch, and vases of flowers from their back yard. But it was still a dump. The fucking landlord wouldn't fix anything.

Rudy turned to see his younger sister emerge from her tiny bedroom. She had made no sound but he knew she was there, her delicate oval face wreathed in smiles and that stupid cat in her arms, lying on its back like a baby. She wore a gauzy broomstick skirt with a pretty blue tee shirt and she looked like a princess from some fairytale he had long since forgotten, her thick straight hair flowing down her back almost to her waist.

"Shall I fix dinner, Rudy?" she said. "I can do it by myself now."

"Sure, little sister, I know you can."

"Will Chipper be coming, or just us?"

"Just us, Camellia. Chipper won't be coming anymore." Her lovely face puckered into a quizzical frown, then the expression faded to one of strikingly mature resignation. She turned toward the small kitchen with head bowed, the cat jumping from her arms and running ahead, looking for something to eat, the lazy bastard.

It was her birthday in a week. He'd have to find something for a gift, as well as a replacement for the freaking monitor. Shit.

She'd be twenty-one on the third of November. He could hardly believe it. Twenty-one. Maybe he would get a cake. They should celebrate. It wasn't anybody's fault; certainly not hers. An act of God his mother had said so many years ago, when he was old enough to understand. Rudy, like his father, had subscribed more to the theory of a nasty trick of fate, but the outcome was the same. Jesus, how long had *they* been gone now? He could barely remember their faces. He sighed and shook his head, clearing the memories.

Yeah, a cake and some nice present. He could handle that. No reason to quit celebrating her birthday just because that sweet, gentle mind had stopped having birthdays when she was seven.

ELEVEN

SUNNY CORTEZ EMERGED from the engine room of the *Emmy T.* on hands and knees, and before lowering the three-step ladder which masked its entrance from the forward cabin, called up to TJ.

"You want to take a look down here?"

TJ, who had been watching Megan Sullivan's purposeful stride down the dock with more than mild appreciation, turned.

"Down where?"

"The engine room. If you're going to keep her and run her, there's some stuff you need to know. You said you wanted some help."

"So I did. Thanks. How do I get down there?" TJ said, peering around the upraised ladder, which blocked the entrance to the forward cabin.

Sunny lowered the ladder and when TJ had descended, raised it again like a drawbridge, fastening the brass hook to hold it in place. He gestured to the brightly lit opening and TJ, hunkering down to get a better view, saw a vast expanse of sparkling aluminum deck plate. At what appeared to be the far end, but was probably just beyond the midline of the boat, stood an enormous engine, silver like the deck plate, with a large metal plate on the front inscribed with the legend BMW MARINE. TJ was struck not only by the cleanliness, but by the almost military order. His idea of a ship's engine room, admittedly owing to Hollywood's questionable interpretations since he had never seen a real one, was of sweating bodies, oil-soaked rags, and clutter.

He'd expected the arterial maze of internal plumbing; large black hoses and small copper tubing, but it was all neatly fastened to the white Fiberglas sides of the hull in artistic symmetry. Four heavy round plates with rectangular handles, each large enough to allow a slender sailor entry, were fitted to the hull in front of the engine, two on each side.

"What are those?" he said, pointing.

"Access doors to the fuel tanks," Sunny said. "In case you have to get in and clean them out. Four hundred gallon capacity; single engine diesel, 160 horsepower. She won't win you any races, and singles don't maneuver like twins, but she has stern thrusters. They're better in some ways than having twin engines."

"Oh, good. What the hell are stern thrusters?"

"Two small props on either side of the stern; they counter rotate, give you precise control in tight quarters. At thirteen tons she doesn't exactly stop on a dime, so you'd better be sure she's going where you want her to.

"Want to take her out?" Cortez said.

"Yeah, I'd like that, if you have the time." He looked at his watch.

"You expecting someone else?"

"No, not really. She'd have been here by now if she was going to. Let's go."

Smiley relaxed on the salon sofa next to Clyde, while TJ and Uncle Beau stood behind Sunny Cortez as he pushed the starter button at the helm and the big diesel coughed into rumbling life. A plume of blue smoke erupted from the stern as the engine settled into a deep-throated hum. Cortez slipped out the sliding door at the helm seat and jumped onto the dock, giving TJ a momentary start until he realized Sunny was unfastening the lines that held the boat securely in its slip and probably wasn't expecting him to solo just yet. He and Beau moved out onto the deck, watching Cortez perform the routine tasks with enviable ease, loosening the sleek lines from their cleats and tossing them over the sides back onto the boat. At the stern railing, TJ looked out over the gently rolling water of the harbor to see an otter the size of a spaniel lolling on its back, drifting aimlessly. When Cortez came back onto the deck, he pointed.

"You're not going to run over him, are you?"

"He'll get out of the way. He's probably smarter than both of us put together."

Back inside the salon, Cortez checked the panel of circuit breakers beside the helm, calling them off for TJ's benefit as he flipped selected ones on.

". . .radio, depth sounder, . . . and for God's sake don't forget the thrusters. You'll play hell getting out of here if you do."

TJ wondered why he couldn't just reach down and correct a lapse of memory if he suffered one until Sunny again stepped out the door, motioning for him to follow, and mounted the steps to the fly bridge. The helm controls were duplicated above, but not the breaker switches—thus the warning. The improved visibility from the bridge was obviously the right choice for tight maneuvering, but if you were caught up here with the thrusters off, she'd be adrift while you sprinted below to correct your mistake.

TJ watched in fascination as Cortez put the boat in reverse and she began to move gently backward. He touched the tiny metal joystick which controlled the stern thrusters, and with a low-pitched whine from the counter-rotating props she began a smooth turn, just like a car backing out of a parking place.

When they had negotiated the other docks and were heading out the mouth of the harbor, between the rock jetties that marked its entrance, Cortez advanced the throttle and finally took hold of the wheel; he hadn't touched it until then, guiding the big vessel in close quarters using only the joystick. As they passed between the red and green channel markers at the end of the jetties, the gentle swell of the water became a decided roll, but the bow of the *Emmy T.* nosed into it steadily, cutting the water into white curls which flung spray onto the decks below.

"Green on your right going out, red right returning," Cortez said, nodding at the markers. "That's how you remember where you are in the ship channels. Or when you're coming back in fog. You don't want to get caught on the wrong side of the red buoy or you'll end up on the beach."

"'Red, right, returning.' I believe I can remember that."

The wind whipped TJ's hair as he turned to watch the land slowing receding. Uncle Beau was leaning lazily over the stern railing, for all the world like he had done this a thousand times. Turning back to look over the bow, TJ saw two tiny specks that were boats on the horizon, and beyond that nothing but sparkling sea, dotted with foaming whitecaps. All the way to Hawaii, he thought.

"A man could get used to this without any trouble at all," he said softly, squinting into the afternoon sun, but the wind snatched his words away and flung them over his shoulder.

TWELVE

"YOU DIDN'T MAKE this lasagna," Lisbee said.

"What makes you say that? What's wrong with it?"

"Nothing; it's great. That's why I said it."

"You think if it's great I couldn't have made it?" Justin said, affronted. "The greatest chefs in the world are men."

He refilled her wine glass, the glowing Merlot winking a reflection from the small fireplace when she raised it to her lips. She wasn't sure what she had expected; not paper plates maybe, but neither the crisp white cloth, heavy blue stoneware and large round-bowled wine glasses that filled your hand. None of it was expensive, but all was somehow right—comfortable and satisfying. She looked up and smiled mischievously.

"True. But that's all they do. There are no sheriff chefs."

"Sheriff chefs? Why not? And what about Spenser? He's a helluva lot better cook than Susan. She can't even boil water."

"He's private. Makes his own hours. It takes time to be a really good cook." Lisbee wrinkled her brow in concentration as she savored the lasagna, spiced perfectly, the clingy cheese melting on her tongue. "And soul. It takes that, too—the soul of a poet."

"Are you suggesting I have no soul?" Justin said stiffly.

"Not at all. I'm suggesting you have very little *time* to cook, with the shifts you work. Or tell me you work."

Highstreet glowered at her.

"I made the fucking *salad*."

Lisbee nearly choked on her wine, and set it back on the table before the inevitable coughing fit could make her splash it in her lap.

"And a very soulful salad it is," she said when she had recovered. "Is there any more?"

Highstreet rose solemnly and disappeared into the small kitchen, returning with a large crockery bowl. He stood behind her, leaning across her shoulder to empty its contents onto her salad plate. She tilted her head back slightly to see a smile twitching at the corners of his mouth just before he set the bowl down, cupped her chin in his hand, and kissed her.

It was Lisbee's experience as a child that if she longed for something so intensely it began to rule her conscious thoughts, the realization was nearly always a disappointment. She smiled fatuously in the darkness of Justin Highstreet's bedroom, contemplating the first instance she could recall of reality outstripping anticipation. She touched the warm length of him beside her, to assure herself this was indeed reality, and he stretched and yawned.

"I'm still hungry," he said.

"That's because you didn't finish your lasagna."

"Who's fault was that?"

"*I* didn't start this," she said indignantly.

"You asked for more salad."

"And that did it?"

"Uhm hmm."

"Amazing. I'll have to add that to my bag of tricks. Do you have a microwave? I can warm up the lasagna for you."

"No."

Lisbee sighed.

"Well, it'll have to go in the oven then. That's going to take a little time."

"We've got time," he said, extending an arm across her body, pulling her closer.

"Who *did* make that lasagna, anyway?" she said, her words muffled against his chest. He didn't answer, and she decided it probably didn't matter.

THIRTEEN

At 5:22 ON SUNDAY morning there was at least another hour before dawn, and the lights in the parking area cast shimmering arcs of illumination around their feet in the damp heavy air. The vintage gray van moved slowly over the speed bumps, its ancient springs protesting mildly. It stopped in the shadows between the darkened side of the building and the fence which bordered the golf course. Rudy Tang got out, closing the door quietly and zipping his tattered fatigue jacket up to the throat. He walked confidently around the building, past the loading dock and the rear door which had been boarded over after the police left, to the employee entrance on the other side where he inserted his magnetized badge into the electronic lock and heard the satisfying click as the bolt snapped back. Pulling the door gently open, Rudy slipped inside into the darkness.

Extracting a small flashlight from his jacket pocket, Rudy made his way down the empty hallway, past darkened offices, to the double wooden doors leading to the rear area of the building which housed both Pan Global's stock room and the Shipping and Receiving cages. The three messages he had intercepted when he'd finally brought the BBS back up for four hours had intimated that the raid had been less than successful. A lot had been left behind due to the ill-timed appearance of a pre-dawn golfer looking for a lost ball. Pan Global's zealous management would no doubt have brought in a clean-up squad by now, but Rudy guessed they wouldn't have made much of a dent in the chaos as yet.

He was right. There was still a lot to choose from. He worked quickly, scanning the toppled shelving and avoiding the litter of boxes on the floor. It almost looked more like vandalism than efficient theft, but he knew that was how they often worked, flinging unwanted booty aside, smashing things that got in the way in their haste, sharing a nervous giggle.

As he had expected, the six new monitors that had arrived three days before and were yet to be installed in the offices of some senior mathematicians, had not been touched. Still in their packing boxes, they were stacked in a corner near the sliding rear doors where the delivery van had left them. Too heavy and cumbersome to fool with on a hit and run raid, their profit margin too small to make the effort worthwhile, they had been ignored by the thieves. Rudy began to sweat as he shifted the heavy boxes, leaving five of them in carefully calculated disarray to match the rest of the scene. It would be days before Pan Global could come up with a full list of what was missing; they would think the one monitor he had chosen, one of the smaller ones, was part of the heist, the rest left because they had run out of time or space to carry them away.

Rudy considered using one of the transport carts to carry the monitor to his van, but he was afraid of the clatter it would make on the asphalt drive. There shouldn't be anyone around this early, but no point in asking for trouble—joggers were known to be about at all hours, day or night. He slid the box against the roll-up door, raised it carefully, and pushed the monitor onto the dock outside, then closed the door gently and slid the locking bolt home.

With a flush of imminent success blunting his natural inclination to get out quickly, Rudy decided to take a few extra minutes to scour the office areas. There could be some loose cash laying around; these guys were dumb enough to do that. They could contribute to Camellia's birthday present without knowing it—a good cause.

Rudy was right for the second time that morning. He had picked up just under thirty dollars by the time he made his way to the executive suite of offices. In the slender beam of his flashlight the rectangular foyer yielded a secretary's desk and four upholstered chairs, all on thick beige carpet. Three doors with heavy brass nameplates opened off the foyer but as he tried each one in turn, he found they were all locked. Turning to the secretary's desk Rudy tugged at the center drawer, the most likely place for loose change. Also locked. They were a little smarter up here, he thought, or maybe they just had more to lose.

He considered prying open the desk drawer but decided it wasn't worth the time it would take and was about to leave, content with his take, when he noticed a small package in the two tiered file tray on the corner of the otherwise empty desktop. It had a red "RUSH" label and a post-it note with a scrawled "*Mail Today!*" stuck on it.

"Her ass is in trouble," Rudy said softly to himself, imagining the chewing out she was in for on Monday morning. In an uncharacteristic gesture of chivalry he picked the thing up, thinking he would drop it in a mailbox somewhere, and glanced briefly at the address label. *Professor Dean Deutch, Bel Harbor Marina, Moss Landing CA 95039.* A little wave of shock ran through him—the Professor was a friend of Chipper's; *had* been a friend he corrected himself.

"Shit," he breathed into the darkness, then stuck the package inside his jacket and made for the exit at the side of the building. Time to load the monitor and get the hell out; way past time, in fact. He'd worry about the package later, maybe deliver it himself, talk to the old man about Chipper. He didn't dare mention him to Camellia anymore because she couldn't comprehend that he was dead, wouldn't be coming back, and Rudy couldn't stand the hope in her eyes. Yeah, the Professor might be good to talk to. He really needed *someone* for Christ's sake.

Rudy Tang slipped out the electronic door and disappeared into the darkness toward the loading dock.

FOURTEEN

LISBEE WHIPPED THE Mustang into the left lane of Highway 1 just south of New Brighton Beach and, nearing eighty, cruised past the offending Toyota, then eased off until she was back to her normal seventy-three or -four miles per hour. TJ smiled, knowing she would only be able to maintain it for half a mile, until she reached the rear guard of the next covey of prudent motorists. She was sure-handed and competent at the wheel, enjoying the exhilaration of speed and motion, the hot little car an extension of her own personality. It was a skill they shared. He wondered idly if it was inherited; if there was a *love of speed* trait hiding somewhere in the gene pool, contributing in centuries past to daring horsemen and Roman charioteers.

"Well *that* was my first mistake," she said, continuing the saga of her meeting earlier that morning with Cory Floyd, Pan Global's *Lothario* among executive officers.

"I should have known he was setting me up, suggesting we go to breakfast. He had to know there's nowhere you can get so much as a bowl of oatmeal around here on a Sunday morning without a 45-minute wait, but I never thought he was that subtle. So when he said 'Come by the house, then,' I thought 'Okay—good, the wife and kiddies will be milling around somewhere' and I walked right into it."

"The wife and kiddies weren't milling?"

"They were not. Off to Grandma's house or a mall walk or whatever wives and kiddies of the young and upwardly mobile do on a Sunday morning—maybe even church. I was suspicious the minute he opened the door with that well-fed grin and led me into his home office. There were book shelves and a PC all right, but there was also a leather couch the size of a double bed."

TJ grinned, feeling a moment of pity for the overmatched CEO.

"How'd you handle it? Did he chase you around the couch?"

"It never came to that. When I gathered he was there alone, I told him I wanted some coffee. He looked sort of alarmed, like he thought coffee came ready made at the end of some feminine hand, so I offered to make some, and said I was sure we'd be more comfortable talking in the kitchen. I figured it would be a lot more difficult to get his libido in gear surrounded by stainless steel and Solarian."

"I don't know about that. Your mother always looked mighty pretty in an apron with her face all pink and a curl falling across her forehead. I seem to recall a few meals that had to be warmed over, before you were around bawling for your dinner."

Lisbee gave him an arch look, then turned her gaze back to the road.

"What's your position on the sensual aspects of salad?"

"Salad?"

"Never mind. Fortunately, Cory doesn't have that much imagination."

"Did you manage to get any information out of him about Chipper Sullivan?"

"I think we can eliminate him as a definitive source. He doesn't remember the kid—I really didn't expect him to. He's not the type of exec to walk the floor and get the real lowdown on how things are going from the people who make it happen. Prefers to run the ship from his mahogany office. But he said I can come by tomorrow and talk to anyone I like. And speaking of ship, do you think this guy Cortez will take us out in your boat?"

"I don't know. Depends on how busy he is."

They drove in silence until the freeway dissolved into the two lane road approaching Moss Landing. In the thick, meandering Sunday traffic, with no opportunity for passing, Lisbee relaxed philosophically behind the wheel.

"When are you seeing Megan Sullivan again?"

"This afternoon."

"You don't believe she really didn't know much about Chipper's life or friends like she told you?"

"No," TJ said.

"What's she like?"

"Hard to say. Could be she and the boy weren't close, like she said. She acts tough, but that could be a front. She's lost her father and her son in a little over a month. You'd have to be pretty damned cold not to be affected by that to some extent." TJ recalled the bark of laughter that had animated the woman's face. Meg Sullivan might be a lot of things—but cold wasn't one of them.

"Beau! How nice to see you," Ellen said as she threw the door wide and reached up to give Beau Billings a hug.

"You're looking mighty fetching today, Ellen."

Clyde Allbright's wife smoothed her denim skirt, a pink flush rising to her cheeks. "I think you'd say that if I was still in my bathrobe with my hair in curlers. Come in. Would you like some coffee? It's fresh."

"That would be fine. And I wonder if you'd mind if I got a cup of water, too. I've got Smiley in the car, and he might get a little dry before I leave."

"Of course I'd mind! You go bring him in here this minute. There's no need for him to wait in the car."

Beau's weathered face crinkled into a smile.

"He'll like that. He's like an old preacher I used to know back in Oklahoma. Likes nothing better than to go visiting and meet folks."

Ellen stood at the door watching as Beau walked back to his station wagon, the black briar cane swinging freely in his hand. The hound exploded from the car when he opened the door, bounded to a small conifer in the neat front lawn, then returned at a curt hand signal to follow Beau, tail wagging and tongue lolling.

"Clyde's on the patio reading the paper," Ellen said as they stood in the sunny kitchen while she poured coffee into thick stoneware mugs.

"Well it never hurts a man to keep up with world events. I still prefer the newspaper; those folks on the television seem to spend more time thanking one another than they do telling me what's going on."

"I'm afraid the only world events Clyde's really interested in are the football scores. Why don't you go join him?"

"I'll do that directly, but I really came to see you," Beau said and smiled at the startled look on her face.

"Me?"

"Yes, ma'am. I've got a nice leg of lamb I'm going to roast this afternoon, and I was wondering if I might get the recipe for those potatoes you fixed the last time we were here for dinner—that is if it's not a family secret or anything."

"Oh, Lord, I don't have any family secrets, but I can't remember what I fixed. What were they like?"

"Well, I think they were baked, only they were cut in half and kind of crispy. Had some kind of cheese on the tops I seem to recall."

"Romano—yes, those *are* good. And there's nothing to fixing them. Just cut them in half, garlic salt and pepper on the cut side, then put them cut side down in melted butter and Romano cheese and bake at—let's see, around 350 for forty-five minutes or so. Here, I'll write it down for you." She began rummaging in a drawer next to the sink for a pencil and paper.

Beau seated himself at the kitchen table, Smiley at his feet. While Ellen wrote out the recipe on a 3-by-5 index card, Beau stroked the hound's ears and he lifted his muzzle and arched his neck to promote a quick scratch.

"Lisbee tells me you're going back to college; that right?"

"Oh, yes! Did she really? I talked to Meg just this morning and she's getting me the admission forms."

"Is that a lady friend of yours? Meg?"

"Megan Sullivan, yes. I've known her for years. We met at a literature discussion group, oh, ages ago. She works at the university, in Career Counseling I think, or maybe it's actually *in* Admissions—I can never remember. She's had a tragic life, poor thing. A really bad marriage, but that was a long time ago, and now her only son committing suicide, and her father dying of cancer, all within a matter of weeks. I don't know how she copes."

"Is that right?" Beau said, reflecting on the blind follies that would let a man search high and low for answers that were to be found in his own backyard. Ellen Allbright was bursting with concern for her friend. A pump barely in need of priming to overflow.

"Poor woman must be beside herself," Beau said and sat back with his coffee, ready to be a most sympathetic listener.

". . . she's got a backbone of pure steel, but there's only so much even a strong person like Meg can take, after all."

"That's true enough. What about her ex-husband? You said it was a bad marriage; does she ever hear from him, you know, get a bad time or anything?"

"Oh I don't think so. No, I'm sure she'd have mentioned it. She's not one to hold things back; not from a friend. I don't think she's even heard from that *bastard* . . . ." Ellen blushed mightily. "Excuse me, please Beau. I don't usually talk that way. Anyway, not since Chipper was very small. She always said the boy didn't remember anything about his father and that was just the way she wanted it. Wouldn't hear his name mentioned even. That's why Chipper grew up a Sullivan."

"Funny the boy didn't press it when he got older, though. You know how kids are. Curiosity of a bear cub, especially about their own folks."

Ellen had started to fix a fresh pot of coffee, having heard a rumble from the direction of the patio which indicated that Clyde probably needed another cup. As the steam began drifting from the coffeemaker, she leaned toward the patio door.

"Beau's here, Clyde . . . I'm just fixing more coffee. We'll be out in a minute."

"Yes, he must have been," she continued, turning back to Beau. "Curious about his father, I mean. I can't recall Meg ever mentioning it though; how she handled it. I wonder if she told him the truth or made up some story?"

"She the kind of woman who'd do that? Make up a story?"

Ellen looked at Beau with a frown clouding her normally cheerful face.

"Oh yes. I think any woman would if she was trying to protect her child from something ugly. Don't you?"

FIFTEEN

Cory Floyd Paced the confines of his study energetically, like he did most things. He had nearly forgotten the morning's missed opportunity with Elizabeth Billings and was struggling with the implications of the break-in at Pan Global. Only occasionally, as his eye caught the expanse of the deep red leather couch, site of numerous amorous successes, did a pang of regret remind him of this recent failure.

"Why now, for God's sake?" he mumbled softly, back on the more troubling topic of what he should do to soften the blow that was bound to come tomorrow when the story hit the papers and the shit hit the fan. He'd have to have a statement for the press; that was obvious. And he could handle that. No real damage had been done, after all. A little embarrassing, sure, but he could smooth it over. No problem. He was good at that kind of gilt-edged bullshit. It was the other thing.

Lowry. The next phase of their talks. Day after tomorrow. Should he call and warn him, or just wait until they met? How best to play it down? Not call because it obviously wasn't that important, or call because there was no way of telling what the goddamned newspapers might print? Reporters loved shit-stirring—especially if it splashed on somebody who could buy and sell them twenty times. Their way of getting even.

Better call. Get his side in first. Make sure that it wasn't pushed out of proportion no matter what the rags did tomorrow.

Floyd stretched out along the leather couch, phone to his ear, and dialed the number he had memorized. When the metallic voice spoke its directions, he punched in his unlisted home office number and hung up. He lay back, hands behind his head, prepared to wait. It could be a while.

With the feel of the smooth leather against the length of his body, Cory's mind returned to more physical thoughts. He wasn't sure Elizabeth Billings was going to be attainable, especially if that big Sheriff's deputy had his oar in. That didn't mean he'd quit trying, but in the meantime there were other avenues. He smiled widely, his square white teeth gleaming through his sunlamp tan. Walking to his desk, Cory picked up the other phone, his regular home number, and began to dial. It wouldn't do to have the private line tied up with a busy signal.

Lowry hated the goddamned West Coast. Hated the sprawling burned out desert that was LA, kept green beneath the poisoned air with unearned money like an old whore winking under an inch of makeup. But LA was a joke, and everybody knew it except the ones who lived there. What he really hated was the Bay Area.

San Francisco, with its improbable skyline and bridges and fog. A stage set. And worse, the arrogant opulence of Silicon Valley, where smart-mouthed twenty-five year olds ran multi-million dollar companies from the cell phones in their BMWs. Glutted with money, leftist ideals, and the unshakable opinion that they were right and everyone else was wrong. There were leftists in the Beltway, too, but they were savvy leftists; they knew how to play the game. These clowns didn't even know it *was* a game. But simple minded or not, they wielded a certain amount of power and that was probably what he hated most Lowry admitted to himself. He was a pragmatist and not prone to self delusion.

The plane circled the sparkling bay and began its approach to SFO, nearly skimming the whitecaps before the gray brown earth and concrete of the landing strip appeared through the window. Though his business was some forty miles south and beyond, Lowry always flew into SFO, rejecting the *nouveau riche* San Jose Airport as the backwater it still was, in spite of its new terminal built for and subsequently rejected by American Airlines as a western hub. Over the last thirty years, the City Council had annexed every inch that wasn't nailed down by its smaller neighbors, and even given the sleepy giant a skyline in a massive effort to renovate the decaying downtown area and take full advantage of the economic boom. But it seemed to Lowry like dressing Cinderella for the ball without first having made sure she took a bath. There remained beneath her skirts an odor of indolent poverty; whole new cultures had arrived to add their own unique contributions to crime in the streets, and in spite of their best efforts, it could not be explained away by the liberal element as merely diversity in action.

The terminal was not overly crowded for a Sunday afternoon—a few vacationers coming home and the usual business travelers getting a jump on the week. The young woman at the Hertz counter was one he had dealt with before. Under neat cornrow braids festooned with multi-colored beads her pleasant face held what might have been a genuine smile, but certainly wasn't the broad commercial one she was paid to display.

"Afternoon, Mr. Lowry," she said as she tapped the computer, then presented him with the contract for signature and the keys to an anonymous silver Taurus 4-door sedan.

When he had retrieved his drivers license and credit card she grinned broadly and said in a husky voice, "See you next time."

He smiled and pushed a twenty-dollar bill across the counter toward her. She tucked it into her skirt pocket and winked. On their first encounter he had explained politely that he was a man who's habit it was to tip generously for a little extra service, and it would be worth her while if she could possibly refrain from telling him to '*Have a nice day*.' She had.

Lowry locked the door of his room at the Santa Clara Marriott as soon as the bellhop departed, well pleased with the man whose habit it was to tip generously. He made one local call announcing his arrival and began unpacking his nondescript canvas carry on. From a padded compartment in the middle of the bag he extracted a laptop computer which he placed on the desk next to the phone.

There was no question of his using the machine while in flight, and Lowry had always transported it tucked safely among his clothing long before the latest wave of airport thefts had begun. The small shoulder bags used by most business travelers were glaring targets at the security checkpoints, where teams of thieves had proved highly successful in separating them from their owners; one snatching the bag as it emerged on the x-ray conveyor belt while the other blocked the unwary victim by setting off the alarm bell in the walk-through arch until his accomplice was lost in the throng of boarders.

A notebook computer snatched from the shoulder of its parent in a crowd was likely to have been stolen for its intrinsic value; they brought top dollar on the black market. But the wave of skilled thefts by more than one person was a hallmark of espionage, industrial or otherwise. It wasn't the machines themselves that were the target, but the data they contained, and Lowry was well aware of this. It was his business to be.

Lowry was the Director of the Electronic Data Integrity Service—EDIS in the ever present world of bureaucratic acronyms—which was a relatively small and highly elite organization tucked safely among much larger intelligence agencies of the Federal government. Because of its mission, EDIS enjoyed a kind of parental protection which was denied its sister agencies by an administration that was in love, however misguidedly, with a dream of the digital future and all the rewards that might be reaped therefrom in the dawn of the twenty-first century. Its budget line item, though inflated, was so paltry compared to its kin that EDIS had never been questioned in Lowry's memory. Which was just as well. He flew first class, stayed in the finest hotels, and never wanted for equipment or manpower, though he used little of either. He liked to think of himself as the governing force that assured taxpayers value for expenditure. Lowry was a patriot.

He was also a realist, and had seen to it that in the unlikely event someone *did* get hold of the laptop, they would be exercised to the limit to get anything from it. He employed screen locks on start-up, and if by chance the intruder got past those, all files on its hard disk were encrypted with the latest and best technology in the commercial field. Though his position provided him access to the tightly held government-developed encryption software as well, he never used it. There were two reasons for this: first, if compromised, it would be a black eye for his service and the government in general; second, and more important to Lowry, it simply wasn't as good as the commercially developed products.

He seated himself at the desk and began the routine of booting up the little machine. Moving swiftly through the litany of checkpoints, he connected it to the telephone jack behind the desk and activated the laptop's internal modem. His call was to a small but legitimate Internet Service Provider in Herndon, Virginia, where he kept a personal account. All communications received through his ISP were encrypted and routed through anonymous remailers. Nothing could be traced back to EDIS.

The messages were routine. He answered those that required it and shut the laptop down. Almost immediately the phone rang. He picked it up and a recorded voice recited a telephone number, which he wrote down. He didn't need to reboot the laptop to check who the number belonged to—there were only two people he was out here to see, one in the 650 area code covering the peninsula south of San Francisco, and one in the new 831 for Santa Cruz county, recently split off from the burgeoning 408 code which encompassed the majority of Silicon Valley. This was an 831 number and would be the private, unlisted line of Cory Floyd, CEO at Pan Global Inc., in the Santa Cruz Mountains near Scotts Valley. The recorded voice, routed through a local office to the number of his hotel, meant that Floyd had tried to reach him for some reason. Wanted to talk before their scheduled meeting. Usually not a good sign.

Lowry sighed, put away the rest of his things, and changed into slacks and sport shirt before picking up the phone and dialing the number.

SIXTEEN

JUSTIN HIGHSTREET GRINNED foolishly as he touched some keys—a little less clumsily than before?—and the screen of his Macintosh bloomed into life. He was still a bit nervous on his own, even after Lisbee's assurance that even *he* would have a hard time breaking a Mac, but there was no denying that against all odds he was having fun. On his first Sunday off for weeks, he had hurried through only the most compelling of household chores that had piled up, just so he could get at the little beast and practice.

Justin rarely watched television and only skimmed the newspapers when the opportunity presented itself, which was infrequently in his line of work, but it was still impossible to miss the Internet craze that had swept the country. It seemed that even the local gas stations had a Web page these days. *Dotcom* had become an overused part of the lexicon, and he had been surprised to find that Internet and Web were not just different terms for the same thing. The Web, as Elizabeth Billings had described it to him, was the commute lane for the bandwagon everyone was jumping on. Powerful and elegant as it was, there was still a teeming world of technological nuts and bolts beneath its colorful facade that Highstreet would do well to understand.

She had set the thing up and had it humming in a matter of minutes that night after they had walked on the beach. He recalled an impulse to apologize for his selection, thinking he might have been foolish to buy the Mac without really knowing what he was getting; only knowing the guy who sold it to him was okay. Instead, he'd merely commented, "This one's good enough then?" as she sat fiddling and tweaking.

"More than that. It's a *Cadillac* Mac. You lucked out."

"Frank said it's obsolete—they don't make them anymore."

"You could say that about any PC more than three months old. It's a cutthroat market; they bring them out every time there's a new bell or whistle that'll get some press and a jump on the other sharks in the pool. Doesn't matter. The older ones still do the job, and do it damn well for a long time."

He'd been grinning and silently congratulating himself, watching her work, until she turned to look up at him with a frown wrinkling her forehead.

"But for God's sake, don't buy anything else until you ask me first. Unless you like throwing money away. Most computer salespeople are worse than used car dealers."

"Yes, ma'am."

He shook his head and brushed the thoughts aside, watching the activity on the screen that indicated his email was being transferred from the local Internet provider's server to the hard disk on his machine. Smiling to himself, he decided to take Lisbee's last word of advice and just relax and have fun with the damn thing.

He began by exercising two of the Internet workhorses she had demonstrated for him—scanning a couple of the more radical newsgroups in the area, and bringing in the latest hacking advisories via FTP. Though she had also set him up with the latest Netscape web browser, which would have made these tasks button-clicking child's play, he followed her written instructions and used the shareware applications she had downloaded for each individual effort. The little programs themselves were elegantly simple to use and he encountered no problems. Flushed with his mild successes, he turned to reading his email.

It consisted of one newsletter on Macintosh topics—most of which he didn't understand—and a three-line note sent off by Lisbee that morning that just missed being downright steamy. Grinning, he clicked the *reply* button and answered it in kind, adding a PS suggesting it was her turn to cook tonight since he'd be back on a long duty cycle in the morning.

Having run through his string of tricks without a slip, he sat staring at the screen, fingers poised above the keys, wondering what new things he could safely try on his own. Elizabeth had said it was nearly impossible to *break* a Macintosh, but he didn't want to bend it either—not when he was just getting started. Then he recalled Jack Delaney's mention of local Bulletin Board Systems that might be used in the sale of less than legitimate computer gear. Real police work, from the comfort of his own cottage. He reached for the phone, remembering as the piercing shriek assaulted his ear that he had to log off and break the Mac's modem connection first. When his ears quit ringing, he dialed. It rang five times before Delaney picked it up.

"Jack, Highstreet."

There was a muffled response from Delaney and some commotion in the background. Music, and another voice in a higher range.

"I know you're not asleep at 1:00 in the afternoon, but I apologize if I got you out of bed," Highstreet said, smiling.

"S'all right. What's up?"

"How do I get on one of those Bulletin Board Systems?"

"What?"

"The ones you talked about yesterday. You said they were sometimes used to unload hot computer gear."

"What're you, at work?"

Rather than explain about his new acquisition, Highstreet just made a noncommittal noise that could have been interpreted as affirmative.

"Well, just dial them up, buddy."

"I gathered that much; where do you get the number? They're not in the yellow pages, are they?"

"Not the kind you're looking for. I'd have to check the files at work. Can it wait?"

"Sure, I guess so. Sorry to have bothered you."

"No problem. I'll do the same for you some time. When's your next date with the lasagna queen?"

"You'll be the last to know," Highstreet said, laughing, and hung up the phone.

SEVENTEEN

"HELLO PROFESSOR DEUTCH. What a lovely boat. Have you had it long?"

Dean Deutch turned with a start, his mail, which he had just collected from the Harbor Master's Office, clutched in one long-fingered hand. The young woman standing on the dock, dark hair flowing in the offshore breeze, was familiar, but he couldn't place her.

"This is my father, TJ Billings," she said, smiling and gesturing toward the tall man with graying hair who stood beside her. Billings. The memory clicked into place.

"Elizabeth! Of course, how delightful to see you here of all places. My pleasure, Mr. Billings. Your daughter was brilliant in my classes, though perhaps not as brilliant as she might have been had she paid more attention to the projects I assigned rather than the ones she preferred to pursue!" Deutch beamed at them.

"Looks like we're going to be neighbors," she said. "TJ just inherited a boat." She nodded at the *Emmy T.*

"Splendid, splendid. Come aboard and have a cup of tea and tell me all about it, won't you? Of course you will. Haven't given up your computers for a seaman's lot have you? What a waste that would be." He waved them on with his hand full of mail, sliding back the door to the salon of the Chris Craft, then busied himself in the galley while they stood just inside the main living space, admiring the old vessel. It was spacious and elegant, the wood paneled walls gleaming richly in the manner of a Victorian gingerbread home lovingly restored. A glass-fronted hutch against the forward bulkhead, filled with antique china and bric-a-brac, projected the atmosphere of an earlier, gentler time.

"Professor of what?" TJ said in a stage whisper as sounds of running water and the clank of crockery issued from below.

"Math department. Computational number theory. Rooms full of supercomputers chunking away in tandem for years to break down numbers with enough digits to run the length of this dock."

"Did you see the name on this boat? It's the *Prime Number*."

Lisbee laughed. "It would be. That's what they use for encryption keys. The prime factors of humungous integers that would take dozens of supercomputers a decade to come up with. Then they change to even bigger numbers every two or three years to keep ahead of the advances in the speed of the hardware—and the hackers. One of the commercial encryption companies runs this contest every year and gives prizes for factoring any of the numbers on their list. To keep on top of the cracking techniques."

"Pan Global?"

"No," Lisbee said, "another one; but *Planned Gabble* keeps an eye on the results, you can bet. Everyone in the business does, including the government."

"How would a hacker get access to a room full of supercomputers?"

"If they're legitimate students, through their universities; otherwise they can crack into them from outside and use someone else's account. It's a game, mostly. One-upmanship. I don't know of a single case where anyone went to all that trouble to steal some credit card numbers. The gain isn't worth the effort, and they could do that a lot easier by breaking into the data files on a commercial website—or rifling trashcans for that matter."

The rich aroma of strong tea began to float from the galley, and was shortly followed by Professor Deutch, tray in hand. An aged *Brown Betty* teapot squatted on the tray, surrounded by mugs, sugar bowl and creamer.

"I'll be Mother, shall I?" he said, pouring the steaming brew into the mugs.

"Jesus," TJ thought to himself, "*Tea* served up by *Mother*. I've come a long way from Caddo County, Oklahoma, and a hip flask." He couldn't think of anyone less likely to be *Mother* than the gangling Professor Deutch, but he smiled and accepted a cup, holding it aloft in a toast.

"Cheers."

"Indeed, cheers. And welcome aboard. The *Emmy T.* How extraordinary. I had no idea Harley Sullivan was a relative of yours."

"He wasn't," TJ said.

"But you inherited her, Elizabeth said, didn't you my dear?"

Lisbee glanced at TJ for a clue but his face was politely non-committal. It was her ball. Might as well run with it.

"Yes, that's what I said. Harley and TJ were old friends. The natural heir, Megan Sullivan, apparently doesn't want the boat. TJ offered to sign it over to her and she refused the offer."

"Did she? How very odd. Or perhaps not. Megan is rather a different sort of person."

"In what way, Professor?" TJ said.

"Oh, I don't mean anything slanderous, believe me. Just. . . I'm not sure I can explain. Aloof one moment, gregarious the next. Rather a bumpy personality if you know what I mean. Difficult to predict."

"What about her son, Chipper? Was he like that too?" Lisbee asked.

"Chipper. Poor child. What a tragedy to be taken so young."

"Not taken so much as volunteered according to what I heard. Did that surprise you Professor Deutch? Was he as unpredictable as his mother?" Lisbee searched the Professor's face and found nothing but apparently genuine sadness.

"Yes, it surprised me a bit. But who can tell, really, with the very young. I surround myself with them, as you know, and the one thing I've learned in my years of teaching is one rarely grasps what they're actually thinking. They're rather like chameleons. Changing to suit the environment until they can develop a suitable shell to present to the world for the rest of their adult lives."

"He spent a lot of time on the *Emmy T.* with his grandfather, didn't he?" TJ asked, setting his empty mug on the polished mahogany table.

"Oh yes, both with and without him. Poor Harley wasn't able to manage many visits in the later stages of his illness, but that didn't stop Chipper."

"Did you know him well?"

"I suppose so. As well as anyone other than Harley. He was obviously a bright young man, but misdirected. Forgive me if that sounds arrogant." The Professor smiled sheepishly. "He could have excelled at the University, but refused to submit himself to the rigors, the structure. Preferred to be his own man, I suppose, or follow the course dictated by his own personal devils. Foolish these days. Even those with degrees find it difficult to establish a career, unless they happen to be one of the lucky few with an entrepreneurial flair.

"Still, he was clever. He would visit me and ask questions. I would venture to say he assimilated several semesters worth of education from me in a neighborly manner without ever having to attend a class." Deutch laughed.

"A teacher is never off duty?" Elizabeth said with a smile.

"Exactly so."

TJ stood and held out his hand.

"Well, thank you Professor. For the warm welcome. I promised Lisbee I'd try to find Sunny Cortez and see if he could give me another lesson on the *Emmy T.*"

"Yes, yes, by all means. Don't let me keep you. You'll not do better than learning seamanship from young Mr. Cortez. Most skilled. I believe you'll find him two docks over, talking to one of the tenants. I passed them on my way here."

The Professor held Lisbee's hand as she alighted to the boarding steps.

"I hope we'll see you again soon, Professor Deutch. Do you spend a lot of time here?"

"You will and I do. One does when one lives aboard," he said and squeezed her hand.

EIGHTEEN

 TJ COASTED TO a stop halfway up the drive and shut the Jaguar down behind and a little to the right of the red BMW 325i. It was nearly five o'clock, and a chill hung in the air. He grabbed his leather jacket from the seat beside him and inspected the distance between the Jag and its high class neighbor. There was plenty of room for it to pass if its owner wanted to leave before he did. The Beemer could belong to Megan Sullivan herself, of course, but he doubted it. Not on a university employee's salary. He cursed under his breath as he approached the wide verandah of the old schoolhouse. It wouldn't be easy to question her while she had company; he'd have to try and get rid of whoever it was.

There were no lights on inside. Since it wasn't yet dark or even twilight that shouldn't really be surprising, but it bothered him just the same. He stood listening a moment on the porch before knocking; no sounds from inside either. TJ sighed and rapped sharply three times on the old double door, then turned to examine the expanse of lawn in the gathering gloom.

A full minute passed with no response. Shrugging into his jacket, he approached the door to knock again when a shuffling sound from within was followed by the snick of a deadbolt lock, and the door opened a bare six inches. Megan Sullivan stared blankly at him. He smiled, hiding the mild disappointment at her lack of recognition, and held out a business card.   She raised a hand as if to push it—and him—away, then her eyes widened slightly.

"Oh God, it's you," she said, closing the door and mumbling from behind it, "Just wait a minute, can you?"

"Guess I'll have to," TJ said under his breath and lowered himself into a wicker chair that stood on the porch to the left of the entrance.

When the door opened a few minutes later, Megan Sullivan emerged wearing an old fashioned chenille bathrobe in a pale green that complimented her dark red hair. It was belted tightly at the waist and swelled softly across her hips. The shawl collar dipped to a vee in the front, and an inch of freckled cleavage was exposed. TJ felt his breath quicken involuntarily when he realized she wasn't wearing a damned thing under it. Slumping into the wicker chair next to his, Meg took a long swallow from the frosted tumbler she was carrying, then set it on the glass-topped table between the chairs.

"If I were a good hostess I'd ask you if you want something," she said. "Do you?"

Her voice was low and husky as if she'd been asleep.

"No, thanks just the same. I'm sorry if I disturbed you."

"Don't worry about it. Time the bastard went home anyway. You saved me an argument."

Glancing toward the drive TJ saw a squarely built man in sweatpants, his striped rugby jersey swelling over muscular chest and arms, emerge from the rear of the house and walk toward the red BMW. He extended a hand toward it and the familiar *chiiirrp* of an electronic lock deactivating filled the still air. His thick dark hair looked wet, like he'd just come from the shower. He didn't turn or wave. Simply got into the BMW and backed it expertly past the XKE and out the driveway.

TJ Billings, Expert Exterminations—rid yourself of household pests and unwanted bed partners, TJ thought, but merely said, "Glad to be of service."

Megan Sullivan smiled faintly.

"I guess you're used to wasting your time in your business," she said.

"Why do you say that?"

"You know, following blind alleys, all that stuff. Or is that only in fiction."

"There are blind alleys in every business, not just mine. I meant, why bring it up now?"

"Because that's what you're doing here. I can't help you. My son Steven was a selfish little prick. I don't believe for a minute he would have killed himself. But he certainly was arrogant enough to think he could get away with mixing pills and booze, if that's what he felt like doing at the time. He'd probably done it before. He liked his little pleasures."

"Like his mother?"

TJ watched her eyes, which gazed steadily back at him without a flicker of resentment or remorse. He wanted to do something to shock her; bring her out of whatever game she was playing with him. He stood, looking down at her as a slow smile spread across her face.

"I suppose his hedonistic tendencies could have come from my side of the family. But not the narcissistic ones. Those came directly from his long lost father."

"What about his father? Where is he now?"

She shrugged eloquently.

"I wouldn't know. Or care. I never asked anything of that bastard except to see the last of him."

"And when was that?"

She looked at her naked wrist as if it were wearing a watch.

"Twenty years, seven months, six days and a few hours ago. Not that I'm counting."

"He was that bad?"

She smiled again.

"We were that bad together, if you want the honest truth. I don't blame *all* my troubles on someone else."

"Why not? It's fashionable," TJ said, smiling slightly.

Meg Sullivan pulled at the shawl collar of her bathrobe, revealing another inch of rounded bosom.

"I'm not much on fashionable, either," she said, rising to stand a foot away from TJ, her nearly empty glass between them. "I need a refill. Sure you don't want something?"

"Okay, sure. And I'd like to look at your son's room if you don't mind."

Megan Sullivan shrugged her disinterest and TJ, taking it as assent, followed her into the house.

The one large schoolroom had been retained as a vast living area, populated with overstuffed chairs and sofas, wooden tables and bookshelves, but to his disappointment the pot-bellied stove was forsaken for a brick fireplace against, and nearly filling, the far wall beyond which the driveway curved to the back of the house. He should have noticed the brick exterior from his earlier visit but his mind had been clouded with memories. The cloakroom beneath the bell tower had been converted to a foyer with a few wooden chairs arranged on the hardwood floor, and three stools lined up before an expensive looking wet bar with a brass foot rail. The bell rope, apparently still functional, hung down from the tower in the middle of the small room and was looped and tied to a reproduction gaslight sconce at the end of the bar, its tasseled end within easy reach.

Megan Sullivan switched on the gaslight and a warm glow filled the foyer, casting the large room beyond into shadow. She refilled her own glass and mixed another just like it without asking TJ's preference, handed it to him in passing, and moved into the large room where she turned on a single lamp.

"Thanks," he said, following her and taking a seat in one of the chairs facing the sofa on which she had reclined against several pillows, kicking off her slippers and not bothering to adjust the skirts of the chenille robe which now revealed a generous expanse of firm white thigh.

"It's my own concoction. Mix yourself something else if you don't like it," she said, gesturing at his glass. He took a sip, expecting it to be sweet, but it wasn't. It had a smoky, nutty flavor with a subtle but definite bite.

"This is fine."

She stared at him for what seemed a long time before speaking again.

"His room's down the hall, on the left," she finally said, pointing to a doorway off the schoolroom which obviously led to the additions which had made the old building into a livable home.

Three doors opened off the hallway; two on the right and one on the left. TJ attempted not to notice the view of rumpled bedclothes through the second door on the right——her bedroom——as he entered Chipper's room, directly across from the bathroom, still damp with steam from the shower.

The boy's room was sparsely furnished with bed, chest and desk, all showing a faint layer of dust, as if she rarely entered it even to do normal housekeeping. There was a computer on the desk, an older one from the look of it with a small monitor. He switched it on and was presented with a black screen containing a white rectangular window demanding a password. Wishing Lisbee were with him, he turned it off and began rummaging in the desk drawers. They contained a few books, some mildly pornographic magazines, and a set of floppy disks secured with a rubber band. The label on the top one read 'backups.' He put them in his jacket pocket and began a methodical search of the closet and chest of drawers.

The clothes were typical; jeans, tee shirts, running shoes, denim jacket and sweatpants. The drawers revealed more tee shirts and underwear. He checked the artwork on the shirts. Most were of various rock groups but one depicted the slogan from a local brewpub in Soquel and he made a note of it. In the bottom drawer, under a pair of striped pajamas that had seen little if any use, he found the only thing of real interest in the otherwise sterile room——a brightly colored silk scarf. Taking it from the drawer and holding it close to his face, he got a faint whiff of a delicate, flowery perfume. Not something Megan Sullivan would wear, either the scarf or the scent. He tucked it away in the other jacket pocket and returned to the living room.

The boy's mother was still on the sofa, the glass beside her half empty. Did he imagine it, or was there just a bit more thigh invitingly revealed? Making a resolute attempt to ignore his accelerating pulse rate, TJ extracted the floppy disks from his pocket.

"I found these in his desk drawer. Mind if I borrow them for a little while?"

She rose leisurely and stood close to him, examining the disks. He didn't mention the scarf; it was definitely not her scent, which was musky and rich, and she probably didn't even know of its existence.

"No, I don't mind. They're of no use to me. Keep them if you want."

"Thanks," he said, turning to go. "I'll be in touch."

She reached out and put a hand on his arm. He imagined he could feel the heat of it through jacket and shirtsleeve, which was impossible.

"You haven't finished your drink."

Her chin was tilted provocatively. He could feel her breath against his throat. Without thinking he bent and kissed her, but when she responded by sliding her hand from his arm up behind his neck, a sudden vision of her rumpled bed made him pull away, gently but firmly disengaging her hand.

"Sorry," he said. "I didn't mean to do that."

"Just for a minute there it felt like you did."

"Maybe you're right, but it's bad for business. Tends to make you lose your objectivity."

"I've changed my mind," Meg Sullivan said. "I do want those disks back. You can bring them back tomorrow or the next day. I get home around six."

TJ nodded. "I'll have my daughter Elizabeth drop them off as soon as she's made copies," he said and turned toward the door.

NINETEEN

Camellia Tang Sat huddled beneath the overhanging vines which spread from their determined grip on the crippled backyard fence across to the trunk of a sprawling plum whose leaves had already made a cushion of yellow on the ground at its feet. She was watching an industrious spider leap from vine to fence and back again, beginning to rebuild a web Camellia had heedlessly destroyed only moments before. Her eyes never left the spider as she sat, hugging her knees to her chest, the flowing folds of her skirt tucked around them. The cat, Pineapple, lay stretched beside her feigning sleep until the spider's movement caught his attention and he tensed into a crouch, eyes widening. Claws unsheathed, his front paw lashed out with deadly accuracy, and the twice disturbed spider scuttled away among the yellow leaves. Camellia smiled.

"Shame on you, Pineapple," she whispered as the marmalade tom rolled onto his back and writhed playfully in the leaves. "Poor spider."

Camellia cocked her wrist and squinted at the golden watch in the shadows. It was a few minutes after six. Rudy had given her the watch when she had proved to him she could tell time on the big wooden clock hanging in the hall, and she loved it. She wore it always, even to bed at night. Telling time was more difficult with the watch; the hands on the house clock were so much bigger and it had all its numbers, while the watch only had four. But she never told Rudy that. Just as she never told him that she sometimes became confused about six o'clock.

It was easy with three, nine and twelve. If you were awake and it was light outside you knew which three, nine and twelve it was. But with six, it could be light whether it was morning or evening. Mostly she knew the difference, but if she'd been thinking really hard about something and six o'clock snuck up on her, well. . . . Rudy would think it was stupid, so she didn't tell him.

This time, even though she'd been thinking hard about the spider and wondering how many times he would keep rebuilding his home, she knew it was evening. And near time for dinner. Rising and dusting the leaves from her skirt, she picked up Pineapple and crossed to the crooked flagstone walk leading to the back door.

Inside, Pineapple leaped from her arms and ran to the bowl of food on the cracked linoleum floor of the kitchen. She followed and saw that it was full. She knew where the bag of dry food was kept, and mostly she remembered to fill his dish if it was getting low. Rudy was very strict about that—it was her cat, he said, and her responsibility to see he was fed. Thinking of her brother, the silence in the house dawned on her. There was no music playing. Rudy always had music and she wondered where he was.

In the living room the small TV was dark. Rudy had been sitting in the old stuffed chair when she had taken Pineapple into the back yard some time ago, his long black hair flowing back from the spiky top, falling loose where the rubber band holding his ponytail had broken. But he wasn't there now, and the sound and dancing colors of the MTV he liked to watch had been extinguished.

The door to the computer room was closed. She wasn't allowed to actually go *into* the computer room with all its boxes on the makeshift shelves, their tangled cords snaking onto the floor, but when he was in there, Rudy left the door open and she could look in and maybe talk with him a bit if he wasn't too busy. Camellia tiptoed toward it, not intending to open the door exactly, but thinking maybe Rudy just forgot to leave it open this time. He did forget things sometimes. As she approached she heard a murmuring sound, and then his voice, much louder.

". . .you weren't fucking there when the fucking monitor died, that's why. . . ."

He sounded angry, but maybe a little frightened too, because his voice dropped again so that she could only hear the rustling hum of it, like the waves coming in when he took her to the beach.

Camellia backed away from the door and turned toward the kitchen. If he was busy, he might not remember what time it was and when he did he'd be hungry. She decided to surprise him and have supper ready when he finished whatever he was doing. As she began her careful preparations, humming to herself and feeling the soft fur of Pineapple threading his way around her ankles, she wondered if she should make enough food for three, in case Chipper was coming.

Jack Delaney pushed an unruly shock of sandy hair back off his forehead and leaned again over the cluttered top drawer of the filing cabinet. It burned him that the ever widening halo of scalp at the crown of his head, the one he masochistically viewed with the help of a hand mirror each morning, kept expanding while the front was forever falling into his God damned eyes. There was no fucking justice.

After several minutes of pawing through papers he found the file he was looking for and extracted it, laying the half-inch thick manila folder on his desk. Down the hall in the coffee room he could hear the duty sergeant laughing at some rude comment from a patrolman just in off his shift, but otherwise the building was quiet. Jack seated himself and began flipping through the pages of the file.

There was no big secret about the BBSs run by a handful of freaked out kids all over the mountains. They were minnows in a very large pool of sharks, and were pretty much left alone except for irregular monitoring when something big went down to see if a lead might pop up. And once in a while it did. It was the Pan Global connection that had jogged his memory when Highstreet called. Somewhere in one of these files, Jack knew, there was a mention of a BBS run by a kid who worked there, or used to.

He was about to give up on the current file and get a cup of coffee before starting on another when the name jumped out at him. *Chamber door.* Email address *Raven*; Raven@Chamber-door.net. He remembered it now; remembered thinking at the time that at least this kid was reasonably literate. The phone number was listed, and next to it, in his hurried scrawl, a brief note: *R. Tang, Pan Global shipping.*

TWENTY

Beau BILLINGS CARRIED his freshly brewed cup of coffee to the great leather chair on the former altar and watched the early November wind whip the branches of the redwood trees through the streaming glass. It was Wednesday, the 2nd, and the rain had begun softly enough after a chill and rather quiet Halloween. It had steadily gained strength until it was now a full-fledged storm; howling wind flinging sheets of pelting rain first in one direction, then another. The second growth redwoods dipped and danced through the wall of glass, their dense foliage absorbing the shockwaves of wind driven water. Beau observed once again that even in the fiercest weather, the trees allowed only a fraction of the outer chaos to penetrate to the forest floor on which they stood. He had never seen anything like it until he came to California. You could stand beneath those trees and it was like being in the eye of a hurricane; dripping wet and misty, but not wild like it was outside of their benevolent protection. He shook his head and settled into the deep leather chair to watch, Smiley at his feet.

He was alone in the old church. Elizabeth had started early to visit a client over the hill in Santa Clara or Sunnyvale or one of those places. She was making a go of the computer end of the business he reflected with a warm sense of pride. Several outfits had her on retainer to keep their computer systems healthy, and she made frequent calls just to touch base or bring them some new trick she'd discovered. Beau understood the basics of the avalanche of technology that had engulfed them in the last couple of years, but he didn't want to know much more than that, really. He was content to watch the swell of the electronic tide jostling the rather complaisant society as it groped its way into the twenty-first century, marveling at the way people adjusted—or didn't adjust—to its new set of rules.

Personally, he had found it easy to take advantage of what was useful and happily disregard the rest, much as he had done things all his life. Elizabeth had set him up with his own little machine on which he could now manage his wide and far flung investments with amazing speed and accuracy. He marveled at this, but didn't think much more deeply about its implications, merely accepting it and enjoying the extra time it allowed him. Although he still used pen or pencil to write, finding a keyboard uncomfortable for his large, somewhat arthritic hands, he wasn't consumed with a *pen and ink* nostalgia as some others his age were.. Being able to use whichever suited you was the best of both worlds in his estimation.

Elizabeth had apparently inherited this sanguine outlook as well, moving effortlessly between the worlds of boundless electronic communication and what Beau like to call *real_reality*, because it made her laugh. There would be very little of whatever she might encounter, he thought, that Elizabeth couldn't handle.

He wished he was as sure about TJ.

When Beau had determined to stay in California after Amelia Billings' untimely death, he had occupied the three-room mother-in-law cottage behind TJ's house on its quiet street in the older residential section north of town. The house had belonged to Amelia's parents and she inherited it when her mother died a few years after her father's murder. Beau could have bought his own place; he had left the oil lease business during a peak and did not want for money. But he preferred to be near TJ and Elizabeth during that difficult time and the cottage suited his needs, which were few.

Over the years it had become his custom, after showering and dressing, to enter the large old-fashioned kitchen of the main house to share a cup of coffee with TJ before they started their day. It was a ritual born of simple companionship rather than a desire for conversation; often they would pass only a word or two, reading the morning paper in silence. But this morning when he entered through the back door he found the house empty. A terse note on the refrigerator informed Beau that TJ had left to spend a couple of days on the boat. Maybe it would do him some good, Beau thought, to get off by himself for a while, but he was surprised and a little hurt. TJ had mentioned nothing about it, and that was unlike him.

He was decidedly not himself these last few days. Kind of quiet and withdrawn. And it had all started with Harley Sullivan leaving him that boat—and what was probably an impossible assignment to pay for it. The case had been thoroughly investigated at the time the boy died and there just weren't any new leads; nowhere to start that hadn't already been covered.

TJ had seemed slightly hopeful after seeing Chipper's mother on Sunday. He'd found some computer disks belonging to the boy and the name of a local beer bar he apparently frequented. But Elizabeth's examination of the disks had turned up nothing of value—a few games, she'd said, and some old software. Nothing more recent than two years ago. When she had returned the disks, Megan Sullivan had let her examine the computer itself, but it was the same story—everything on it was nearly two years old. If he'd had Internet access, email, personal files, they were somewhere else, not in his mother's house.

TJ had visited the brewpub earlier in the week and found that the owner recognized Chipper's picture, but not much more than that. He didn't know him by name and couldn't recall anyone in particular who'd been with him. None of the semi-regulars TJ questioned were of any help either. Dead end.

Beau knew this unwanted job weighed heavily on TJ and it worried him. What would he do if he couldn't complete it; couldn't pay for that boat? Sell it and donate the money to charity? Or manage to give it to Harley's daughter some way or other though she insisted she didn't want it? Or keep it and carry the guilt around with him like he'd been doing with the unsolved murder of Jim Locksley all these years? A month or two ago Beau could have predicted TJ's actions with a fair amount of certainty, but now he wasn't sure. Maybe there was something else gnawing at him beside the Sullivan case. He hadn't felt this shut out of his nephew's life since Amelia died.

Finding his coffee had grown cold, Beau rose from the leather chair and started for the kitchen in the old vestry. He had one report to write for a client on the backburner, and then he would call Clyde, he decided. See if he wanted to have some lunch. As he headed back toward his office to compile the handwritten report which Lisbee would then transfer to the computer, the phone rang.

"Anadarko Grace, good morning," Beau said into the handset, placing his replenished cup on the trestle table next to his yellow legal pad.

"Mr. Billings?" a feminine voice asked.

"Yes, ma'am. How may I help you?"

"I'm not at all sure you can, young man, but I'd like to talk to you anyway. Are you available for a consultation?"

Promptly at 10:30 the woman stood in the vestibule, daintily shaking a sodden umbrella which Beau took from her and placed on one of the brass hooks on the mahogany hall tree. She began unbuttoning her raincoat, turning slightly in an elegant, feminine gesture which suggested she would wait for the gentleman to help her off with it. He hadn't seen the likes of that for a long time, and he smiled as he slipped the coat from her shoulders.

She was a small woman with an easy grace and the natural poise borne of long experience in authority. Her white hair, curling closely to a finely boned skull, was slightly ruffled from the effects of the storm, and she patted it unselfconsciously as they walked down the wide aisle toward Beau's office. She wore a woolen suit in a deep crimson shade, mid-heel calf leather pumps, and carried a pair of soft kid gloves. The bright blue eyes in her lined face gathered in the stained glass, subdued carpeting, and finally the wall of glass with its view of the storm still raging outside. As Beau stopped and gestured toward the cushioned pew in his office, she said,

"May we sit up there? It's really quite lovely."

"We surely may, Miz Sims. May I offer you a cup of coffee? It's freshly brewed."

"Please call me Aurelia. I've been addressed as Miss Sims for so many years I'm beginning to grow weary of it. Coffee would be fine, thank you. Black please, no sugar."

When he returned with the cups, she was sitting comfortably in one of the leather chairs, the gloves on her lap, gazing at the swaying limbs of the redwoods.

"I wonder that you ever get any work done," she said. "I could sit here watching for hours. I imagine squirrels play out there when the weather's fine, don't they."

"Run right around those trunks, chasing one another. They do have a time."

Beau studied her face and decided she could be sixty or eighty; her old-fashioned manner favored the latter, but she wore her age well. She finally turned to him, a slight frown creasing her brow.

"As I said when I called, I'm not sure you'll be able to help me, but I thought it was worth the effort. I'll try to be brief; I'm sure you're very busy."

"Just take your time. I don't have anything going on right now that'll suffer for the wait." She nodded, sipped her coffee, and straightened in the chair, her hands clasped in her lap. She looked like a school girl preparing to recite a lesson.

"There is a young woman, a girl really, I'd like you to observe for a time sufficient to satisfy yourself that she is well and not in harm's way. Surveillance. That's something you can do isn't it?"

Beau hesitated a moment, but when she didn't continue he concluded the question was not rhetorical.

"Well, yes ma'am, there have been occasions when surveillance became necessary in a case. But I'm afraid I'll have to have a little more to go on. I take it there are reasons why you feel this young woman might *not* be well. Can you give me some background?"

Aurelia Sims sighed and closed her eyes. Beau noticed the lids were lightly dusted with blue eye shadow.

"Yes, of course. Stupid of me. I'm sorry, it's rather difficult to explain. You see I have no really good reason to think she may not be all right; it's just a feeling I have. We were quite close for a time, or so I thought. And then, a few months ago, she simply dropped from view. When I called to inquire about her I was told by her brother, quite rudely I thought, that she no longer wished to see me. My first reaction was to press the issue myself, but on consideration I became convinced that could do more harm than good.

"I was a teacher until I retired ten years ago. Toward the last it became very disheartening; I nearly quit on several occasions, but then there always appeared some special student who made it worthwhile for a little longer. When I finally did leave I was somewhat concerned about what I would do to fill my time. I have no hobbies to speak of, and my family is widely dispersed, what's left of them. I've never married." She said this last in a practiced way, as if she'd said it many times before.

"So I did the obvious thing and began tutoring in my home. Just one or two youngsters at a time; ones who were deserving and made an effort. It wasn't for the money; I've saved enough over the years to keep me comfortably along with the small pension I receive. In fact, some of my students didn't pay at all—because they didn't have the means."

"It was more for the company?" Beau asked gently.

Aurelia Sims smiled.

"Yes, and for the small sense of accomplishment, I suppose. I became very fond of my charges and enjoyed observing their eventual success, feeling I'd had some small part in it."

"Is that how you met the girl you're worried about?"

"Not exactly; I did meet Camellia through one of my students, but I was never an official tutor to her, poor child, although I did what I could to help. She's retarded, you see. Mentally challenged, I believe they like to call it today. I know so little about those things, really, but she's not the victim of a congenital birth defect like Down's Syndrome, where there are physical disabilities as well as mental. She's quite beautiful; just childlike in her ability to cope with everyday tasks. It's very sad."

"She lives with her brother? The one who was rude to you on the phone?"

"Yes. Rudy Tang. Her parents are dead I suppose; she only mentioned that they had *gone away* a long time ago, which could certainly be a euphemism for death to an immature mind."

"Do you think the brother might harm her?"

"I don't know. I don't think so, surely. He has apparently taken care of her for many years. That can't have been easy."

The woman sighed and glanced once more at the rain streaming along the glass wall. "Perhaps I'm just a foolish old woman. I told you I have no real cause for concern. It's just a feeling that things are not as they should be." She looked back at Beau with a steady gaze.

"Will you indulge me? I can pay whatever fee you normally receive. It would be worth it to me to know she is all right."

Beau rose and offered his hand to Aurelia Sims.

"Well, I don't see how it could hurt to do a little checking up for you. If you'll step down to my office now, I'll write up all the particulars."

TWENTY-ONE

CORY FLOYD SAT behind his massive desk, his steepled fingers the only object which marred its pristine surface. He liked the bare expanse of it, the shining wood uncluttered with the paraphernalia of business. It lent an aura of executive status, he thought. No clutter of papers, pens, or coffee cups for one in his position. The few items of necessity to his business day rested on the table behind him, where his computer terminal also sat, its screen silently reviewing the day's stock performance. A sleek, fat, Mont Blanc pen; a daily planner in black Italian leather; a telephone; and the framed photograph of his wife and twin daughters, smiling artificially into the camera's lens.

A collarless teal silk shirt was tucked into carefully faded denim jeans above sockless feet in black Cole Haan loafers. The gold-rimmed glasses perched on his nose he only needed for reading, but he liked to wear them as much as possible for he believed they lent him a *Steve Jobs* look, although he didn't resemble that legendary entrepreneurial mystic in the least, being dark and stocky rather than lean and aesthetic in appearance.

Across the desk in a chair which nearly engulfed her sat a young woman in tight black leggings and baggy blue tunic. Her thin legs were crossed and she repeatedly pushed strands of long brown hair back from her face as she read from a report spread open on her knees. Her nasal voice droned against the soft background of New Age Celtic ballads issuing from the computer's CD player, adding to the somnolent effect that was carrying Floyd toward the edge of sleep. He was about to cut her off and tell her to leave the report with him when something she said caught his flagging attention.

"Say again."

"What?" She looked up, startled.

"That part about the private key cache."

"Oh. Um, the Bonded Private Key Bank log showed several attempts at unauthorized access last Sunday night? Is that what you mean?"

"Yeah. Isn't that unusual?"

"I don't know. I guess, maybe. But it could have been just a mistake, you know, some new employee trying to log into the wrong place? It's happened before."

"When has it happened before?"

"Um, I'll have to check. Do you want me to check?"

"Yes I want you to check. How long will it take?"

"I don't know. A day or two?"

"Can't you do it any faster than that?"

"I guess. If I let some other things go. Shall I let some other things go?"

Cory Floyd sighed. "No, just get it to me as quick as you can. And don't mention it to anyone else, all right?"

"What? Oh, sure. I won't say anything. Do you think it's important? They didn't get in or anything."

"No, probably not. Just humor me, okay, Melissa? Now I've got another appointment. Tell Judy to hold my calls on your way out, will you?"

The young woman rose, gathering the report to her bosom, cradling it like a small child.

"Sure, Cory. Whatever you say," she said and smiled wistfully.

Cory Floyd felt it was important to be on a first name basis with his subordinates. It helped close the gap.

The office door at the end of a hall in one of the new cinderblock buildings at the north end of Scotts Valley looked like any other with the exception of the small video camera mounted on the ceiling above it and the telephone handset on the wall beside it. The name "Bradley Young Associates" in raised gold lettering looked the same as all the other businesses in the building, and was listed in the lobby directory next to its suite number, just as they were. When Cory Floyd lifted the handset and pressed the button beneath it, a smooth voice intoned, "Bradley Young, may I help you?"

"Cory Floyd."

"Yes Mr. Floyd, just a moment please."

There was a metallic buzz indicating the door lock had been released and Floyd pushed it open and entered a small reception area. The door clicked heavily closed behind him. A gray-haired woman in horn-rimmed glasses sat unsmiling behind a large desk that was remarkably free of clutter. The backs of several framed photographs, surrounding a vase of harvest-colored dahlias, met Floyd's gaze, though the receptionist did not. She was busily writing in a desk diary and only looked up after he had been standing on the burnt orange carpet for more than thirty seconds.

"Please have a seat, Mr. Floyd. Mr. Lowry is running a bit late. He just called and should be here shortly; he was at the summit." Cory assumed, correctly, that she meant the summit of the Santa Cruz Mountains on Highway 17. On his way over from Silicon Valley. He sat and began leafing aimlessly through the stack of magazines on the coffee table—*Newsweek*, *House and Garden*, the much revamped *New Yorker*.

When Lowry appeared some ten minutes later, it was from the hallway to Floyd's right leading off the reception area. Without speaking, he motioned for Floyd to follow him. They entered a large anonymously furnished office and Cory took a chair while the other man closed the door firmly behind them. When he had seated himself behind the vast empty desk, Lowry gazed levelly at Floyd for what seemed a long time, his expression bland, unreadable. He was a man of sharp edges; hawk-nosed above a pointed, clean shaven chin, his nearly colorless hair cut close to a square skull.

"So, it wasn't that bad after all," Floyd finally said to break the silence. "Just a paragraph on page two in the *Sentinel*; the *Mercury News* didn't even pick it up. They've got bigger fish to fry over there."

"You were lucky."

"Yeah. It was obviously amateurs. No organization, nothing but some hardware missing."

"Is that what the police said? Amateurs?"

"Well, not in so many words. They didn't say much of anything if you want the truth, except it's unlikely we'll be getting any of the stolen property back. Bottom line is we write it off; it's not enough to make a blip in the quarterly earnings. No big deal."

Lowry was silent again, turning to look through the window behind his desk at the mountains shrouded in misty rain. Cory Floyd felt he should say something more, add to his reassurances, but some instinct told him that for once he might be better off keeping his mouth shut. Finally the other man turned back to him, resting his elbows on the desk.

"Cory, we both know it wouldn't take very damned much to make a blip in your company's earnings, but that isn't what concerns me. Your products are good; I'm using them and I've had them checked out. They're as good as or better than your competition."

A bloom of relief flushed Floyd's face and he began to speak, but Lowry held up a hand.

"Wait until I've finished. I'm in a position to take the earnings problem off your back. Government cutbacks aren't just empty campaign promises anymore, as you probably know. That's why I've been given the authority to contract for the best encryption tools available. It's just too damned expensive to keep building our own classified networks; things are growing too fast. And the biggest, fastest networks are already being paid for in the private sector. We have to be able to take advantage of them while maintaining the integrity of sensitive information.

"The problem is publicity. That is precisely why your competition has lost this particular race—they're in the public eye. All that high profile squabbling over the export laws in an arena with a global audience that doesn't miss a thing. We can't afford to be even close to that kind of scrutiny."

Floyd took a deep breath and let it out. His hands were tingling and he found it difficult to sit still in his chair. He wanted to shout.

"So are you offering . . . ."

"What I'm offering is a trial. A demo. Nothing moves fast in government, not even in my section, but I have some ears on the Hill and in the Pentagon. A six-month demonstration, using benign data and your best products. Then another three-month evaluation period. That's close to light speed in these circles." Lowry paused, his silver eyes pinning Floyd in his seat.

"Think you can handle that?" he finally said, almost in a whisper.

Floyd, for the first time he could recall, had lost his power of speech. He nodded.

TWENTY-TWO

THE MAN WITH the duffel bag slung on his shoulder and three plastic grocery bags swinging from his arm moved carefully along the dock, limping slightly, as if from an old injury protesting the weather. The hood of his windbreaker was pulled forward against the rain. Sunny Cortez didn't recognize him at first; he was rising from his chair in the warmth of the marina office, ready to intercept the stranger, when a gust of wind snatched at the man's hood, pulling it back from his face. It was TJ Billings. Grabbing his navy blue slicker from its peg on the wall, Sunny stepped out into the rain, glancing at his watch and wondering what in the hell Billings was doing here at 6:45 in the morning on a day like this.

"Not going out in this shit are you?" he said, reaching to relieve the older man of one of the grocery bags.

"No."

They walked along the dock, the howl of the wind precluding any further conversation. It was barely light and the sleeping boats swayed and jostled at their moorings. There was the occasional lamp glowing from behind a shuttered window, left on by an absent owner to protect against the damp, but otherwise the vessels were dark.

When they had negotiated entrance to the *Emmy T.* and stood in the salon, their streaming coats dripping on the faded carpet, TJ bent to the panel of breaker switches and turned on the heavy marine batteries before flipping on the breakers that would bring the boat to life in its tethered berth—salon, forward and aft stateroom overhead lights; radio so he could listen to the weather channel; water pump and heater; and finally the battery charger. Sunny watched, mentally congratulating the new owner on his memory after only one lesson. The cold was numbing, and when he had finished with the breakers, TJ turned on the electric heater that stood on the deck behind the helm seat, powered by the shore connection that stayed on at all times while the boat was berthed, keeping the refrigerator running and juice flowing to the wall sockets. The heater looked like a small radiator, the kind that used to heat apartment buildings in cold weather climates, but it was electric and instead of the hiss of steam, small sharp crackling sounds began to fill the cabin as the oil within it came up to temperature.

"Thanks," TJ said, indicating the bags Sunny Cortez had deposited on the galley counter.

"Sure. Got any more?"

"No, that's it."

"Going to stay for a while?"

"A day or two."

"Well, give a holler if you need anything. I'm usually around somewhere."

TJ nodded as Cortez slipped out the sliding door and into the rain.

By 10 o'clock TJ had gone through every drawer, cupboard, and hanging locker inside the trawler. While he had found nothing of an intimate personal nature belonging either to Harley or his grandson, he discovered that Megan Sullivan had not removed the essentials for life on a boat—it was fully stocked with everyday necessities; dishes, towels, bedclothes, even extra jackets and foul weather gear in the hanging lockers. That didn't really surprise him. She had no need for such items unless she wanted to have a garage sale, and somehow he couldn't see her sitting on a folding chair in her long driveway with a cashbox on her knees. He pushed away thoughts of what he could see her doing, remembering her standing naked beneath the soft green bathrobe when he had kissed her.

His feelings about Harley Sullivan's daughter were untidily mixed; pity, irritation, mild suspicion, and, most uncomfortable of all, a highly unprofessional physical attraction. He couldn't decide if the image she was trying to project was that of bold, uncaring innocence, or shameless corruption. What was painfully clear was the delight she took in her ability to shock. TJ found he felt a grudging admiration for this woman who regularly insisted on calling a spade a fucking shovel. The only other woman he knew with that questionable quality was his daughter, Lisbee, but the two were entirely different. Lisbee's was the open, genuine expression of feelings with a youthful disregard for propriety, while Megan Sullivan maintained a more mature, calculating manner, however blatantly uncaring it might appear on the surface. He decided his randiness in the case of the latter was purely that, and not some unconscious incestuous longing from the dark side of his personality. It made him feel a little better.

But not much.

"It's that goddamned will that bothers me," he said churlishly, interrupting the crackling static of the weather station on the marine radio.

That brand new shiny spanking clean will that left everything but the boat on which he stood to Harley's only child, Megan. Brand new because, of necessity, it had been rewritten after Chipper died. In order to leave the boat to TJ and lay the task on him of finding the boy's murderer, if he existed. But what was the disposition of Harley's goods prior to that? He could find out easily enough, but he didn't really need to. TJ was ready to stake his reputation on the supposition that Harley's original will—before he knew he was terminally ill; before his much loved grandson died—had left everything to Chipper. By her own admission, Meg had been the odd man out in that threesome. And once Harley's illness was known, the timetable was the driving factor. No time left to work on the old man, convince him the boy was a selfish, grasping little shit. What to do?

What indeed. Much as the circumstances might point in that direction, he simply could not believe the woman would hastily arrange her son's death in order to benefit from her father's will. He knew his own feelings were probably clouding his judgment, but he still couldn't swallow it. And what about Harley? Even if father and daughter had never been close, would the old man really have wanted TJ to finger her as the killer of his grandson? Maybe. If he couldn't bring himself to do it, but couldn't die with his suspicions on his conscience either. Or maybe he'd hoped TJ could prove him wrong.

"Shit," TJ said aloud, and opened a can of beer from the refrigerator just before he noticed the pale face framed in damp, dark red hair peering through the glass of the sliding door to the salon.

He motioned Meg Sullivan in, and when she stood before him, in jeans topped by a yellow slicker, clasping her arms across her chest to forestall the chill, he said lightly, "I thought you didn't like boats."

"It's not the boat I came to see," she said, her mouth curving in a smile.

TWENTY-THREE

Beau BILLINGS AND Clyde Allbright sat in the bar of Orlando's, ignoring the view of the clamoring surf through the wide window. A fire burned in the mammoth stone fireplace and a few desultory conversations murmured from several tables away, but it was not especially crowded. The weather would keep a lot of folks away, Beau thought. He had continued his patronage of the restaurant at the end of the pier, even after the tragedy that had sent its owner to prison and his wife to the hospital.

That had been in the Spring, and the vision of the pale blond woman lying in Justin Highstreet's arms, his shirt soaked with her blood, was still fresh in his mind. And her husband, Orlando Cruz, eyes dimmed of rage and brimming with tears, on the floor of Highstreet's cottage after TJ had hit him and taken the revolver from him. A simple case of jealousy; attempted murder of his wandering wife and her reluctant lover, the deputy.

It had changed Highstreet, left him missing a certain spark of liveliness he'd possessed before; or perhaps just left him a good deal older, shriveling the bloom of youthful naiveté for good and all. Sandra Cruz had recovered and moved to San Diego, leaving the restaurant in the capable hands of yet another man who'd loved her, although he had never crossed the dangerous line of doing anything about it.

Alex Gordon, formerly the business manager at Orlando's, was smooth and professional. The food was still excellent and the atmosphere as conducive to good digestion as it had always been. Beau had not noticed that the notoriety hurt the restaurant's popularity any. He surmised it just might have added a little something for some folks.

"So she got those forms or whatever and it looks like she'll get signed up all right. I shouldn't bitch, Christ, it's only money. And I've gotta say, I've never seen her happier. She's even quit nagging about my smoking." Clyde took a long haul on his draft beer, belched quietly, and caught the eye of the barmaid, who nodded and began drawing another.

"Well, Clyde, a man's got to allow some time in his life for what really interests him, and I expect that applies to women too. Seems only fair."

"Yeah, that's what I thought. She stayed home most of the time I was working, and didn't complain all that much. Not like most cops wives, anyway. If she wants to go to school and be the next Danielle Steel, what the hell."

The barmaid, a tall, conventionally pretty woman in her thirties with a full, rounded bosom which complimented her height and graceful carriage, bent to place two frosty glasses on the table.

"Thank you, ma'am," Beau said, smiling. "We'll eat lunch right here I think, if that's all right."

The woman returned the smile. "I'll bring you some menus."

When she had gone, Clyde leaned back in his chair.

"So what's this new case or client or whatever you wanted to ask me about?"

Beau related the facts of the morning visit he had had from Miss Aurelia Sims without embellishment.

"You think she's on the level?" Clyde asked after he had finished.

"If she isn't, she's awful good in the part," Beau said.

"You want me to run a check for priors on this kid, Fong, I guess."

"Tang. Rudy Tang. Might as well run them on his sister and Miss Sims, too, just for thoroughness sake. I'd also like to know what happened to the parents, and when, if you can find out without a lot of trouble."

Clyde laughed.

"Oh I can find out if it's on a sheet somewhere. Or County should have something if the kids were minors when their parents died. How much trouble it'll be depends on who's on duty when I ask. I'll get back to you in a day or two."

"Fine. That's just fine. And I've got something for you out in the car. Don't let me forget when we leave."

Clyde looked slightly dubious.

"What?"

"Well, it's for Ellen, really. Elizabeth asked me to bring it along. It's a little home computer. Ellen's going to need a word processor, she said, though from what Elizabeth tells me this machine can do a lot more than that." Clyde's expression had progressed from dubious to incredulous and was bordering on panic-stricken.

"Who's going to set it up? I don't know anything about those goddamned things."

"Neither do I, but Elizabeth says a child of eight can do it. I suggest you just hand it over to Ellen and let nature take its course."

Professor Deutch had been brewing his morning coffee when he noted the arrival of Sunny Cortez and TJ Billings. He wasn't surprised to see Sunny, who was often to be found along the docks at any hour, but the man in the hooded jacket was unfamiliar and it wasn't until they boarded the *Emmy T.* that he realized it was the new owner. Cortez stayed only long enough to deposit the bags he had helped carry and then retreated to the comparative warmth of the marina office.

Deutch watched the lights come on in succession in the cabins of the *Emmy T.* and decided Billings was conducting a thorough search of the vessel. Throughout the morning the professor maintained a discreet watch, noting that Elizabeth's father was, at least, methodical in his methods. Deutch admired that. He had despaired in the last decade or two at the lack of application in his own circles of the scientific method, and was disproportionately pleased at its application by this man who was decidedly not a scientist. Still, it made him more threatening. Disciplined intelligence was always a threat if one couldn't be sure in what direction it was aimed.

He nearly missed the mid-morning arrival of Megan Sullivan. She had slipped quietly down the dock, and it was only by a fluke that he had raised his head from the laptop to see her standing momentarily at the salon door, dripping rain from her yellow slicker, before Billings admitted her.   Deutch felt something of the voyeur as he peered through the glass, their figures clearly outlined by the interior lighting in the gloom of the stormy day; but he couldn't help himself.   Ordinarily a man of impeccable discretion, he felt pinned by the pantomime unfolding before him.   Slightly ashamed, he nevertheless continued his vigil.

Megan Sullivan stripped off the yellow slicker and hung it on a brass peg near the sliding door of the salon.

"Want a beer?" TJ said.

"Yes, thanks, I'd love a Bass."

"How'd you know I'd have one?"

"I didn't, but I thought it was worth a try. You don't strike me as the Bud type."

"Glass?"

"No, the bottle's fine."

TJ pulled the Bass from its shelf in the apartment-sized refrigerator and proceeded to make a mess of opening it. After three tries at the ornate brass opener affixed to the teak beneath the galley sink, more decorative than functional, he finally succeeded in parting the bottle from its cap and handed it to Meg Sullivan.

"Cheers," he said, lifting his own half empty bottle of Fosters.

"Cheers."

She took a long draught of the Bass and leaned back against the couch, running a slim-fingered hand through the damp mess that was her hair. It was only damp, having been partially protected by the hood of her slicker, but it was a rat's nest of snarls from the wind. She didn't seem to care.

"Why are you here?" TJ asked bluntly.

"To keep you from finding incriminating evidence?"

"Is there some to find?"

"Lord, I hope not." She laughed, throwing her head back to reveal a lovely white throat.

"I'm not looking for anything," he said. "Incriminating or otherwise. I'm just down here to get away for a couple of days."

"That's good. Want some company?"

"No. That's what I came here to avoid."

She looked steadily into his eyes. He held the greenish amber gaze as long as he could, then finally looked away.

"Am I supposed to take that as a dismissal and trot obediently off weeping salt tears into my lace hankie like a good girl?"

"Take it as whatever you want."

"What I *want* is the problem."

TJ stared hard at the woman, his face grim.

"If I had to guess, I'd say what you want has always been the problem," he said at last. She smiled.

"Touché."

"Was Harley leaving everything to Chipper before he was killed?"

"You really think he was killed, Sherlock? By person or persons unknown?"

TJ waited for her to answer her own question.

"By God you do," she said at last, the smile gone from her lips. "And you've penciled me in as suspect number one. Well, good for you. I probably deserve to be. Sure, he was leaving it all to Chipper. Harley always did have a blind spot when it came to his precious grandson. But you could have found that out easily enough; did you just want to see if I'd admit it?"

"Something like that," TJ said.

"Okay, I admit it. I'd hardly be stupid enough not to." Her smile returned slowly. "He was leaving the whole ball of wax to the kid, and when he got sick and we knew he was going to die, the only alternative was for Chipper to pre-decease him. 'And so, your honor, being the greedy, grasping, uncaring bitch that she is, she arranged her own son's murder.' 'So you may say, counsel, but can you prove it?'" Megan Sullivan's smile faded once more. "Well, can you?"

"No."

"It is a nice fit, though, isn't it? Maybe that's even what Harley thought, but he left the dirty work to you because he didn't have the stomach to open that little sack of filthy family laundry himself. That would have been like him. He couldn't stand unpleasantness—probably why he avoided me all those years."

Her gaze was still steady, but no longer mocking.

"Do you ever quit playing games?" TJ asked.

"Hardly ever as long as I get to make up the rules."

Setting her now empty beer bottle on the table, she began descending the steps to the master stateroom, then stopped to look back over her shoulder.

"Are you coming, Captain?"

TJ lay on his back in the dimness, his breathing nearly steady now and his mind a fog of dark thoughts. Beside him, Megan Sullivan was making a barely audible sound, like a quiet growl in her throat. He didn't want to open his eyes, but he did, turning his head slightly. She had covered herself with a cotton throw from the shelf next to the bed, and even in the gloom he could see goose pimples rising on the white flesh of her arms. His hand had fallen asleep, was tingling with the pins and needles of returning circulation, but he reached out clumsily and grasped the top of the flimsy blanket, wrenching it down to expose her full, round breasts, the perfect pink aureoles taut with the cold. He raised himself on one elbow and touched them, feeling the heat radiate through the cool, dry skin. She grasped his wrist and held it there, rolling slightly as the noise she had been making grew louder, finally swelling into a recognizable chuckle.

TWENTY-FOUR

"HE JUST TOOK off? What do you mean he just took off? He's too old to run away from home."

Elizabeth's face was contorted into a scowl as she stood in Beau's office, the umbrella in her left hand dripping desultory drops on his carpet.

"Don't do that; you'll get wrinkles before your time," Beau said in a gruff voice.

"No man—nor a woman either I suspect—is ever too old to run away if enough grief has been piled on him." He watched Lisbee's scowl soften to a frown of concern.

"Anyway, I don't think this is a case of running off exactly; more like he just needed a couple of days to himself."

"It's this Chipper Sullivan thing, isn't it?"

"That'd be my guess."

"But what if the kid really did kill himself? No one can find a murderer when there isn't one to find. Not even TJ."

Beau rose from behind his trestle table desk and handed a sheaf of yellow hand-written pages to Lisbee.

"That's the Calcott report, when you get a chance to type it into your computer." She nodded absently as he looped her umbrella over a wall peg to dry and stretched a long arm across her shoulders. Together, they moved out of his office toward the library, Beau's voice rumbling off the rafters as they walked.

"It *is* a dilemma, this Sullivan thing. If Harley was alive, TJ could explain to him that everything that could be done has been, and let it go at that. But with him gone, and his bill paid in advance, so to speak . . . well, there's just no way of knowing when the job is finished. Not without some kind of proof, one way or the other. Now that wouldn't bother a lot of folks; they'd spend a little time to satisfy themselves and say to heck with it."

"But not TJ."

"No."

Lisbee had taken her favorite leather chair in the library, her wool trousered legs curled beneath her. The rain was starting to diminish in the late afternoon gloom, the redwood branches through the glass nearly still in the dying wind, dripping their weight of water on the forest floor. Her left hand, still holding the pages that were the Calcott report, was draped over the arm of the chair and Smiley gave it a tentative lick with his long tongue. She smiled and dropped the papers to stroke his head while he sat leaning contentedly against the arm of her chair.

Another orphan ripe for rescue, Smiley had been. A mixed breed with the long ears and sad eyes of at least one of his more noble hound ancestors, he'd been the only companion of a nasty character named Murdock Jones until Jones got himself murdered. Unlike his former master, Smiley was naturally affectionate and had responded to Uncle Beau's kindness like a parched sponge, soaking up love like water, only to give it all back to anyone who administered the slightest squeeze. He nuzzled Lisbee's arm again and looked up at her beneath drooping eyelids.

"Well, what are we going to do about it? We can't just leave him dangling out there," Lisbee said, looking down at Smiley, who'd been in a dangling situation himself six months ago.

"I thought you might have some ideas."

She closed her eyes and leaned farther into the leather folds of the chair. "*Planned Gabble*," she said after a few minutes.

"I beg your pardon?"

"Where Chipper worked. Pan Global. There has to be more there than I've been able to find out so far. Cory Floyd doesn't know jack about anything in that company unless it reaches the executive boardroom. But somebody else does."

"Who?"

"Professor Deutch, for one."

"He the one lives on his boat down at the marina? What's his connection with the company?"

"Advice and consultation, but that's not as important as his connection with the boy; apparently he was fairly close to Chipper from the way he talked. Maybe he knows more than he thinks he does."

"Okay, the professor for one. And for two?"

Lisbee's face took on a rosy bloom which she tried unsuccessfully to mask with her best no nonsense consultant's voice.

"Justin Highstreet could be two. He was first on the scene of that burglary at Pan Global; he'll have access to whatever they've dug up, if anything. Something might be of interest."

Lisbee rose and started down the aisle, then turned.

"You going to help?" she asked.

"I think you'll do fine," Beau said. "And I've got a new case to get started on anyway. You going to start with the professor?"

"Well, there's time to get to the marina before dark and I . . ." Lisbee stopped as the thought that was in Uncle Beau's eyes hit her squarely. " . . . Oh. TJ. He'd think I was checking up on him or horning in or . . . would he?"

"Hard to say, but you might be better off starting with the deputy. Or the Calcott report."

Lisbee looked at the yellow pages, still laying on the carpet beside her chair.

"How do you always do that?" she said as she started back to pick them up.

"Do what?"

"Tell me I'm about to make an ass of myself without saying a word."

A fire crackled lazily in the small stone fireplace. It cast flickering shadows across the hardwood floor of the cottage, the only other illumination coming from the door to the kitchen, where the remains of a beef, mushroom, and onion pizza cluttered the hefty butcher's block table. Justin Highstreet, in jeans and plaid flannel shirt, sat in a straight-backed kitchen chair at the makeshift office squeezed between the telephone table and his aging recliner, trying to concentrate on the computer screen. He would have managed just fine if it hadn't been for Lisbee's warm, round rump resting on his thigh. She was trying to type, but the angle was all wrong sitting on his lap and she was cursing under her breath and repeatedly stabbing the delete key. He slid his hand up to cup her breast and she made a throaty sound, then sat back against him.

"Shit. This isn't working," she said.

"I thought it was."

"Oh, *that's* working all right. That's the problem. Listen, let me sit here and you stand behind me and watch over my shoulder. There isn't enough room for two chairs."

He pulled her long hair aside, kissed her neck, and got up.

"Yes ma'am, whatever you say. You're the expert."

Arms leaning across the chair back, Justin forced his concentration back to the screen, where he was immediately lost. Lisbee would normally tell him each step she was taking, explaining carefully and concisely as she went. But tonight she was silent.

"Just exactly what is it you're doing?" he said at last.

"Something highly illegal, unless you happen to be hired by the target as a consultant. I'm trying to break into Pan Global's intranet." She frowned. "And I see they haven't done everything I advised them to, or I wouldn't be doing this well."

"You got in? You actually broke into that high tech outfit with this piddling little computer?"

"This piddling little computer doesn't know what a lowly place it occupies on the social register. It only knows 1's and 0's. You can break into Lawrence Livermore Nuclear Labs with a laptop if you know the right back doors to use."

"Jesus, that's scary."

"Yeah. Isn't it."

"What was that databank you just got into? Private key something?

"Private key escrow accounts. The most common means of encryption is by using a public key and a private key. The public key is just what you'd suppose; it's in the clear, both parties in a transaction have access to each other's public key. It's like a name tag or a mailbox number. But the private key only you have and you'd better keep it in a safe place. You and the issuing escrow agent, in this case Pan Global."

"And you use both these keys to encrypt the message or whatever?"

"Right."

"But how does the guy at the other end decrypt it?"

"With his own private key, issued by the same agent."

"And it's also in this escrow bank?"

"Um hmm."

"This bank that you just broke into with my piddling home computer? Shit, it's worse than I thought. Could someone else do that, someone who wasn't working for them?"

"Not necessarily; at least not without some social engineering." Highstreet raised his eyebrows. "Con games. Pretending to be an employee trying to fix some problem on the system—getting someone on the phone to go through a login process and stealing their account name and password—that kind of thing."

"That's not what you're doing now."

"No. I have root access, so I can get the account names and passwords without going for an Oscar."

"Then what was it they didn't do? That you advised?"

Lisbee didn't answer. She was typing rapidly, half words and symbols dancing across the screen. Finally she stopped.

"There," she said and turned to look at Highstreet.

"What they didn't do, and I'm not really surprised, is go to a one-time login for everyone with root access or access to the key escrow bank. That's where you change your password every time you access the system. It's a real pain in the butt for the users. They hate it. The only one who's been doing it is Professor Deutch when he does a remote login, but he's a pro. I'd have expected that from him."

"So what did you do just now? Change it for them?"

Lisbee grinned.

"Yeah. Cory Floyd's going to walk into a pack of howling scientists in the morning. If he doesn't like the flak, he can always fire me and have his system administrator change it back. I sent him a message telling him to get ready for the uproar."

Highstreet stood and stretched to loosen the muscles in his back that had tightened from stooping and peering over her shoulder, imagining the ruddy faced Floyd being besieged by disgruntled mathematicians.

"So is Pan Global bullet-proof now?"

"No one is bullet-proof, but they're as good as I can make them at the moment. It's still people who are the biggest threat—employees with an ax to grind. What's the latest on the break-in? Was there someone on the inside?"

"No evidence of it. Not that that means much. I had Jack Delaney at Scotts Valley PD check his files; there's one guy works there who runs a flaky BBS at home; *Chamber Door*. Could be used to advertise hot items if you knew what to look for, but they haven't been able to get anything solid."

"Name?"

"Rudy Tang. He's no scientist; some kind of gofer, probably not smart enough to hijack the computer system, but not above picking up a little extra cash on some borrowed hardware."

"You want some coffee?" he said, turning toward the kitchen.

"Sure, if you're having some."

When he returned with the mugs, Highstreet saw a screen filled with color and neat, old-fashioned script. In one corner a large black bird seemed to hover over the messages, its bright yellow eyes piercingly alert as the wings fluttered in the animation.

"Now what are you doing?" he said.

"Now, I'm playing. Our Mr. Rudy Tang, lowly employee of Pan Global and master of the flaky BBS called *Chamber Door*, has built himself a page on the Web. Looks like he's an Edgar Allen Poe fan."

TWENTY-FIVE

Eᴌɪᴢᴀʙᴇᴛʜ ʜᴀᴅ ꜱᴘᴇɴᴛ the second half of Wednesday night badly after rousing herself from the warmth of Justin Highstreet's bed shortly before two to make her way through the dimly lit deserted streets to her own apartment. She had left plenty of food and water for Hester, but was nevertheless assailed with guilt at the rush of meowing, slithering, rubbing welcome she received from the cat on unlocking her door. After this highly emotional display Hester subsided into a sulk, as was her habit on such occasions of perceived neglect, though they were few, and proceeded to ignore Lisbee's attempts to make up. Well acquainted with this routine, Lisbee still made a few feeble attempts to comfort the cat and when they were rebuffed, felt even guiltier.

She undressed in the dim glow of the night light and slid between her own cold sheets, hoping she could catch a few more hours sleep, but her crowded thoughts continued to tumble over one another in the darkness. As she listened to the chiming clock in the living room strike three, then the quarter hour, she finally gave it up and padded barefoot into the kitchen to make some tea. Hester, thinking it was close enough to breakfast time to come out of her snit, followed and stood at Lisbee's feet, looking up expectantly. Smiling, Lisbee dropped two treat's in Hester's dish, and having completed the reconciliation, the two returned to the bedroom where the cat settled into the rumpled bedclothes and her mistress into the worn chair in front of her

Macintosh. She placed the steaming cup of tea out of harm's way, just beyond the mouse pad with Hester's imperial face emblazoned on it—a gift from Ellen Allbright.

Bringing up the Internet connection, Lisbee decided to take a closer look at the Web page Rudy Tang had authored. She had a vague and completely unfounded feeling that it simply didn't fit him. Ridiculous, since she didn't know the man—how could she know what did or didn't fit a total stranger? But whether or not its content was his doing, there were things she could find out about him from it.

The crimson red background flashed onto the screen followed by the laying in of its pattern—flocks of ghoulish black ravens with amber eyes in a geometric proximity reminiscent of M. C. Escher. Pretty sophisticated for a stockroom clerk, or whatever he was at *Planned Gabble*. A white frame in the upper left corner of the page held the single raven animation, dark wings aflutter. In the main frame a large graphic of Poe's distinctive silhouette slid into place beneath a stark title listing only his years of birth and death: 1809 - 1849. Under that, a bulleted list of hypertext links in bold black script directed the Poe aficionado to a few of the myriad sites on the Web where biographies, history and his best known works might be found. And near the bottom of the page, a quotation:

"It may roundly be asserted that human ingenuity cannot concoct a cypher which human ingenuity cannot resolve."

The word *cypher* was another underlined link, and when she followed it, Lisbee found herself at the home page of Pan Global, Inc.

Clicking back to the Poe page, Lisbee's gaze fastened on its address—*WWW.CHAMBER-DOOR.NET*. Rudy Tang, or someone, was paying the fifty dollars a year it cost to maintain his own domain name, *CHAMBER-DOOR*. A custom domain name was the digital equivalent of a vanity license plate. And in the credits at the bottom of the page, comments on the site were invited to be sent to its actual author; *WEBMASTER@LOTREALM.COM*. L...O...T... REALM. *Lord of the Realm.* Another vanity domain name—this time Mick Deering's, her old friend from Santa Cruz University days. It was Mick who had actually designed and built the web site.

Though she would rarely admit it, and then only to herself, Lisbee was a little afraid of Mick Deering. Not physically—Mick was the gentlest of creatures with his lean, handsome face and lazy smile. It went deeper than that, and was somehow more compelling. A fear of what? Mental domination? Rather a melodramatic description, but it was all she could come up with.

They had known one another when they were both undergraduates at the private, and consequently expensive, SCU. It was exciting then, being in his inner circle. His was a type of genius that was not unknown on other college campuses across the country, but where most of his fellow hackers with similar gifts cracked forbidden computer systems from boredom or from some real or imagined slight by the academic bureaucracy, Mick's escapades were characterized by their lack of malevolent intent and, to an even greater extent, by his bizarre sense of humor. These factors had not kept him from being suspended on three occasions, but they had figured prominently in his never being criminally charged.

Lisbee had resisted joining Mick Deering in his projects, though it had taken more determination and will power than she imagined she possessed. That was where the danger lay. It would have been so easy to fall in with him—let herself be persuaded by his charm and good looks, his sense of fun. As it was, she had been privy to each of his *campaigns* as he had called them. He could not resist sharing the excitement of each victory with someone who could appreciate its subtlety and flair.

His favorite had been the attack he dubbed *The Compensatory Adjustment Campaign*. Having found he could gain access to the mainframe where the University's personnel files resided, he was able to substantiate his own views that certain professors and teaching assistants were underpaid for the work they performed, and using a highly sophisticated algorithm he developed himself, managed to double their paychecks by subtracting matching funds from the wages of those professors deemed less deserving, again based on his personal evaluation of their performance. Since the total funds allocated to meet the payroll were never exceeded, it was only through the outraged cries of the faculty members who were victims of pay cuts, and to their credit a few who were beneficiaries of unexpected salary increases, that the ruse was made known to the administrative staff. Having made his point, Mick owned up and obligingly removed the offending algorithm under the watchful eye of the Dean of Computer Science. In a spirit of generosity, he even pointed out the defects in the system that had allowed him access so that they could be patched to preclude future invasions. He was suspended for one semester.

During his third suspension, with only four units outstanding for graduation, he made the decision not to return. His horizons had expanded far beyond campus life, even beyond national boundaries, to the world at large—through the labyrinthine corridors of the Internet. In the intervening years, Mick had gained a reputation as a sort of hot-wired Robin Hood, traveling at will every path in the global Sherwood Forest, rubbing electronic elbows with lawful and lawless alike. His band of merry men—and women—grew steadily, and though he remained true to his own peculiar code of ethics, virtually nothing went down in that shadowy world without him knowing about it.

Lisbee closed the Internet connection and carried the cordless phone to the bed, moving Hester gently aside so she could lie back against the mound of pillows. It wasn't quite four AM, but she knew Mick would be up, and indeed, the phone rang only once before a mellow voice came on the line.

"Bess?"

"How'd you know it was me?"

There was a soft chuckle on the other end.

"You're the only one who'd have the gall to call me at this hour—or the insight. You've never lost the need for vocal contact. Everyone else emails."

"What are you doing for breakfast?"

There was a pause on the line.

"Are you cooking?"

Lisbee thought of her tiny kitchen, her ineptitude with a morning skillet, and sneaking in the back door of her mind, a vision of the proximity of her bedroom to said kitchen, with Mick standing there, eyes smiling, watching her every move.

"No, but I'm buying."

A nearly inaudible sigh.

"Okay. Where?"

"Denney's?"

"My God."

"Can you think of anything else open at this hour?"

"My place."

Lisbee hesitated.

"Are you telling me you can cook?"

"No, but I can call out for pizza."

"Pizza for breakfast? There's no all night pizza place around here."

"There isn't for the general public. Bring your checkbook. Thirty minutes."

He hung up.

A lamp glowed dimly through the bow-fronted window of the two-story frame structure as Lisbee mounted concrete steps toward the wide covered porch, which was unlighted.

"If he does get somebody to deliver pizza, they'll probably break a leg and sue," she thought as she reached to rap on the door. It opened before she could touch it and she jumped involuntarily.

Mick Deering stood languidly in the door frame, backlit so that his impossibly white teeth were framed by the fair curls surrounding his long saturnine face. He wore gray sweatpants and a black tee shirt with some kind of glowing surreal landscape on the front, and his feet were bare. Lisbee suppressed a shiver and managed to smile.

"Come into my parlor," Mick said and she laughed out loud. He hadn't lost his ability to read thoughts.

"I'm no fly, you arrogant bastard," she said lightly and ducked beneath his arm and into the room.

After closing the door, he turned and surveyed her, still smiling.

"The Queen Bee, come home to the hive at last." He made a courtly bow from the waist. "Your servant."

"Jesus, Mick, come off it. It's me, remember? Save it for your raw recruits."

Deering looked wounded.

"I never recruit, Bess. Can I help it if . . . ah well, never mind. You're here, that's the important thing."

He moved gracefully across the room and reached for her jacket, slipping it from her shoulders, managing to caress them lightly as he did so. She began to turn, ready with a reproachful glance, but he was gone, disappearing into the darkened hallway with the coat over his arm. God knew what she would have to ransom it back with. *Damn* him. He was as compelling as ever—maybe more so.

Lisbee sat in a bamboo chair, its fat cushion enveloping her, and called up an image of Justin Highstreet, lying beside her. Had it been only a few hours ago? It might have been years—she was in another world, another time, and though she tried to hold on to it, the picture faded.

"Not still seeing the troglodyte, I trust?"

He was back. And once again, slipping unnoticed into her mind's back pocket.

"Kyle? No. That was over before it started. I'm afraid I wounded his delicate ego."

Mick set two glasses and a bottle of red wine on the low glass table at her feet.

"Wine for breakfast?"

"I'm sorry. It is breakfast for you, isn't it? I've been up all night, so it's dinner for me. A little time trick. Would you rather have tea?"

With the sense of having stepped into a bog of benevolent quicksand, Lisbee realized that she would rather have wine. She would rather it were dinner for her too, regardless of the clock. She wished fervently to be a part of Mick Deering's airy timeless world that didn't mock convention so much as simply not notice it.

"Yes, I'd better stick to tea. I have to be at the office in a little while. Mick . . . ."

He held up a hand.

"Let me get your tea and then we'll talk business. I know that's why you're here."

"I'm sorry."

"Don't be. Another time, another place, and who knows? Mine is an optimistic nature." He stooped to kiss her lightly on the mouth, then disappeared into the darkened hall again.

When they were seated over red wine and chamomile, Lisbee spoke without preamble.

"Rudy Tang and Chipper Sullivan. I saw the web page you did for Rudy. Chipper's dead. What can you tell me about them?"

"Other than what's readily available? I'm not sure there's much. Chipper died from overconfidence. That's the word that's out. Are you investigating his demise or the smash and grab at *Planned Gabble*?"

"I'm investigating whether there's a connection between the two—or rather TJ is. I'm helping out."

"I doubt there's a connection other than Rudy being close to both of them. And the web page was originally Chipper's idea, not Rudy's. Rudy can't *spell* web. He's at his technical pinnacle running that BBS for his friends in the trade."

"Black market trade?"

Mick Deering stretched his long legs beneath the glass-topped table and adjusted the pillow behind his back, then took a sip of wine.

"Bit of this, bit of that. Your friend the deputy can help you out there, or more precisely his friend Jack Delaney at Scotts Valley PD."

Lisbee stiffened in her chair, then relaxed, her face breaking into a grin.

"You really are a bastard, you know that?"

"Yes," Mick nodded, returning the smile. "But optimistic, as I said."

"Was Chipper involved in the BBS?"

"Only as an intellectual exercise, I gather. He provided upfront money and managed to lift some pre-release encryption software from *Gabble* and set Rudy up as a key master to impress his friends and get the backing he needed. Make them feel safe."

"Why couldn't they get *PGP* off the 'Net?"

"Oh they could, but the name is everything, isn't it? *Pretty Good Privacy* doesn't give a warm feeling to a bunch of paranoid street merchants who don't know any better. Or so I would imagine."

"So Chipper was the brains, and now that he's gone, Rudy's limping along on his leftovers. Where did Chipper get all his background? He refused to go to college and his system at home was just juvenile junk—I checked it out."

"You're not becoming a bit of a snob, are you Bess? The best and brightest in that league are rarely to be found on the honors list. And he wouldn't have left any trace in a nest he'd flown from. Didn't get along with Mom, our Chipper. The BBS hardware is the obvious place if he left a trail at all, which is questionable.

"As to the late young Sullivan's prowess, I think you'll find the answer at the knee of our mutually esteemed friend, Professor Deutch."

A scarcely audible tapping caused Mick to rise gracefully.

"Did you bring your checkbook? Total is $19.68; make it out to Nehi Nguyen," he said moving into the shadows toward the front door.

TWENTY-SIX

BY 9:30 THURSDAY morning, the rain had disappeared completely and a watery sunlight filtered through the trees, splashing pale yellow light on the freshly washed shrubs which clung to the gap-toothed fence. The homely little rental house on Ferris Lane in Felton, where Miss Sims had said her young friend lived, was silent. Beau Billings, with a large cardboard cup of cooling coffee, sat in the front seat of the old station wagon thinking it was a lovely morning to put in a little peaceful surveillance. He would see if he could catch a glimpse of the girl, but if he didn't by, say, noon, he'd find a phone booth and call Clyde Allbright to see if anything had come through on the brother or the parents. In the seat beside him, Smiley watched through the half-opened window. When nothing bigger than a songbird moved for a full minute, he sighed and lay down to take a little snooze.

There was no traffic in the lane, it being well off Highway 9 which was the main thoroughfare of the mountain community. Highway 9 was the main drag of all the towns strung along its length like knots in a rope as it meandered northeast through the Santa Cruz Mountains, curving sometimes gently, but more often sharply through dense forest to eventually emerge at the village of Saratoga in Santa Clara Valley. It then continued across the flats, changing identities every few miles like so many streets in the South Bay—Saratoga-Sunnyvale Road, De Anza Boulevard, Mathilda Avenue—finally traversing the Lockheed Martin facilities near the southern tip of San Francisco Bay to turn full circle and head back toward the mountains as Lawrence Expressway, formerly known as Lawrence Station Road.

In an hour and a half of watching, Beau observed three joggers, all female, a homeless man with a shaggy gray beard pushing a grocery cart laden with what Beau supposed amounted to the sum of his worldly possessions, and a school-age boy, glancing nervously over his shoulder as he darted across the lane to disappear into a field of high, wet grass; a truant probably. The rental house where Camellia Tang lived remained closed and silent until about ten minutes after the last jogger had passed, when a marmalade tomcat of impressive proportions jumped lightly through the tangle of weeds in the front garden to sit in a patch of sunlight on the cracked walk leading to the front door.

The cat remained there, sunning himself, until a noise distracted him and he turned as the door to the house opened slightly. A lilting sing-song call, barely discernible, floated on the still air, but the cat stayed stubbornly seated, head cocked at the sound, but unmoving. The door opened further and a young girl stood on the tiny porch, hands on hips in the ultimate feminine gesture.

A soft blue sweater topped the full flowing denim skirt which reached her ankles, slender above ludicrous work boots and heavy socks. What was it Lisbee called that particular aberration of fashion? *Prairie chic*. Beau thought there must have been worse modes of dress throughout history, bent on detracting from a woman's natural beauty and grace, but he couldn't recall one offhand. A boldly colored scarf tied back her long black hair from a high smooth brow. Though he was too far away to see her features clearly, his impression was that they would do. Grace, he decided, was her strong suit rather than conventional beauty. Grace so pronounced even that garb couldn't hide it.

When it became clear that the sing-song was having no effect on the recalcitrant cat, the girl uttered a word which sounded like nothing Beau had ever heard. He was slightly startled and searched his memory of the interview with Aurelia Sims. The girl was retarded, yes, but he was sure nothing had been said about a speech impediment. Was it Chinese? She repeated it, then spoke a third time in exasperation as she started for the cat. This time Beau got it and laughed to himself. *Pineapple.* The cat's name, apparently, and a darned good one, too. As she bent to scoop the animal up in her arms, Beau clipped the leash on Smiley's collar and stepped onto the verge where the wagon was parked, the hound bounding down to sniff the virgin terrain.

He fully expected the young woman to disappear back into the house as he walked slowly down the opposite side of Ferris Lane, letting Smiley explore, nose to the ground. It was only to establish himself as unthreatening, an old man walking his dog, that he had decided on the spur of the moment to get out of the car. But when he was close enough to look up naturally and take in the view of the yard where she had been standing, she was still there, the cat resting in her arms on its back like a baby. Beau smiled and sketched a gesture that would have tipped his hat if he'd been wearing one.

"Morning," he said.

The girl watched him somberly for a moment, then smiled and raised her hand in an answering wave. It was early days yet, but she sure didn't appear to be in any trouble, Beau thought as he continued walking Smiley down the lane.

TWENTY-SEVEN

 T J FELT HIS stomach lurch as the *Emmy T.* hovered on the crest of one roiling green wave before dipping into the trough between it and the next. The vivid blue horizon teetering on its axis through the vast windows at the helm became progressively thinner until it disappeared completely, replaced by a wall of white-flecked, angry water. The boat, engine whining steadily at twenty-eight hundred rpm, began its climb of the next hurdle and the unsettling sequence was repeated again, as it had been since they'd left the safety of the harbor.

It wasn't *mal de mer* that was affecting his insides, TJ decided. He didn't feel that he was in imminent danger of losing the Danish and coffee he'd had for breakfast—it was the zero gravity sensation that was the core of every amusement park attraction worth its price, the thrill of controlled, well-engineered danger—only the control was missing. He stood at the lower helm, grasping the spokes more for balance than anything, as Sunny Cortez calmly issued directions into his left ear.

"Bring her back a bit—to port, this way—this is a following sea; you want to keep the stern ninety degrees to the set of the waves. That's it."

TJ cramped the spokes too hard, realized it as the bow began to angle too far left for the stern to be at ninety degrees to the waves coming up behind, and reversed the wheel. Sweat was popping out in beads on his forehead and his thick, gray-streaked hair clung damply to his scalp. The gray had never bothered him overly much; he'd always smiled derisively at the TV commercials for exotic formulas that whisked it away and gave you back twenty years everywhere but in your joints, but maybe he'd been too smug. By the time this was over—if he survived—he might be in the market. The way things were going his hair was likely to be as white as Uncle Beau's.

The trawler crested the next wave and began the descent once more. At a little over seven knots, the *Emmy T.* was moving slightly slower than the eight foot seas so that the swells rose up from behind, lifting her to teeter on the brink of the crest before moving on to rise up and block out the horizon once again. It was claustrophobic, that wall of nothing but water.

"You're doing fine. How do you like it?" Sunny Cortez was smiling, standing spread-legged in the middle of the cabin, one muscular hand nonchalantly holding the grab rails that ran most of the length of the salon's ceiling, the grab rails from which a large, old-fashioned brass lantern was suspended. It hung from artfully knotted quarter-inch nylon line so that it swung freely with the motion of the vessel in an arc that was approaching a hundred degrees, TJ estimated. Maybe one-twenty. He tried not to watch it, though the motion grabbed his attention every time he glanced toward his instructor. And against the forward bulkhead a brass bell sounded melodically without benefit of human intervention, its knotted pull rope dancing, another reminder of the vessel's roll—as if he needed one.

"This is pretty smooth, huh?" TJ said hoarsely.

"Sure. It's not bothering you, is it?"

"Oh, hell no. At least only when my heart beats, and it stopped about twenty minutes ago. I expect this kind of thing takes some getting used to . . . although right now I'm damned if I know why a guy would want to."

Sunny Cortez laughed.

With each trip to the top of a cresting wave, TJ could see for what seemed to be miles in all directions. Clumps of fishing boats dotted the whitecapped water both in front of and behind the *Emmy T.* They looked small and vulnerable, but he supposed they were not. The fish were there in spite of the sea state and if your livelihood depended on them you'd better be out there in everything but blatantly foolhardy conditions, like a real storm or dense fog. As they began slipping into the trough before the next wave, a flash of light struck TJ's eyes. He thought it must be the sun's reflection off the water until they crested again and he saw it was coming from one of the fishing boats, well apart from a group off their starboard bow. On and off again. Then back on, like some kind of signal.

"Are they signaling to us?" he asked Cortez over the roar of the engine. Sunny looked in the direction TJ had indicated.

"Don't know why they would be," he said lazily. "Probably one of the other fishing boats."

"Why would they signal at all? Wouldn't they use the marine radio?"

"Should. Unless their radio's out. Wheel her around and we'll start back; that is, if you're ready."

"I believe I am."

When the red and green channel markers at the entrance to Moss Landing Harbor came into view, Sunny moved toward the port side door.

"Just hold this course. I'll take it from the fly bridge, then you come on up. Docking lesson time."

"Red, right, returning—don't run into the beach. Gotcha."

The seas subsided noticeably as they neared the red and green buoys and TJ managed to climb the ladder to the fly bridge with no trouble. The two men stood side by side at the helm while Sunny Cortez guided the trawler, reducing speed when they had passed the entrance markers. He grinned at TJ and spoke into the whipping wind.

"I wouldn't have taken you out in this for your first lesson, but you seemed determined."

"You mean it's not always like this?"

"Not always. But it didn't hurt to get your feet wet—metaphorically. This is nothing the *Emmy T.* can't handle."

"It wasn't the *boat* I lacked faith in."

"You'll do fine. Don't worry about it."

TJ shook his head.

"I'm not. I've got other things to worry about."

"Meg giving you trouble?"

"I don't know. Is she prone to giving people trouble?"

Sunny's eyes, which had been smiling along with the rest of his face, suddenly changed; became hooded, blanking out what he was thinking.

"Depends."

"On what?"

"On whether people are giving her trouble, I guess," he said flatly.

"Now when you get to this point, you need to keep her going slow and steady—take your hands away from the wheel and just use the stern thrusters to guide her. Like this." Sunny touched the tiny joystick and a thin whine reached TJ's ears as the boat began a smooth turn toward the fingers of Bel Harbor's docks. Slow and steady, hands off the wheel. Maybe that would work on Meg Sullivan, too.

TWENTY-EIGHT

HE HAD FALLEN into an exhausted sleep after the second time even though it wasn't yet noon, and when he awakened more than two hours later Meg Sullivan was gone. Except for a lingering scent of her musky perfume she might never have been there.

"Jesus. Love 'em and leave 'em," he'd said into the quiet, before he realized he was glad she wasn't there. He got up and began straightening the rumpled bedclothes, whistling tunelessly. He hadn't asked her here; had even told her he didn't want her company. Maybe she'd finally gotten the idea. He didn't know what he would have said to her if she had stayed, and he sure as hell wasn't up to a third go-around.

Entering the salon, he headed for the refrigerator, suddenly aware that he was ravenously hungry. He made two sandwiches and when he found he could only hold one and a half, flung the remains through the salon door to a gaggle of soggy seagulls, who seemed surprised but grateful for the windfall.

The rest of the dismal day he spent working; polishing every inch of interior teak on the vessel, which was considerable; exploring the engine room; making an inventory of tools that were aboard and noting what few things were missing that he would have to supply. He continued his efforts into the evening, finding things to do, until the salon and both cabins gleamed. When there was nothing left undone that he could think of, he put a TV dinner in the microwave and ate at the small table, his dinner companion the latest Elmore Leonard. After clearing up, he returned to the master stateroom with the book, thinking he probably wouldn't sleep after the nap he'd had. To his surprise he dropped into a dreamless sleep, waking six hours later to watery sunshine streaming through the spotless windows. It was then he'd determined to take the boat out, in spite of the whipping wind and cresting seas.

Sunny Cortez made the docking maneuver look easy, and as the *Emmy T.* slipped gracefully into the berth, Lisbee's old professor stood smiling fatuously, reaching to take the bow line that TJ tossed him to secure the boat. Sunny cut the engine and TJ leaped ashore to tie the other lines, feeling awkward and clumsy, his hands not yet used to the fluid motions of dogging a cleat that Sunny had shown him. It would take time, he knew, but that didn't keep him from suffering the frustration of the fledgling, especially with someone looking over his shoulder.

"Fine, fine," the professor chirped, his smile still stretched wide across the lantern jaw, exposing large, square teeth. "Was the excursion to your liking? A bit rough, perhaps? Not for this fine vessel, of course; nothing for her. Now mine. Poor old *Prime Number* would be tossing like a cork on a day like this. Better off staying at home where we belong."

When he'd secured the last line TJ stood, returning the professor's smile.

"It was a little choppy," he said, thinking that the understatement would make him sound like an old salt who could take that kind of gut-wrenching sea state in his stride.

"But I did enjoy it," he added quietly, slightly astonished to discover this was true.

"Of course you did. Made for this kind of thing, I would say, just getting rather a late start. It happens all too often, don't you think? We run along busily tending to business until we stumble across our real calling, sometimes too late to do anything about it, only not in your case, of course. Plenty of time."

That old boy's not a mathematician, TJ thought, he's the village philosopher—and historian too, probably.

"I'm not all that sure it isn't too late in my case," TJ grinned, "but I doubt it's going to stop me."

The professor nodded happily, his head bobbing on his long neck, bright dark eyes missing nothing.

"I was just going to make some tea. Would you care for some? When you're finished here of course. Or I have beer if you'd prefer something a little stronger?"

"I believe that tea of yours could become addictive, but if you've got a beer I'd sure appreciate it."

"Beer it shall be, then. I'd join you myself, but I've still work to do. Tea for me, I'm afraid. I'll just run along then," Professor Deutch said, lifting a hand in greeting to Sunny Cortez, who was descending from the fly bridge.

The *Brown Betty* teapot, a thin wisp of steam issuing from its curved spout, sat on the salon table flanked by a plate of shortbread cookies, napkins, a spoon and matching creamer and sugar bowl on one side, and on the other a frosty glass of beer and bowl of pretzels. TJ Billings took a seat on the corduroy-covered settee. Deutch, having shouted 'Come aboard,' to his hail, was not in evidence when he sat down, but his dome-shaped skull, spiky gray hair awry, popped up from the galley well a moment later. He clambered into the salon, another plate, this one heaped with what appeared to be ham sandwiches on cocktail rye, in his hand. TJ was about to protest at this largess on the part of his neighbor, but on consideration decided against it. He was hungry.

"Looks good," was all he said.

"Please help yourself," the professor said, bobbing and smiling while he poured his tea. "Do you a world of good. It's the salt air, you know. Not a cliché, what they say about it—it does make one ravenous."

After TJ had finished two of the ham sandwiches and was starting on the shortbread cookies, the professor fixed him with an avian eye over the rim of his teacup.

"It's all about the boy, isn't it?"

"Beg pardon?" TJ said after a brief hesitation.

"Chipper Sullivan. The tragic demise of that poor young man. That's why you're here."

"What makes you think that?"

Deutch leaned back against the settee, crossing his long legs at the knee, resting his bony hands on his lap.

"That sort of death is an unfortunate commonplace among the young these days, of course. A bitter commentary on our little triumphs of technology, our arrogant advancements along the road of evolution, that our children become so lost on the way." TJ watched the older man's eyes, trying to read behind them, but said nothing.

"Still, it's hard to accept. Hard for any parent—or grandparent—to believe in the senseless waste. Much better to be able to focus on someone or something as a direct cause. Especially for a man of Harley's generation." He poured more tea and added self-deprecatingly, "Mine, too, of course. But Harley was a man of action, while I've been satisfied to hide beneath the shell of academe and merely observe. Cowardly, really, but there it is."

"Did Harley tell you he didn't think Chipper killed himself?"

"Oh, no. Nothing that overt. I only saw him once after the boy died. His illness was far advanced; he was gray and shrunken, weighed down with the tragedy and too weak to fight back himself. That's why I naturally supposed he chose you as his champion."

"Why me?"

"Not you particularly, not at the time. Of course not. I didn't know you then, did I? But later, when you first appeared here, with Elizabeth."

"Why me even then? Because he left me the boat?"

"The boat? No, I hadn't even thought of that, though now you mention it, it makes sense, of course. Silly of me to miss it. No, it was because of Jim Locksley. I didn't know him myself—I came here much after his time—but Harley spoke of him often. His tragic death, and the son-in-law who never gave up trying to find his killer. Billings. It's not all that common a name, really. And when Elizabeth entered my class, I presumed she was Locksley's granddaughter, which made you the son-in-law who took over his investigations agency. Who else would Harley have called on when he was in need?"

"I don't know," TJ said wearily, "but I wish he'd found somebody else. This whole thing is a dead end as far as I can see."

"And you're uncomfortable with being paid in advance for something you don't believe you'll be able to accomplish? That's what the *Emmy T.* is—payment in advance. It's the way Harley would do things." The professor lifted the *Brown Betty*, swirling its contents, then put it down, deciding against the remains for himself. He looked at TJ's empty glass and raised an eyebrow, but TJ shook his head.

"I must commend your sense of responsibility in the matter—it seems to be lacking in so many these days—but my advice, if I may presume to offer it, is to look at the thing objectively. It's nearly a lost art, you know, objectivity; but it's essential to problem solving. Personal bias, in whatever form, merely serves to cloud what may already be murky waters. But you know that, of course you do, or you wouldn't have made a success of the business you're in. Still, even the best of us succumbs occasionally without realizing it."

TJ looked at this elderly man with the cartoon face, contorted by exaggerated expressions to accompany his stilted speech, and was struck by what a fine teacher he must be. He wondered if the students who were lucky enough to attend his classes knew what they had come across. Or if the University paid him what he was worth. Probably not, in either case.

"All right, professor, you've made your point very nicely, and with a great deal more consideration for my ego than it deserves. You should have just said it's time I stopped brooding and got off my ass—that's what I would have done."

"You know, I believe you would," the professor said, his eyes nearly disappearing in the wrinkles of a wide smile.

"It's going to cost you though, me getting off my duff. I need to know more about Chipper Sullivan; who his friends were, what he did in his spare time. His mother doesn't know, or says she doesn't. They weren't close, apparently. But you must have seen him a lot. Who were his friends? Did he bring them to the marina, take anyone out in the boat? I'd pick you for a pretty keen observer."

"Not the keenest, perhaps. My vision isn't what it once was, but I might be of some assistance in that regard. Chipper spent a good deal of time here, mostly with his grandfather, but there was one boy who accompanied him occasionally. Someone he worked with, I gathered, at Pan Global. You knew he worked there, didn't you?"

TJ nodded.

"Yes, well, this boy, as I said, was an infrequent visitor, but they seemed to be close when he was here. An Asian boy, but tall, nearly as tall as Chipper himself, and with long hair tied back in a ponytail."

"Do you know his name?"

"As it happens I do. Chipper told me during one of our discussions on the vagaries of the Internet that he runs a Bulletin Board System out of his home in Felton. His name is Rudy Tang."

TWENTY-NINE

Cory Floyd stabbed at the button on his intercom as it buzzed angrily for the fifth time in less than twenty minutes.

"What is it, Judy?" he said shortly.

"Dr. Petersen and Ms. Mathis. They can't get into their accounts on ZED. Kevin again?"

"Yes, Kevin again. And tell anyone else with the same problem to see him. He's the System Administrator. And get me Melissa Collins. Now."

"In your office or on the phone?"

"Here. Is she in yet?"

"I don't know; I'll find out."

He turned back to his computer and reread the short email message from Elizabeth Billings, a carbon copy of which she'd sent to Kevin Pogue, the SysAdmin, so he'd know how to deal with the one-time login she'd put in place.

"*. . . assumed it was an oversight so in the interests of security I plugged the hole. Apologies for the flack, but thought you'd rather be safe and hassled than vulnerable and possibly breached. Regards, EB.*"

Well, he certainly didn't need the flack, but under the circumstances he was glad she'd made the move. When the Memorandum of Agreement with Lowry's service was executed, his people would be all over the system looking for things just like the one she'd fixed. He deleted the message in clear and copied the encrypted version, the one that had traveled the Internet, onto a Zip disk with his other personal files, then locked it in his desk drawer.

He was undecided on how to handle the reports Melissa was gathering; the hacking attempts. Would it be better to shred them and not advertise their existence, or would the fact that the attempts had failed be more in their favor? Maybe the latter, but to be safe, he'd see that she shredded the printed copies and only kept the on-line files—encrypted and locked away, like his email.

That only left the Professor. And the biggest hole of all. That genie, if it ever got out of its bottle, would bring them all down. He scanned his email once more. He should have had a reply from the old bird by now—the latest test algorithms had gone out to him last week. The irony of sending the most sensitive information by *snail mail* was not lost on Cory Floyd, but he agreed with the Professor that it was unwise to put any development work out on the 'Net, even encrypted. He decided to send a veiled inquiry to Deutch, asking how his evaluation was coming. In this case bad news was better than none at all; they could keep working at it, eliminating one more direction so they could try another.

He had just finished his query when the buzzer sounded again.

"Melissa's here, Cory."

"Send her in."

Lisbee had decided to bypass Cory Floyd and catch him on her way out. She let herself in at the employee's side entrance with the company badge she still possessed as a cleared contractor and made her way down the central hall to the large double doors that opened into the rear area of the building. The couple standing in conversation by a spring water dispenser near the doors took no notice of her; in jeans and tee shirt, with the badge clipped to the pocket flap of her denim vest, she was just another denizen of Pan Global. The cardboard cup of Starbuck's coffee in her hand was yet another piece of effective camouflage; it might as well be useful for something—the coffee had had little effect on her tired eyes, still scratchy from lack of sleep after her predawn visit with Mick Deering.

In the warren of cubicles beyond the doors a few heads appeared over partitions and someone laughed as she made her way among them, checking the nameplates outside each one as she went. A voice behind her made her start involuntarily.

"Help you find someone?"

She looked around at what appeared to be a spotty teenager, surely no more than fifteen, with a scraggly growth of blond beard struggling mightily across his thin cheeks.

"Rudy Tang. Is he in today?"

"Yeah. That's his desk," he said, pointing to a surface stacked with papers, cardboard boxes, and a computer monitor swirling the random colors of a screensaver.

"He was here a minute ago; I'll go see if I can find him," the boy said and moved away before she could thank him.

Lisbee was debating whether to move a stack of magazines from the only chair in the cubicle so she could sit down when the blond boy returned and scooped them up.

"They're mine," he grinned. "He's on his way."

"Thanks," she said and remained standing, looking over the partition to follow a dark head that was moving in her direction.

Rudy Tang stopped at the doorway and rested an arm along the cubicle wall. His face was almost expressionless; only a slight tilt at the corner of his wide mouth that might have been the beginning of a smile.

"Back again?" he said in a low voice.

"Lord, I didn't think I was that memorable," Lisbee smiled. "That was months ago."

Rudy nodded noncommittally.

"Help yourself," he said, gesturing toward the computer.

"Thanks, but it's you I came to see this time. Do you have a few minutes?"

He shrugged and dropped into his chair, flipping the ponytail with one hand so it hung over his back as he slouched down, feet extended, legs crossed at the ankle.

"Shoot."

"It's about a friend of yours; Chipper Sullivan," she said, watching his face closely. She was hoping for some reaction, but there was nothing. Rudy Tang merely continued to stare at her with his quarter-smile, waiting for her to go on. Lisbee had the sinking feeling he could stay like that, stolid, emotionless, for hours at a time.

Lisbee's Mustang in the parking lot at Pan Global was unmistakable, and under ordinary circumstances it would have brought a slow smile to TJ's face. But at this particular moment, he would have preferred his daughter to be elsewhere. Minding her own business. He chided himself for the thought, admitting that she probably was minding her business—she was the consultant for the firm and he wasn't—and pulled the XKE into the slot next to hers. He would give it ten minutes and if she hadn't appeared go make himself known to someone who could grant him an interview with Rudy Tang.

About five minutes had passed when Lisbee came out a door at the front of the building, in deep conversation with a man in jeans and a banded-collar shirt. He was short and stocky, and even though he wasn't wearing sweats and a rugby jersey, TJ had no trouble recognizing him. The red BMW driver who had overstayed his welcome at Megan Sullivan's house, or so she would have him believe. They stood talking for another two minutes, then the man went back inside while Lisbee started toward her car, registering a slight double-take when she saw who was parked next to her, but recovering quickly.

She leaned both elbows on the Jag's passenger windowsill, unmindful of the provocative view her rounded behind provided to two young men exiting the building.

"Hi," she said from behind a broad smile. "How's the boat?"

"It's okay. Who was that you were talking to?"

"Out here? Cory Floyd."

"Chief Executive and errant husband?"

"That's him."

"Where you headed?"

"Back to the office. Are you coming?"

"In a while. I've got to see a guy in here; friend of the Sullivan boy."

Lisbee's face clouded.

"Oh shit," she said in a small voice.

TJ knew at once that his initial assessment had been right after all. She'd been minding his business, not her own.

"Fuck," he thought, barely managing not to say it aloud. But his momentary wish that his goddamned family would just back off and let him handle it must have shown on his face.

"Listen, I'm sorry. I didn't think you knew about Rudy Tang."

"I didn't until an hour ago."

"Buy you a beer at the vestry?"

TJ sighed and started the Jag.

"I may need something stronger," he said, putting it in gear as Lisbee dashed for her Mustang.

THIRTY

LISBEE SAT WITH her head bowed, resting on one closed fist, feet curled under her in the seat of the big leather chair. It was a posture she used to adopt when she was young and on his bad side, or thought she was. TJ was by now over most of his anger, having released some frustration by leaving rubber on Pan Global's asphalt and making it to the old church in just under fifteen minutes.

"Look, don't worry about it. If you couldn't get anything out of him it's not very likely I could have either."

She made a dismissive gesture with her other hand and lifted her head to take a sip from the large glass of milk beside her.

"It's the pepperoni. Don't ever have pizza for breakfast at four AM," she said enigmatically.

TJ started to laugh but caught a warning look from Uncle Beau and restrained himself.

"That's not a temptation I'm faced with on a regular basis, but I'll keep it in mind."

Clyde Allbright returned from the vestry with his second glass of beer and turned a cheery eye on the company.

"If you ask me you'll be lucky to get the time of day out of that kid. He's a tough nut."

Beau turned from his perusal of a pair of squirrels scrabbling around the trunk of one of the larger redwoods.

"I thought you said you couldn't find anything on the boy, Clyde."

"I said he didn't have a criminal record—at least nothing since some petty stuff when he was fifteen or so, and that's been sealed. He did leave a trail, though. Him and his little sister. Quite a sob story among the ladies over at County."

"You found out what happened to the parents?"

"Yeah. The quake. Killed 'em both. Didn't find the bodies for days in all the rubble."

"God," said Lisbee, shivering at the memory of that bright afternoon in October, 1989, when most of the downtown area had been demolished in a matter of seconds. "They were downtown?"

"In their store. They'd just opened it a few weeks before; poured all the money they had into stocking it. The kids got a little insurance money, but not much. The girl wasn't even close to sixteen yet and Social Services tried to convince her brother she'd be better off in an institution, but he wouldn't have it. Got a job and held them off, said he'd take care of her, their parents would have wanted him to. Like I said, he's no pushover."

"Was there any connection between him and Chipper Sullivan then, or earlier, when they were kids?" TJ asked.

"None that I could find. Doesn't mean there wasn't, but not for the record."

TJ sighed and drained his beer glass.

"Well, without any more information about who his friends were and what he might have been mixed up in that could make him an enemy pissed off enough to kill him, I'm right back to zero. His mother's the only one who gains by his death and even if she'd wanted to get rid of him, which she might, I don't see her doing it that way. A gun or a knife or a tire iron alongside his skull maybe. Goddamn Harley! He wouldn't have set me up to finger his own daughter."

"You said the Professor thought the Tang boy and Chipper were close, from what he could tell." Beau was ruminating aloud, gazing into the trees.

"Might just be another way in, if Rudy insists on being uncooperative, and I gather he's not likely to change much."

"Spit it out, Uncle Beau," TJ said. "This pie's already so full of fingers it looks like an infielder's glove."

Beau ignored his nephew's uncharacteristic sarcasm and smiled benignly.

"It just occurred to me I've yet to tell you about my latest client."

THIRTY-ONE

THE SEAT SPRING threatened once again to burst from its moorings in the van's driver's seat as Rudy Tang hit the speed bump in the parking lot of *Planned Gabble*, some fifty yards behind a red BMW, waiting for traffic to subside before scooting onto Mt. Hermon Road heading east. Its transmission grinding ominously, the van lurched into the stream of oncoming cars in second gear and rocked along on aging springs before Rudy was able to coax it into third and negotiate his way through the traffic into the left turn lane at the light. Ordinarily his head would be nodding rhythmically as he drove to the heavy metal beat coming through the earphones attached to the Walkman in the seat next to him. The van's radio had given out three weeks ago. But the Walkman lay silent, nearly slipping to the floorboards as he whipped the van into the shopping center when the green arrow appeared. He parked next to a woman loading groceries into an aging Honda and strode purposefully into the U-Save Liquor Store, where he purchased two six-packs of Rolling Rock, a pack of generic ultra light cigarettes, and a red silk rosebud wrapped in cellophane from a jar on the counter.

Making his way next to the bakery section of the supermarket adjacent to the liquor store, he eyed the ready-made cakes behind the glass partition and finally decided on an eight-inch double layer with red icing roses to match the silk one. The bored blond girl behind the counter asked if he wanted HAPPY BIRTHDAY written on it, but he could tell she didn't really want to bother, and it didn't matter anyway—the roses were the thing—so he shook his head and she placed the cake in a pink cardboard box, taping it shut with cellophane tape.

When he returned to the van he put the liquor store bag on the passenger seat and set the boxed cake carefully in the foot well so it wouldn't roll around. As he did so, he noticed the corner of a small package sticking out from under the seat.

He pulled it out and set it beside the sack of beer, its red address label staring up at him. He had forgotten about it; forgotten his sentimental thoughts of delivering the thing to Professor Deutch himself so they could reminisce about Chipper. Stupid. The Professor might be one of them, even though he'd been Chipper's friend. That Billings woman had mentioned Deutch, knew him, and she wasn't to be trusted no matter what she said. He didn't believe for a minute she was just investigating Chipper's death. What was to investigate? He'd OD'ed. It happens; even to the smart ones. You have a couple of drinks and get careless. But God, he'd hated it to be Chipper, in spite of the circumstances.

Rudy considered dropping the damned thing in a mailbox on his way home, but decided he'd better check it out first. He thought he knew what was in it—the same as some they'd lifted in the past—encryption software; new stuff for testing. If that was all it was, he'd seal it back up and mail it in the morning. The Post Office was always losing stuff; nobody would think anything of it. He'd wait until Camellia was asleep, open it carefully so it could be resealed. Unless it might be worth something to somebody. He sure could use a little extra cash.

Camellia Tang could scarcely believe the rose would stay like that forever; not open into full flower and then turn brown and have to be thrown away. But that's what Rudy said, so it must be true. And it didn't need water—shouldn't have water, he said. She had placed it in a small glass vase and set it by her bed and her eyes kept returning to it, to drink in the deep red color of its perfect petals. Silk, like her scarves. Only not like them; very different, for the leaves and petals were stiff not soft.

At first she had not wanted to destroy the twin roses on her birthday cake, but Rudy insisted that's what they were for, you couldn't save them and she still had the other one. So she had eaten one; smooth and buttery, it had the same flavor as the white icing on the rest of the cake, even though it was a different color. Then she had started to cry. When he asked her why, she didn't know if Rudy would understand that she was happy and sad at the same time; thought he might just say that was stupid. But he didn't. He'd felt that way too sometimes, he said, only it had been a long time since it had made him cry. That made her laugh because she could not remember Rudy ever crying and when she imagined it he looked so funny.

Camellia wanted desperately to tell someone about the rose and her birthday cake. She'd shown it to Pineapple, even given him a bite of the cake without frosting, but he didn't want it and left it in his dish. Miss Sims would love to see it and she thought about suggesting that she visit her tomorrow, but knew somehow Rudy would say no. Miss Sims was too busy now to see her anymore, Rudy said. She had new students and a nephew had come to live with her and she was sorry but there just wasn't any time for Camellia. That made her sad too. She liked Miss Sims.

She lay awake in her bed long after the time she would usually have been asleep, thinking of the rose and Miss Sims. And Chipper, of course. Pineapple was asleep beside her, but he woke up when she threw back the covers to go into the bathroom. The light was still on in the living room and she could hear Rudy fumbling around in the kitchen. It sounded like he was looking for something in the silverware drawer. Maybe he'd decided to have another piece of birthday cake. When she returned to her bed, Pineapple was on his back with his feet in the air, purring loudly. She smiled and scratched his furry stomach, which was what he wanted when he did that.

THIRTY-TWO

IF STEVEN "CHIPPER" Sullivan had really been given a push into his early grave—and TJ was not too far from conceding that he probably had been, if only because everyone connected with the damn thing was so insistent he hadn't—it all boiled down to the hackneyed old standbys; motive and opportunity. The only motive he'd been able to come up with so far was his mother's, and combined with her frank dislike of her only child it left her at the top of the list, whatever his gut feeling about her innocence in that particular regard might be.

Opportunity was a little trickier. Access to the *Emmy T* didn't rule Meg Sullivan out, but that was just where the boy had finally died—it didn't mean shit about where, or even when, he'd gotten the drugs that had killed him. And that was the other thing that bothered TJ. The method. Women were notoriously more likely to be poisoners, but the downers he'd OD'ed on weren't exactly the same thing as traditional poison. How did she get them to him? They hardly saw each other according to her, and Harley's attitude toward his daughter the last time TJ saw him tended to confirm her lack of position in that strange family group. Did she leave the stuff on the boat in a small box marked *Eat Me*, and hope he'd go for it like Alice did when she went down the hole after the White Rabbit?

Unfortunately, Meg Sullivan was still the best starting place. It was an unnecessary and messy complication that he'd ended up in bed with her, but that was nobody's fault but his own. He sure as hell wasn't the only one. And that was another thread he'd have to chase down eventually—Cory Floyd. Probably nothing there, but the kid had worked at Pan Global and its top executive was screwing his mother. Jesus, what a snake pit.

Toweling his hair as he stepped from the shower he decided to call Meg Sullivan at the University and offer to buy her lunch. It was time he started calling the shots, and his first call was to choose his own ground.

The morning overcast was beginning to recede and a cold November sun cast brittle shards of light on the gray swell outside the narrow entrance channel to the Santa Cruz Marina. The Crow's Nest, perched at the end of the pier where the neck of the channel swelled into the harbor itself, was catering to a normal Friday lunch crowd; noisy, relaxed, sporting only a few obvious tourists. In more clement weather, TJ would have chosen a table on the deck surrounding the upstairs bar, not for the atmosphere so much as for more privacy, where the winds off the sea snatched conversation away from neighboring ears. But the door to the deck was closed. The corner window table, away from the serving bar and not facing any of the televisions provided for its patron's amusement, would have to do. He wasn't expecting a confession out of Meg Sullivan. Wasn't even sure she had anything to confess to. But he was banking on her knowing more than she was telling, even if she didn't realize she knew it.

He had finished half his glass of draft beer when he spotted the auburn head moving up the spiral staircase. She wore dark marine blue wool slacks and a lighter blue bulky sweater that subtly accentuated her figure, swelling over the full bosom and clinging at the rounded hips. She was smiling slightly and the smile widened as TJ rose and held out her chair, a habit so ingrained from his youth under Uncle Beau's tutelage that he was unconscious of it.

"Nice outfit," he said.

"Thanks."

"How long do you have before you have to get back?"

"As long as I need. What did you have in mind?" Her eyes crinkled at the corners and TJ was glad he'd chosen a crowded restaurant. He smiled involuntarily.

"Just some questions. The service can be a little slow on Fridays, that's all."

"I know. I've been here a few times."

"With Cory Floyd?"

He watched her face carefully, but she displayed no particular reaction; a barely perceptible widening of her eyes maybe, but it could have been a trick of the light.

"No, not with Cory. That's not for public consumption. Image, you know. With Ellen Allbright, mostly."

She glanced at the menu.

"What would you like?" TJ said as a waitress moved toward their table.

"A double martini, up. I've got a feeling I'm going to need it."

When the waitress had gone to fetch their drinks and turn in the order for artichokes stuffed with shrimp and smoked salmon linguine, Megan Sullivan reached a slim white hand into the basket of warm sourdough rolls, and spreading one thickly with butter, took a bite. She must have the metabolism of a teenager, TJ thought ruefully, and restrained himself from doing likewise.

"Okay, Marlowe, shoot," she said a moment later when the martini was placed before her. "This should fortify me against the best you've got."

"I'm just doing a job, lady. One I didn't ask for in the first place, if that matters."

"It doesn't."

"Somehow I didn't think it would," TJ said and smiled. "Let's start with the easy stuff. What about the marina? What are you going to do with it?"

"Bel Harbor? I don't know. Sell it. Give it away. Keep it and rake in the money it doesn't make. I haven't made up my mind."

"It's not making a profit?"

"I suppose it is. Sunny keeps sending me checks—small checks—but I've yet to go over the books with him."

"He does the books? How long has that been going on?"

"Since he bought in for thirty per cent a year or so ago. Harley wanted to turn it all over to Chipper then so he could retire and not worry about it, but the kid didn't want to do it.

Took too much time away from his other projects. Said he'd hire a bookkeeper when it was his."

"Harley told you that?"

"No. Sunny. Like I said before, Harley didn't tell me the time of day."

THIRTY-THREE

THE LEATHER SOLES of Cory Floyd's loafers made walking on the still damp dock like walking across a frozen pond and he held his arms slightly akimbo, for balance in case he slipped. It made him look something like a penguin out of water. He was not unaware of this and wished he had changed into the Nikes he kept in the car, but he hadn't thought of it. He hadn't thought of anything since he received the Professor's email at 8:30 that morning except getting to him and finding out what the fuck had gone wrong. It was past 11:00 by the time he'd been able to get away from the office and was now well after noon. A thin film of sweat covered his upper body, making the silk shirt cling annoyingly under his jacket, though the temperature was barely into the sixties.

The professor had never received the package. It had been mailed more than a week ago, but still hadn't arrived. Judy was sure she must have mailed it, she'd said. If he'd put it in her out box, that's where it went—out. She'd been a little prickly and defensive about it which made Cory think she probably didn't specifically remember doing it. He didn't like to imagine what might have happened to the package if she had screwed up. The test software could be pirated if it got into the wrong hands, but that didn't worry him as much as the cover letter to Deutch.

Cory couldn't remember it word for word, and he hadn't used Lowry's name, of course, but he had mentioned something about *our mutual friends in DC*, or some such veiled reference that could be trouble, depending on who might read it. That was why it hadn't gone out over the 'Net, encrypted. Because even with the best Pan Global had, the top of the line that was being considered for use by the government to save money on their classified transmissions, there could be a hole big enough to let a train through. It was almost laughable, but Cory Floyd wasn't laughing.

The thin face at the salon door was expressionless as Professor Dean Deutch slipped the latch and slid it open, beckoning with a long-fingered hand.

"Cory. I thought you might be on your way here. Come aboard. I'm just fixing tea."

"I really wouldn't be overly concerned, you know," Deutch said when they were seated at the salon table with the teapot between them. "Packages go astray often even now, with all the improvements the Postal Service has implemented. It could turn up here any time. You've no reason to suspect anyone at your office would have taken it, have you?"

Floyd just frowned, shaking his head.

"Well, then, there you are. What news of our Mr. Lowry? Your meeting with him went well, did it?"

"Better than well," Cory said and recounted the proposition Lowry had made for a contract with Pan Global.

"Splendid! There, you see? Things are not as bad as you feared."

"What about the hole?"

"My *Hole in the Dike*? Oh, I'm much more encouraged on that account. Not a whisper anywhere that I can find, and

I've been most diligent. I do wish you were a mathematician so that I could explain to you how very unlikely it is that my little discovery will be repeated independently. It's all a matter of style, you see. The current style in factoring is using brute force, and it's understandable in a way because computers continue to become so much more powerful—able to compute so much faster. It's only natural to take advantage of their power, but it tends to stop one from thinking, doesn't it? From appreciating the elegance of simplicity. And that's what my little *Hole in the Dike* is—simplicity in its purest form.

"We're not ready for it yet, of course. It would be catastrophic with virtually the entire globe wrapping all its secrets in the current encryption technology. Not until a new approach can be developed by people like yours at Pan Global."

"What about the Sullivan kid? Have you found out where he hid the copy he stole off your laptop?"

"My dear Cory, as I've told you before, I'm not positive the boy did steal a copy. It's only that the directory it was in was accessible to him, and working for your company he could have ferreted out the necessary key to decrypt it. I blame myself, of course. I let him use my machine because he was such an avid pupil. An old man's pride of accomplishment, I suppose."

"But you haven't found anything? On the boat?"

"No. And I've searched everywhere he could possibly have concealed a floppy disk. The single fault of simplicity, that it fits in so small a place."

Professor Deutch considered the morose expression on Cory Floyd's face.

"If he did take it, and knew what it was, what would he have done with it?"

"I've given that a great deal of thought and I'm sorry to say, humanity being what it is, I would have expected him to try to make a profit from it. I'm not sure he had the wisdom or experience to do it successfully, however. And now the poor boy is dead. That may well be the end of it."

"But we don't know, do we?"

The Professor rose and, picking up the aged brown teapot, shook it briefly.

"No, I'm afraid we don't. More tea, Cory?"

THIRTY-FOUR

AT TEN MINUTES to one on Sunday afternoon, Justin Highstreet had called to say they'd made an arrest in the Pan Global break-in. He had some paperwork to finish up and would come over in about an hour to tell her about it. The morning mist had cleared to reveal fine fall sunshine, so Lisbee ducked out to the market two blocks away for steaks to cook on the small grill she kept on the deck at her apartment. She enjoyed the little deck, with its flower boxes and bright folding chairs. There wasn't enough room for a table, and the view was not of the ocean, but the thickly wooded green of the mountains rising behind town—that was why she could afford the place. For the same price, with an ocean view, the apartment would have been barely a studio instead of the large living room and bedroom, with full kitchen and six-foot walk-in closet. It was no contest.

Justin had been guarded on the phone, saying only a few words and giving no hint of what the outcome of the investigation had been. She had a vague hope there might be something that would shed light on the Chipper Sullivan-Rudy Tang connection, but was not expecting much. Just being able to eliminate that avenue would be enough, she told herself, and came within an inch of believing it.

The crisp knock on the door came as she finished applying the last brush of mascara to eyelashes that had never needed it. With a swipe at her hair, she gave up on lipstick and was rewarded for her foresight when Justin kissed her soundly while standing in the doorway in full view of two neighbors who pretended not to notice. He seated himself on the couch, legs stretched out beneath the predictably littered coffee table, and initiated a boxing match with Hester, who responded by swiping his knuckles with unsheathed claws, leaving a thin trail of blood.

"Unruly bitch," he said, scratching her ears to change the tempo. The cat rolled on her back, purring.

"You're the only one I know who can get away with that. She's usually incurably hostile. Beer?"

"God, yes."

When they were both seated on the sofa with Hester, acting as chaperone, ensconced firmly between them, Lisbee looked expectantly into Highstreet's square, tanned face.

"All right, let's have it," she finally said when he didn't speak, but just sat smiling at her.

"You wouldn't consider bribing a police officer, would you?"

"Yes, certainly. But not until I know what I'm getting is worth the sacrifice. Give."

"It was just a piece of luck. San Jose PD worked a sting Friday night; picked up thirty or so who'd been dealing in the valley. We weren't in on it, but one of them dropped the name of a small fry over here, hoping for a bargaining chip. Couldn't turn one of his own or he wouldn't live to see his next birthday. But we'd put feelers out over the hill and some smart detective remembered and gave us a call."

"So who was it?"

"Nobody you know. I can't give you names until they're arraigned tomorrow. You know the drill."

"But no connection with Pan Global? Or Rudy Tang?"

"Doesn't look like it. Not right now anyway. It's possible they were using Tang's BBS, but that would be a bitch to prove. And we don't have anything yet that could get us a legal look at his setup."

"No hope of them talking, I guess?"

"They weren't talking *before* they got their lawyers. If we hadn't found some of the stuff they weren't able to get rid of, we wouldn't have shit. County's running their prints, and if we're lucky we'll get a match on some of the ones the lab picked up at the scene, but I'm not holding my breath. Even street kids know enough to wear gloves."

Lisbee rose and gathered up the empty glasses and a basket with a handful of dime-sized blue corn tortilla chips in the bottom.

"Well, I'm happy for the Sheriff's Department, but I'm damned if that was worth the price of a bribe. You'll have to earn your keep."

Highstreet looked dubious.

"Doing what?"

"Well, I'm cooking, so I thought maybe dishes? Or can you think of something else of value you can contribute?"

"I can think of something, and I'm more than willing to pay in advance."

THIRTY-FIVE

"IT'S NOT SO much a question of ethics as it is of just being neighborly; showing a genuine interest in the welfare of your fellow man, you might say."

They were seated at a small wrought iron table on the flagstone patio just beyond the kitchen door, and Aurelia Sims had finished filling Beau's coffee cup for the second time.

"And by that I mean fellow woman too, of course."

"But you've told me Camellia appears to be all right."

Beau smiled. The November sun was springtime warm as it sifted through the branches of a tree studded with fat lemons, just beyond the neatly trimmed square of lawn that bordered the patio.

"Well, yes ma'am, that's right as far as I could tell. Physically she seems to be just fine. Not being mistreated or held prisoner or anything. But is that all you really wanted to know?"

Miss Sims gazed intently into the old man's clear blue eyes, the laugh lines etched deeply into the leathery skin stretched over high cheekbones. His white hair was neatly combed and he smelled faintly of Old Spice.

"Mr. Billings, you are either a very wise man or a complete bounder," she said at last. "Perhaps both. You recognize me for what I am—a lonely old woman—and you have no compunction whatever in taking full advantage of it. Yet at the same time, I feel confident that your aims are predominantly unselfish. That Camellia Tang's welfare, and mine too I suppose, are uppermost in your mind."

Beau's smile didn't waver.

"I don't know about being wise, but I do think the two of you would be better off for seeing one another again. Having a little talk. The thing is, as I see it, if you just happened to be in the neighborhood and decided to drop by—when brother Rudy is at work, I mean—why, it's Camellia's house too. If she invites you in, what's the harm in that?"

"None if you put it that way, except my own guilty knowledge that it is against her brother's wishes. That's what has been troubling me. Why? Why should he not want her to see me? I can't begin to fathom what there was about our friendship that would be cause for alarm."

Beau sipped his coffee and leaned back as far as the small chair would allow, lifting his gaze to the lemon tree in a parody of contemplation.

"The only thing I can think of is that Rudy might have something to hide. Something his little sister is aware of, whether she knows it or not, and could reveal to a friend in all innocence. Maybe, say, a word here or there about a young man called Chipper Sullivan."

The elderly woman's thin white hand stopped on its way to her coffee cup and leaped involuntarily to cover her mouth in a gesture so quaintly old-fashioned Beau had nearly forgotten its existence. A quintessentially genteel expression of feminine surprise.

"Chipper? Oh my dear. Is that what this is all about?"

"She's mentioned him before, has she?"

"Mentioned him? Oh, Mr. Billings . . . Beau. That poor child is in love with him."

As gently as he was able, Beau recounted to Aurelia Sims the circumstances of Chipper Sullivan's death and Anadarko Grace's involvement in the case. The fact that there had been a close relationship between the dead boy and Rudy Tang and his sister was now established beyond doubt, but he wondered if Miss Sims would be willing to carry it any further considering the effect it might have on Camellia Tang. Her expression of sorrow had deepened as he spoke, and now she sat, head bowed, as a chill breeze began to ruffle the leaves in her neatly manicured garden.

When she raised her eyes, Beau was relieved to see they were clear and steady, her small chin set firmly.

"It's getting cool. Why don't we go inside," she said and stood, beginning to gather cups and saucers.

"Here, let me help with that," Beau said, taking his own cup and the plate that now held only the crumbs of a lemon cake he suspected had originated from the fruit of the tree in Aurelia's back yard. He held the screen door for her and when the dishes had been deposited on the kitchen counter, followed her into the living room where she switched on a brass lamp to dispel the gloom of the swiftly fading afternoon.

"So my task, as I understand it, is to call on Camellia while her brother's at work and find out as much as I can about what he and Chipper Sullivan were up to," she said without preamble.

"Well, now, . . ." Beau began.

"Please don't take me for a fool. This is a matter that could well involve a crime or crimes, isn't that right? I'm really not a shrinking violet, though I may look like one."

"That's not something I would ever take you for," Beau said.

"Good. It is a nasty bit of work, I'll admit, but I can't think of anyone who would be more suitable to do it than I, considering Camellia's involvement in it. I know her quite well, and I believe I can spare her feelings as much as is possible under the circumstances. Certainly more than any stranger could."

Beau nodded.

"That's what I thought. Otherwise, I wouldn't have asked you."

"That's settled then. I'll begin tomorrow." She hesitated, and Beau wondered if she might be rethinking just what it was she had agreed to do. He needn't have worried.

"But don't you expect miracles, Beau Billings. This may well take several visits; it's a delicate matter, after all."

"Very delicate," he agreed, smiling. "You take just as long as you need."

THIRTY-SIX

THE MONTEREY BAY Aquarium Research Institute, occupying most of the spit of land across the channel from the Moss Landing municipal harbor, would have covered more than a city block had it been located in one. MBARI, as it was known locally, had replaced a rather sleazy string of aging fisheries and bait shops, yet surprisingly did not seem out of place for its surroundings. The architect must have been a genius, TJ thought, for the multi-tiered facility, painted a soft sea green with weathered brown shingle roofs, showed subtly through the maze of masts of the fishing fleet as if it had been there for decades instead of months. A huge square vessel, the *Western Flyer*, snuggled against the far dock. It was the mother ship to MBARI's latest robotic submarine, financed through the still cushy David Packard grant that had established the institute ten years before, and looked like a modern day paddle-wheeler waiting for passengers. But even that didn't affect the overall impression of a working fishing port.

The village of Moss Landing itself was unchanged from pre-MBARI days. One street long, it was crowned at its intersection with Highway 1 by a garish pink stucco Mexican restaurant which had changed hands several times over the years and was currently, if rather predictably, dubbed *The Whole Enchilada*. Then followed a marine supply store, several antique shops in various stages of economic decline, school district building, post office, and the most prosperous looking structure, with its fresh yellow paint trimmed in white, the Chamber of Commerce. About a hundred yards beyond the restaurant, the main street of Moss Landing curved south at a right angle to parallel the highway. From this elbow stretched a narrow road leading to the one-lane bridge that crossed the slough, just beyond the entrance to the municipal harbor parking lot. Across the bridge, the road meandered past the Institute to end at the tip of land forming the southern leg of the harbor entrance, which was still occupied by the remaining fish packing facilities.

The harbor district's lot was nearly full late on a Monday morning. As Clyde Allbright maneuvered his ten year old Cougar through the lanes in search of a parking slot, TJ recalled Meg Sullivan's lack of surprise or rancor when he'd asked flat out how much money Bel Harbor was bringing in. She continued to amaze him. He hadn't met anyone he was so poor at outguessing since he'd been a raw college kid, anticipating having a friendly drink with one of Uncle Beau's oil field hands, but ending up on the wrong end of a quick left jab in the mouth instead. She'd told him frankly what money she'd banked since Harley died; money sent to her by Sunny Cortez as her seventy per cent share of the profits. It didn't seem like much to TJ, but he was, admittedly, ignorant of the business and its economic potential.

"Fucking seagulls are gonna give me a new paint job if we stay here very long," Clyde said, eyeing the circling scavengers as they followed two boats that were sliding in to dock after the morning's fishing.

"I know," TJ grinned. "That's why we're in your car and not mine."

Clyde managed to give him the finger while simultaneously wheeling the Cougar in between a rusting Chevy van and a GMC pickup with canvas concealing the lumpy cargo in its bed.

The two men wandered leisurely along the grassy verge, watching the activity below. Most of the slips were occupied by commercial fishing boats of varying sizes, and those that weren't showed signs of habitation—lines attached to the iron cleats, crates of gear, long yellow electrical cables that would provide shore power to the boats when they returned.

"Looks like they've got a pretty full house," TJ said. "I wonder what they do with drop in trade. You see anything that looks like guest docks?"

"If you mean empty parking places, it doesn't look like it. Why? You going to bring yours down here for a visit?"

"Just curious," TJ said and started walking toward the Harbor Master's office. "Let's go find out."

They stood in the small foyer for five minutes before a young man in Levi's and denim shirt, with shoulder length hair that needed washing, emerged from the back to stand behind the counter. He seemed friendly enough, but explained that the harbor master was gone and wouldn't be back for at least an hour; he was just helping out. TJ knew the answer to his question before he asked, from studying the maps and brochures that were on the wall and in a rack on the counter. But he asked anyway.

"You got any guest docks? I've got my boat up at Pillar Point—thought I'd bring her down for a week or two, try the fishing down here."

"Our guest docks are at the yacht club," the man said, pointing to the map TJ had already seen. The Elk Horn Yacht Club was north of the municipal docks, south of Bel Harbor. On the map two rows of penciled fish backbones indicated about fifteen slips of varying lengths for guests. "Or there's probably space available at Bel Harbor," he added. "You could check."

"What about a permanent berth? You got anything?"

The young man scratched his week's growth of beard.

"We'd have to put you on the waiting list. It's pretty long. But you could check with . . . ."

"Bel Harbor?" TJ finished for him. "Thanks. I guess we'll do that. Sorry to take up your time."

"No problem," the young man said, smiling.

There was no sign of Sunny Cortez as TJ approached the Bel Harbor office, but he found the door unlocked, so he went in. Like the Harbor Master's at Moss Landing, there were maps and charts on the wall, but there the resemblance pretty much ended. This office was, if not cozy, at least homey by comparison. In one corner two aging wicker chairs sat on either side of a table stacked with boating magazines. Three small but cleverly painted watercolors of ships and harbor scenes hung on the wall above them. The glass-topped counter that divided the foyer from the office area was a repository for maritime memorabilia, apparently collected by Harley Sullivan himself—ship's lanterns, an aged brass porthole, and several items TJ couldn't put a name to. All were displayed with museum-like precision.

The office area itself was unremarkable; two desks, a small, clunky looking though no doubt adequate computer, and three five-drawer filing cabinets. A door to the right, which was closed, might lead to some kind of living space, or at least a kitchenette containing a coffee maker, for there was a rack of mugs on the wall of the office, some with names painted on them.

TJ found the latch on the half-door that separated the office area from the foyer and went behind the counter. He wasn't sure what he was looking for; if Sunny Cortez was skimming from the marina's profits he would hardly stash the money in one of the filing cabinets and leave the office door unlocked. Two of the cabinets produced predictable contents—receipts for marina supplies and contract work; a file for each of the slips that were currently rented, containing sparse but pertinent information about the boat that occupied it and its owner. But no account books. Those were probably kept on the computer, he decided as he tried the third cabinet's top drawer. It was locked. They all were—all five drawers. TJ inspected the lock plate in the middle of the top drawer, under the handle, and decided he could probably pick it. But better not. Not in broad daylight, when Sunny might reappear any time.

He had just stepped back from behind the counter when his good judgment was vindicated by the sight through the glass pane in the office door of Sunny Cortez strolling leisurely along the dock. By the time he entered, TJ was seated in a wicker chair, leafing through a two-month old copy of *Passagemaker*, a magazine dedicated to trawler yachts.

"Looking to move up to something bigger?" Sunny asked.

"No, I don't think so. Not just yet, anyway."

"What can I do for you? It's a good day to take her out if you want."

"Can't today. I just wanted to talk to you a minute. About berth rent, mainly. I suspect I owe you some money, don't I? I never thought to ask about the freight around here. What do these slips go for a month?"

"Well, the going rate is $6.50 a foot; that includes electricity and water. Gate keys are $10.00 apiece, refundable if you decide to leave and turn them back in." Sunny opened the file drawer that contained the slip rental folders.

"Fact is, I don't even have a folder for that slip. The owners don't pay themselves rent. I'll make one up later, but there's no hurry."

TJ did a quick mental calculation while pulling his checkbook from a hip pocket.

"I'll give you a check now anyway, so I don't forget. Seems pretty reasonable. Upkeep must be kind of steep on an operation like this, isn't it? Does that kind of rent cover it?"

Sunny Cortez gave him an unblinking gaze, his dark eyes taking on that hooded look TJ had noticed when they first met, before his face relaxed into an easy grin.

"Barely. The profits really come from fishing parties and launch fees. When its salmon season you can't poke a needle into this place for miles around for the boat trailers. And

I take groups out party fishing—like Harley used to do before he got sick."

It seemed a perfectly plausible explanation. Of course the profits from fishing would be seasonal, and TJ just hadn't thought of it. So that was that. He thanked Sunny and left, walking slowly up to the parking area where Clyde had dropped him off on his way back home. The XKE had been expertly targeted by at least one seagull. As he wiped the excrement from the otherwise gleaming hood with a rag from the trunk, TJ wondered why his irritation at the random attack barely approached what it normally would have been under the circumstances. Because he was thinking of something else?

Because *that wasn't that* maybe? What was wrong with Cortez's story about the income from Bel Harbor? Nothing. Nothing at all, except that look in his eyes before he told it.

THIRTY-SEVEN

THE PLACE WAS buzzing with the news by the end of his shift. It was going to hit the fan, Rudy knew; the only question was how soon. Stupid, rotten, pure bad luck that Nehi's little brother had been fingered by some cokehead in San Jose trying to save his own skin. When they'd asked him to help in the inventory of what had been stolen from Pan Global, he'd thought he might be able to fix it so the monitor didn't show up on the list, but that was blowing smoke. It was there all right. And Nehi knew it wasn't part of the stuff his kid brother Jimmy and his dipshit friends had lifted. He'd really been pissed when Rudy told him, though he'd explained it was a matter of necessity—the BBS was going down unless he did something, and Nehi, the money man since Chipper died, hadn't been around—he'd had no choice.

None of this would have happened if Chipper was still alive. Chipper had money falling out of his pockets, from the old man or wherever. The BBS had been his idea and he'd set the whole thing up, got all the gear. All he'd needed was a place to run it from and that's where Rudy came in. And it was working—the fucking thing had taken off like a rocket, but when Chipper died Rudy had no choice but to go to Nehi. It wasn't self-supporting yet, wouldn't be for another six months or so Chipper had said, but Nehi had enough of a stake in its operation by then that he'd come through. Rudy wasn't sure if it was just referrals Nehi provided for his friends and their friends, or if he actually moved some of the hot items himself, and he didn't want to know. The less he knew the better.

But all that had changed now and the shit was definitely going to hit the fan, with Jimmy Nguyen picked up by the cops. Normally, those guys wouldn't open their mouths to eat, let alone tell the pigs the time of day, but the monitor was on the list and Nehi knew Rudy had taken it. It wouldn't take the brain of one of *Planned Gabble's* scientists to figure out that little brother might be able to make a deal—toss them a bone named Rudy as the inside man, even though he hadn't had anything to do with it.

Rudy was sweating slightly inside his camouflage jacket, though the temperature in the van was in the fifties. Fucking heater hadn't worked since July when nobody needed it. He had the Walkman on, headphones blasting in his ears to try and drive away the thoughts, but it wasn't working. The parking lot was emptying out, but the red BMW was still there, at the front where the execs parked; he could just see it's shiny rear fender from the back of the lot where he always left the van.

If he had given any thought to Cory Floyd up until now, it had been a throwaway opinion that he was just another flashy Yuppie who liked to be seen tooling around in the Beemer, talking in acronyms so people would think he was savvy, that he'd earned his position in the company instead of knowing somebody or buying in, which was more likely in Rudy's opinion. But the letter in the package addressed to the professor had changed all that. He hadn't understood most of it—Chipper would have, but there was no use thinking about that now. It was a lot of stuff about private keys and escrow accounts and all that shit *Planned Gabble* managed for the customers that bought their encryption software. Chipper had lifted some of the software so they could use it on the BBS. It was supposed to be better than the stuff you could download free from the 'Net, that's why they made money selling it. Rudy didn't know if it was or not—he'd trusted Chipper to handle that end and there hadn't been any problems as far as he knew.

Then the letter got really heavy. Math stuff. Something about the professor testing what was on the CD in the package, like Rudy had thought. He'd almost shit-canned the whole thing right then. But something made him glance down toward the end, just before that loopy scrawl that was supposed to be Cory Floyd's signature. Even then, he hadn't got it at first.

". . . . counting on your continued discretion in the matter of our friends in D.C."

He'd thought it referred to just what it said—some mutual friends of theirs—until he remembered what Chipper had told him just before he died. That something big was going on. Something that could be very profitable if they played it right. Something to do with the Feds. That's who the *friends in D.C.* were. The fucking Feds.

It had never bothered Rudy Tang that he lacked Chipper Sullivan's gift for learning—they were friends. And it didn't bother him now that he hadn't a clue what it was that was going down. The important thing, as Rudy saw it, was that none of those dorks had any way of telling what he knew and what he didn't. His guts told him that letter had to be worth something.

And right now he needed to disappear for a while, and to do that he needed a stake and needed it bad.

The message sent through the anonymous remailer had been brief. *'Be in your office at precisely 5:47 and be sure you're alone.'* Even without the digital signature, Cory Floyd knew it was from Lowry; knew he would be calling on the private line. At 5:50 Floyd was beginning to get nervous, wondering if something had gone wrong. Five minutes later he was pacing the office, hands in his pockets to keep them still, when the jangle of the phone made him jump. He forced himself to let it ring twice more before he answered.

"Floyd."

"Everything clear there? No company?"

"No, I'm alone."

"Good. Listen carefully, but don't take any notes. I've got the Memorandum Of Agreement set up but the Contracts assholes back here are being a little sticky. I told them if anyone's legally authorized to make contractual agreements for Pan Global, it's the fucking CEO, but they want to know if there's a Contracts organization you have to get in the picture. Is there?"

Floyd was not expecting the question and hesitated for a moment. The voice on the phone was overly patient.

"I don't want to bring anyone else in at your end just yet if I can help it, but Contracts won't budge without all the i's dotted, and without their say so I can't break the funding loose. Bureaucratic bullshit, but they've got me by the balls."

"I can sign without them in the picture," Cory said, finding his voice.

"That's something. What about Fedex? You open your own, or does your secretary do it for you?"

"Judy gets them, but I can probably . . . ."

"No *probablies*. I'll send it to your house. Your wife doesn't open your mail does she?"

"No, of course not."

"Good. Sign it and Fedex it back to the address it comes from. There's another thing."

Floyd waited expectantly, hoping it wasn't something he didn't have a ready answer for. He'd never come across a man like Lowry. It wasn't just the magnitude of the opportunity he was offering, the unthinkable consequences if he suddenly decided to withdraw and let Pan Global founder in its own red ink. It was the sheer force of the man's personality. He intimidated the shit out of Cory Floyd.

"I want you to decide how many people you're going to need to do this demo. The absolute minimum; no frills, no hangers-on. Understand?"

"Yes. Sure."

"There'll be some forms with the MOA package. Security stuff. I want you to hand pick these people. They'll have to go through a background check; not the full ride—there's no time for that. But I've got a shortcut I can use if I don't overdo it. So make it easy on all of us. No dopers, nobody who's on the verge of bankruptcy, and no one with any close contact with aliens. Non-citizens, not the flying saucer kind."

Lowry barked a little laugh at his own joke. It was the first time Cory had ever heard him laugh; the man never even smiled, and he wondered what he looked like when he did. His imagination failed him.

"Got all that?"

"Yes, I've got it. No problem."

"Good. Get it back to me within ten days. I'll be in touch after I get things rolling."

The phone went dead. No social amenities for Lowry. But then even Cory Floyd, who was inured to it and guilty himself of inflicting it on others without giving it a thought, would hardly have expected him to end their conversation by saying *'Have a nice day.'*

It had grown dark by the time Rudy saw the stocky figure emerge from the building's main entrance and disappear in the direction of the red rear fender that was now only a luminous gray in the fading light. He had stopped sweating and the cold was beginning to bite through his jacket. Coaxing the van to life, he left the headlights off in the nearly empty parking lot until the BMW had turned east onto Mt. Hermon Road, then lurched forward and pulled into the still heavy traffic five cars behind it.

THIRTY-EIGHT

THOUGH SHE WAS grown-up enough to know it was only make believe, Camellia Tang preferred to think that the almost magical appearance of Miss Sims was the granting of a wish she had made on her birthday—the wish to show her the equally magical silk rose that didn't require water and would never turn brown and withered. She had shyly confessed this and watched the smile bloom on Miss Sims' face, although her eyes, which usually twinkled when she smiled, stayed the same. Almost sad looking.

They had talked for a long time, and Pineapple, who usually only let Camellia get close to him, purred and rubbed against Miss Sims, showing off, and finally curled up to sleep in the old lady's lap while she stroked his soft fur. It was mostly about Chipper. That was another wish granted, for Camellia longed to talk about Chipper but knew somehow, especially lately, that Rudy didn't want her to. But Miss Sims was different, interested, seemed almost to encourage her ramblings about the fun they had had, she and Chipper, how he was nearly always there helping Rudy with the computers, but still had time for her.

Time for walks in the woods behind the back fence, holding hands, Pineapple leaping in front of them, climbing-running half way up a tree trunk and back down again, pouncing into the grass or piles of leaves after some small woods creature, but they always got away. Chipper would eat dinner with them often, smiling and helping her in the kitchen, laughing as she giggled when the arm he slipped around her waist tickled.

Miss Sims had complimented her on their house, the bright scarves Camellia had draped to hide the old furniture, and wondered if they had other friends over, like Chipper. There'd been no one. No one like him. It had just been the three of them until Chipper stopped coming. Camellia explained that she was sure he would be back soon, that he'd had to go somewhere far away for a while but would be turning up for dinner any time now. He'd always said he would never leave her, not for very long. Miss Sims had nodded and smiled, but again not with her eyes.

There were so many things she wanted to say, to tell, but some of them were almost like secrets and she wasn't sure she really ought to, so when Miss Sims put Pineapple gently on the couch beside her and said she must be going, Camellia asked if she would be coming back, thinking that she would know next time and could decide what it would be all right to talk about. She would come back, of course, if Camellia wanted her to, she'd said. And then she had passed her a small piece of light blue notepaper with her telephone number on it. Nothing else, not even her name; just the number.

She must call, Miss Sims said, if she needed anything, or just wanted to talk.

Aurelia Sims was a practical woman with a mind normally uncluttered by indecision. She had accepted this without thought during most of her life and only recently had she realized this state was rather rare in most individuals, especially those a generation or two behind her. She did not dwell on the matter and if she gave it consideration at all, she charitably postulated it might be because those younger people had so very many more choices in their lives than she ever had.

It was different this evening. As she moved around her familiar and well loved kitchen, preparing a fresh green salad to go with the Cornish game hen that was roasting in the oven of the old yellow gas range, she found herself overwhelmed with doubt about what she should do in the matter of Camellia Tang.

Aurelia was not a craven woman either, but she had been unable to bring herself to explain to the girl that Chipper Sullivan was dead and would not be coming back. She blamed that partially on not knowing what exactly she had been told by her brother; whether he had told the truth and Camellia simply chose not to believe it, or whether he too was postponing the inevitable, not yet willing to bear the grief it would cause her. Though her opinion of Rudy, based on their one telephone conversation, was not high, the young man obviously cared deeply for his sister. That mutual affection shone in the girl's face when she spoke of him.

The other possibility for her hesitation Aurelia Sims was most reluctant to contemplate. It smacked of using the girl; transforming her into a pawn. There obviously was a great deal more Camellia Tang could, and eventually would, reveal about her relationship with the Sullivan boy. Throwing her into a state of bereavement now might well mean that knowledge would be lost forever. The difficulty lay in divining whether that as yet untold body of information would have any bearing on the young man's death. Could what Camellia had yet to say provide proof—or even point to something that would prove—murder rather than suicide? It was impossible to tell.

She fussed about the small table, carefully setting her place with old china and well polished silver plate, pouring a half glass of fume blanc to complement the game hen. A growing frustration was building in her over her inability to deal with this situation. Perhaps she was just getting too old. It was only after she had sat down and begun to disjoint the small fowl that it occurred to her the decision was really no longer in her hands. She had left her telephone number with Camellia Tang; it would be up to the girl whether she returned or not. There would be no valid reason for another visit without a summons.

Feeling somewhat relieved, she decided she would phone Beau Billings as soon as she had finished her meal and report what had occurred, making it clear to him that further investigation on her part depended entirely on the girl. She was sure he would understand her position.

THIRTY-NINE

THE DINNER, LIKE Ellen Allbright herself, was overly generous. Lisbee was helping her store away the mountains of leftover pork roast, mashed potatoes, rich brown gravy, and apple crisp in the kitchen after TJ and Uncle Beau had retired to the homely den with Clyde, having been refused admittance to the feminine sanctuary to help with the clean up.

"I really do pay attention to what I cook for Clyde, and me too of course, most of the time, but I don't know—it seems like a little celebration with the things you really love shouldn't hurt once in a while." Ellen turned the dishwasher on and beamed at Lisbee.

"I mean, have you ever really studied those heart people's recommended diet? Maybe I'm just too old-fashioned, but it seems to me a person could starve to death on that kind of thing all the time. You might actually live a little longer, I suppose," she mused. "At least it would seem longer, without any treats ever."

Lisbee grinned.

"Don't look at me; I live on greasy hamburgers and pizza. The medical pundits come out with something new that's bad for you every day, so I figure stay with what you like and what the hell. If everyone starts living to be one hundred it's going to cause a worldwide economic collapse anyway," she said, scooping a dollop of apple crisp that had escaped its container into her mouth.

Ellen gave her a hug and Lisbee thought how fortunate she was to have this unworldly yet infinitely wise woman for a friend. There had been numerous times when she was growing up after her mother died that she'd needed the special understanding only another female could provide, and Ellen Allbright had always been there as confidant and advisor. She'd not had any children herself, which Lisbee personally considered a terrible loss to her own generation, but she had a natural empathy that benefited everyone close to her.

Mugs of freshly brewed coffee in hand, they started down the hallway, Ellen talking back over her shoulder as they went.

"I did everything you told me over the phone and it just came to life, just as you said it would. It's a wonderful little machine and I've done a bit of playing with it, but I'm really such a novice, so if you could just show me a few things . . . ."

Even in the subdued light from a shaded lamp in the room that had been converted to an office, Lisbee could see the glow of pride and excitement in Ellen's plump face as she switched the computer on and pulled a second straight-backed chair within viewing distance of the monitor. They sat together, shoulders hunched, fingers moving on the keyboard—one set expertly, the other somewhat tentative—for the next twenty minutes, while Lisbee ran through the catechism of commands that would allow Ellen to operate the word processing software she needed for her upcoming class. When she felt the older woman was comfortable with her lesson, Lisbee changed some system settings, explaining as she went what she was doing and why, then did the installations necessary to connect the machine to the Internet through the University's network, using the information provided in the student's packet Meg Sullivan had given Ellen *under the table* so she could get a head start.

The fact that it was not yet strictly sanctioned under the rules and regulations imposed by the University's system administrator didn't bother Lisbee overly much. They'd never miss the bandwidth; it was like following in the draft of a lead car on the straightaway at Laguna Seca. She smiled to herself as she set up the account, thinking of Mick Deering's forays into the bowels of those hallowed fiber optics. And when she did a quick remote check of her own email account, it was almost like some kind of electronic telepathy. There was a message from Mick, sent not two hours before.

"So you think he's skimming a little cream and maybe the kid found out more than was healthy for him?"

Clyde's incongruously dainty size seven and a half stocking feet were propped on the edge of the redwood burl coffee table he had succeeded in salvaging from Ellen's inevitable garage sales and charitable drives for more than twenty years. His father had made the thing; layered coat after coat of clear varnish over the swirling rings of multi-colored wood until it gleamed like glass. His wife's objections to it were purely aesthetic. Though handsome on their own, the burls stood out among standard furnishings like misbegotten children. They had become clichés, carted from California to grace living rooms across the nation by enthusiastic tourists with more money than taste. But Clyde liked it and stood firm, winning the continuing disagreement by insisting it was a family heirloom.

TJ sipped his after dinner coffee which Clyde had liberally laced with a fairly good local brandy.

"I don't have one damned good reason to think any such thing."

"But that's what you think anyway."

TJ shrugged.

"*Think* might be too dignified a word. Hunch maybe, or gut feeling. But one locked filing cabinet isn't much to base it on."

"No good cop ever ignored a hunch, whether there was anything to base it on or not. What about the daughter? Could she be in on it with the Cortez kid?"

"Meg? Why would she?"

Clyde stretched and re=crossed his ankles on the offending table.

"I don't know. Just a thought."

"Spit it out, Clyde—nothing's ever *just a thought* with you."

"I got the impression they were pretty friendly, that's all. Kinda close, for owner and employee. Probably nothing."

"He's not just an employee anymore, he's a partner. Bought in for a third back when Harley was alive."

"Oh yeah? Where'd he get the money?"

"I don't know. That's one of the things that's bothering me."

Beau Billings had been sitting silently, hands folded across his stomach, eyes closed as if he might be dozing, though TJ was sure he wasn't.

"What does Ellen think?" Beau interjected, leaning forward to reach for his cooling cup of coffee on the table beside his chair.

Clyde looked surprised.

"About what?"

"Isn't Megan Sullivan a friend of hers?"

"So what? Hitler probably had friends."

Beau smiled.

"You'd never met her before? Until we saw her at the marina, I mean."

"Naw, I don't know most of Ellen's women friends. When they come in the front door, I go out the back."

FORTY

LISBEE HAD MAINTAINED her composure and made her good-byes while TJ and Uncle Beau were still talking with Clyde, not disabusing their good host when he hinted that she must have a hot date. Ellen knew better; had noticed Lisbee's reaction to the email she'd read, but being Ellen, had asked no questions. The message itself was innocuous enough, but it was so unlike Mick that it had frightened Lisbee.

You'd better come by. Mick

Something was up and she had better go by—as soon as she could get there.

It wasn't far, no more than four miles with little traffic after 10:00 PM on a Monday night. When she parked on the street she could see a dim light through the windows, but this time the porch light was on as well. And Mick was standing at the door when she reached it; he'd been watching through the window and seen her arrival.

He kissed her lightly, his fair curls brushing her cheek, and led her into the living room, his arm around her shoulders. She sat in a chair, but when its soft cushions nearly enveloped her, rose again, flinging her shoulder bag into it instead.

"Well, I'm here. What's going on?" she said rather crisply, trying to bolster the sinking feeling the look on Mick's face was causing her.

He smiled then, and she felt slightly better.

"Sorry, Bess. I wasn't thinking. It was important I see you, that's all. I didn't mean to frighten you."

"Who says you frightened me?"

He didn't answer, but poured a glass of what looked like orange juice from a carafe on the low sofa table and handed it to her. It *was* orange juice, cold and sweet.

"The traffic's been buzzing and there are some things I thought you'd want to know——should know. Sit down and relax. The world's not ending just yet."

Ridiculously relieved by his last statement, Lisbee sat cross legged on a cushion and leaned against the arm of the offending, too soft chair, convinced that *should* the world be coming to an end, Mick Deering would be among the first to know. He dropped gracefully to another cushion on the floor some distance from her and in the dim light his face was covered in shadow. She waited impatiently for him to speak, fidgeting, winding and unwinding a strand of hair in her fingers. When he finally spoke, it was uncharacteristically inane.

"I haven't seen you do that since high school. I thought you'd outgrown it."

"Oh for God's sake, Mick . . . ."

"All right then, back to business. You'll know about the arrests from your resources at the Sheriff's Office I suppose."

She hoped her face was shadowed too, as she felt the blush rise to her cheeks.

"The Pan Global job? Yes, but I don't know who they picked up."

"Glad to hear your friend has some integrity. It hasn't been advertised yet. Not officially. Unofficially, it was the younger brother of a man of some influence in certain circles. Along with one of the boy's schoolmates. They're probably guilty as hell, but that's not the point."

"What is the point?" Lisbee was feeling a growing frustration as Mick paused to sip from his glass of orange juice. He was usually more forthcoming than this. Was he involved somehow? Protecting himself, even from her? She pushed the thought aside.

"The chain reaction that's been set off. That's the point. I'll have to give you some background—you can tell your friend if you like, but I don't think it will do him any good. There's nothing that wouldn't be laughed out of court for lack of evidence.

"Nehi is what you might call a contact man. If you want to know something or find something that's not available through normal, legitimate channels, he can get it for you. Or tell you how to get it yourself—for a finder's fee."

"Nehi? The pizza guy?"

Lisbee could see the gleam of Mick's white teeth as he grinned through the shadows.

"Only one of many enterprises."

"He's the big brother?"

"Yes. It was Jimmy Ngyuen they arrested on a tip from someone the San Jose Police caught in a sting operation. Nehi wouldn't have known about the job. If he had, he would've put a stop to it. Too amateurish and dangerous."

"All right, but what does all that have to do with me?"

"That's what I'm trying to explain to you, Bess. I said I'd have to give you some background."

Lisbee waved a hand in acquiescence and settled back against the chair arm.

"When Chipper Sullivan set up his BBS at Rudy Tang's house, he didn't do it just to collect subscription fees. There was money to be made as a black market warehouse source, but he needed to get the word out to the right people, so he brought Nehi in as contact man. I don't know if Nehi made an initial investment in the equipment; probably not. Chipper never seemed to lack for cash, from his grandfather or wherever he got it. But when Chipper died, the whole situation changed. Rudy Tang doesn't have a bean. And Nehi, recognizing they had a good thing going, took over backing the BBS.

"This much I know. The rest I'm going to tell you is educated guesswork, from some of the traffic I've been intercepting in the last few hours."

Lisbee raised an eyebrow.

"I thought you'd given up that sort of thing."

Mick's grin gleamed again in the dim light.

"I'll always use any of my resources in the cause of justice."

He rose and stretched, the muscles of shoulders and arms well defined under the thin tee shirt. Mick was like a modern vampire, rising at sunset to begin his electronic rounds of the planet and retreating to sleep before dawn. Lisbee wondered how he kept himself in such good shape. He must work out, she decided, wondering where in the rambling house he stowed the exercise equipment.

"The take from the Pan Global burglary was just what you'd expect from some kids on their first try, except for one thing. A fifteen inch monitor, still in its packing box. It was the only thing stolen that wouldn't fit in a jacket pocket or duffel bag. Add to that the shutdown of Rudy's BBS on Saturday for more than twelve hours; nighttime hours—the prime hours of his kind of business. And the last factor in the equation—Nehi wasn't around that weekend; gone off to investigate expanding his business base, according to some. If he had been around, Jimmy's little excursion never would have gotten off the ground.

"I think Rudy brought the BBS down because his monitor died on him, and when he couldn't reach Nehi, he decided to take advantage of the break-in and lift one from Pan Global. Nehi wouldn't have been too happy about it when he found out, but he'd have let it go. Until Jimmy got picked up, that is. Now the whole picture changes."

"Rudy becomes the scapegoat to get the kid off?" Lisbee said.

Mick nodded.

"And Rudy's disappeared," he added.

"How do you know?"

"Because his BBS went down again three hours ago, only this time there were no warning messages. Which means it crashed. And there was no one there to bring it back up."

FORTY-ONE

RUDY WOULDN'T LIKE it. She had tried, but for some silly reason Camellia just couldn't remember where she had left the can opener, so the big can of chili sat waiting by the stove. Dinner wouldn't be ready and Pineapple was meowing his displeasure at only dry food in his bowl. Stupid, stupid.

He would find it when he got home and tell her it was all right; he wasn't mad. He didn't like her fixing dinner on her own anyway. But he wouldn't like it that she forgot something so easy. Camellia stamped her foot in frustration and the big orange cat jumped from its position near her ankles, startled. That made her feel even worse and she reached for him and carried him with her to the couch.

"I'm sorry, Pineapple," she said softly.

They sat together, watching the muted television, Camellia enjoying the antics of the soundless people as they scurried across the screen. It was a game she played, trying to figure out what was going on without having to turn the volume on. It took her mind off the unopened can of chili, and more important, it kept her from looking at her watch. Because it got dark early now and she could pretend it still was early if she didn't look at her watch. Still early and Rudy would be coming in from work any minute. He was a little late sometimes but never this late that she could remember, so she concentrated on the silent people jumping around and pointing at each other and laughing, and made sure she didn't sneak a look at the watch he had given her. The watch she never took off.

They were sitting in almost total darkness, in deep chairs in the conventionally furnished living room that had remained virtually unchanged since Amelia Jane's time, with only the glow of a hurricane lamp shimmering from the doorway to the kitchen. It was the first time in weeks they had sat in companionable silence, and Beau began to have the feeling maybe things were going to sort themselves out. He decided to risk it all to see if he was right.

"She's a mighty attractive woman," he said, knowing he didn't have to put a name to her.

"Lord, yes," TJ finally responded in a husky voice after a pause so long it left Beau thinking he might have made a serious misjudgment. With a silent sigh of relief, he left another space of quiet before speaking again.

"And not a thing wrong with that, either, except maybe the timing."

"It's a little more than poor timing."

Beau waited for him to go on.

"Meg Sullivan could very well be involved up to her lovely backside in Chipper's death."

"But that didn't make her, ah, *backside* any less desirable? Is that what's eating at you?"

TJ smiled in the dim light.

"Maybe. I guess I think it should have made a difference, but I'm not a kid back at Norman cramming for exams. Real life has a way of tempering ideals, even if it never quite gets rid of 'em altogether. It's not as high-minded as that."

"Well, there's only one thing I can think of that's not high-minded, but is pretty much inescapable when you're a man. You have reason to believe that her virtue lack's a little of being what it ought to be?"

The laugh, when it came, sounded like the old TJ. In full appreciation of his own folly.

"It's pretty ridiculous when you come right out and say it, isn't it? It's one thing if she might be a murderess, but something else again entirely if she's sleeping around," TJ said.

Beau smiled.

"Hardly an attitude that would gain much support today I suppose, though that doesn't make it any easier to wrestle with. The ladies have come into their own and they surely deserve to, but it did happen kind of sudden for some of us."

In the next few minutes TJ recounted his visit to the home of Megan Sullivan; the exit of her dark, stocky guest, freshly showered, who TJ later discovered was none other than Cory Floyd. He didn't mention Meg's appearance when he was staying on the *Emmy T.*, partly because he assumed Beau had guessed as much, but mostly because one gentleman didn't discuss the details of such a meeting with another gentleman. At least, the *'some of us'* for whom the ladies coming into their own had been kind of sudden, didn't.

The sharp burr of the office phone filled the room like a shout. Like most businesses, Anadarko Grace had an answering machine to take messages during off hours, but because of the nature of the work, Lisbee had installed an option to forward calls in case of emergency; first to TJ's second home number added for the purpose, then to her cell phone. Beau was closest. He picked up the receiver.

"Anadarko Grace."

"Mr. Billings? It's Aurelia Sims. I'm sorry to bother you so late, but . . . ."

"No bother at all, Miss Sims. What can I do for you?"

"I'm not sure, really. I just thought you ought to know. It's about Camellia Tang."

"What about her? Is she all right?"

"Well, yes, under the circumstances. She's here with me now."

"What circumstances are those, Miss Sims?"

"It's about her brother, Rudy. He seems to be missing."

Beau motioned with one large hand and TJ rose to stand beside him, listening in to the conversation.

"How long has Rudy been missing?"

"I suppose, technically, since this morning when he left for work. That's the last time she saw him. He just didn't come home this evening. She became frightened when he was so late and called me. I went over to their house and we tried his office number, but there was no answer. I didn't like to leave her alone like that, so I brought her home here with me. I didn't know what else to do."

"I'd say you did the right thing. Has he done this before? Maybe gone out after work with some friends?"

"She says not. At least, not without calling to let her know. I left a note, explaining that she got frightened and is staying here with me. I hope it doesn't make him angry. It seemed the only thing to do."

"I wouldn't worry too much about that. You just take care of the girl and we'll look into it. Probably some simple explanation. I'll let you know as soon as we find out anything."

Beau replaced the receiver and looked at TJ.

"Should we wake Clyde?"

"Not yet. You start calling the hospitals and I'll see if I can get hold of Lisbee. If Highstreet's not on duty, she'll be able to reach him quicker, see if any accidents have been reported."

"You think he was in some kind of accident?"

"No, but it's the easiest thing to eliminate."

FORTY-TWO

T HEY WERE AS close to a full blown row as they had ever come when her cell phone rang—Highstreet's normally sunny face darkened in a frown of frustration as he stared at the stubborn set of Lisbee's sharp chin. Private cops. They were all the same; a royal pain in the ass. When they weren't underfoot they were being obstructive, keeping him from doing his job. Only this time it was worse because he couldn't kick this private cop in the butt and threaten her with the mighty arm of the law.

She had arrived a little before eleven, just a few minutes after the call from her cell phone to announce she was on her way. He hadn't asked what it was all about until she got there, and then she would only say she needed him to use his position to find out if anything had been reported about Rudy Tang, who was missing. When he asked all the obvious questions; how long had he been gone, who'd reported it, when was he last seen, she'd just waved them away saying there was no time for that and couldn't he just trust her and get on with it. He had tried to explain that even if he trusted her, no one at County was going to launch any queries without some answers first. Things had deteriorated from there.

He stretched and ran a hand through his close-cropped hair before heading for the kitchen and a cold beer as she punched the button to answer her phone. When he returned, handing her a glass of wine in a vaguely conciliatory gesture, he was relieved to see that her expression had changed from mulish to thoughtful. She even smiled as she took the glass from him.

"Thanks."

He nodded.

"Peace?"

"Peace," she agreed and took a sip.

"That was TJ. Looks like it's official now. Rudy's sister's reporting him missing. He hasn't come home from work."

"Did he make it to work?"

"I don't know."

"Maybe he's just gone out with some friends. It's not that late yet."

"I don't think so. There are other things. . . ."

"Which you're not going to tell me because you've got some misplaced sense of loyalty to your source. Listen, I can't help if my hands are tied. You're going to have to trust me."

Lisbee looked into the cool green eyes. He was right, of course. And she did trust him, or at least believed she could.

"All right," she said and gave him an expurgated version of what Mick Deering had told her, without revealing where she had come by the information.

"So he may just be in hiding, although I'd think he would have done something about his little sister besides leave her to fend for herself. He's apparently watched out for her for a long time; I don't think he'd leave her to the wolves to save his own neck. Which means it could be a lot worse. For Rudy that is. He's running in some pretty rough company."

"What's your big interest in Rudy Tang? Is it just that he was a friend of the Sullivan kid?"

"More than a friend. Chipper set up the operation Rudy's now stuck with and he's in over his head. It's the best indication we've had so far that Chipper's death might not have been an accident. If he tried to get cute with the wrong people, or found out more than was good for him . . . ."

Highstreet shook his head.

"It's pretty weak. All conjecture and no facts. Or is there more you're not telling me?"

"It's a place to start, which is more than we've had up until now." Lisbee rose and stood looking at Highstreet, seated in his lumpy overstuffed chair. Her face was solemn.

"We're approaching this from different sides, but our purpose is the same—to see justice done. I don't expect you to bend any rules, but anything you can do to help short of that . . "

Highstreet's face relaxed into a grin.

"I never could resist pure, cool logic, especially coming from someone who looks like you. What do you want me to do?"

"Was Rudy's name brought up when they questioned the Nguyen boy?"

"Not that I know of. Not yet, anyway."

"Is he still being questioned?"

"No. His brother showed up with an attorney and got him released. Minimal bail. If they're going to shop Tang it will be when they start talking deals with the D.A."

"Then the only other thing is to see if anyone matching Rudy's description has figured in a police report this evening.

Can you do that? Even though he can't be officially reported missing until tomorrow?"

Justin Highstreet reached out to touch Lisbee's hand. It was cool and sent an electric charge through his fingertips. She sat on the chair arm, sliding slim fingers behind his neck, then bent to kiss him.

"It's a very serious offense," he said in a voice muffled by her thick dark hair.

"What is?"

"Bribing an officer of the law."

"It's worth the risk," she said and handed him her cell phone.

FORTY-THREE

WHEN CORY FLOYD left his office after speaking with Lowry his mind was whirling with possibilities, both good and bad, for his future and that of his company. He automatically headed the BMW toward home, easing into the stream of traffic on Mt. Hermon Road, but before he had gone a mile on the familiar journey he realized that what he really needed was a stiff drink. The thought of his wife's mundane conversation and his daughters' shrill bids for his attention seemed suddenly intolerable. He was not, by nature, a drinking man; only occasionally did he patronize one of the many brew pubs that had sprung up in the past year or two, and that more for the atmosphere than the brews themselves. But a brew pub was not what was called for now. He needed to relax, get a grip on what was happening. Ignoring his usual turnoff for home, he accelerated and headed the 325i toward Soquel.

The welcoming smile on Megan Sullivan's face faded quickly when she saw Floyd on the porch.

"Oh, it's you."

"What kind of a greeting is that?" Cory said a little testily.

"An unenthusiastic one. What do you want?"

"I thought I'd surprise you; maybe we could have a drink and a little pleasant conversation. But if you're expecting someone else . . . ."

"It's probably too late now. You might as well come in. But just for a drink; I'm going to bed early tonight. Alone."

Cory started to make a stinging reply and retreat with his pride nearly intact, but decided the drink was more important. He walked past Meg and sat on a stool at the small bar in the foyer.

When he had taken his first swallow of the scotch and water he felt a little better. Eyeing Meg, who was standing behind the bar like a bored barmaid waiting for her last customer to drink up and leave so she could close up for the night, he knew that he should take advantage of the silence and say something urbane about it being nice while it lasted. Make the break first, before she finished it for him. But he didn't. It would be a whole lot better if he could jolly her into bed and then do it. In spite of her attitude when he arrived, or perhaps because of it, he found he wanted her almost desperately. Just one more time, at least.

"Aren't you having one?" he finally said.

She eyed him sardonically, then sighed and reached behind the bar for the half full bottle of Jameson.

"Oh hell, why not," she mumbled, pouring the amber Irish whiskey into a tumbler.

"'To absent friends,'" she toasted, lifting her glass aloft.

"'And those that aren't'" he added, giving her his best smile.

It almost worked. Meg had become mellow after finishing the Irish, and he'd managed to get her sitting beside him on the long sofa with a second drink, but then her mood had turned when he tried to slip a hand under the yellow chenille sweater she was wearing. If she'd made a scene, spit bitter words at him, it would have made him feel a little better; at least that would have shown some feeling. But she merely rose with a resigned look on her face and walked him to the door, like she was getting rid of an overly eager salesman, polite but firm.

The scotch was causing bile to rise in his throat as he walked stiffly down the steps toward his car, silently mouthing words he should have said to the bitch; cruel, stinging words that hadn't come to him at the time they would have done any good. He flipped the alarm switch on his key ring and was about to open the driver's door when a shadow slipped from the shrubbery lining the driveway, and a hand reached out to touch his arm.

"What the fuck . . ." he said, turning to see a young Asian man in a ratty fatigue jacket, long straight black hair held back in a pony tail. He looked familiar, but Cory couldn't place him, and he raised a muscular forearm ready to defend himself from a presumed mugging.

"Take it easy," the man said, blocking the raised arm. "We need to have a little talk."

Adrenaline rising, Cory started to turn into the man for a quick jab to his midsection when he spoke again, stepping back barely out of reach.

"About your friends. In Washington, D.C.?"

The man's face was expressionless and it finally clicked into place. He worked at Pan Global. Cory didn't know his name, but that didn't matter. He had access to the building, and from what he'd just said, the words falling like ice chips into the chill night air, he must have the package. Judy had indeed been grandstanding. She hadn't mailed the damned thing to the professor and somehow this kid had gotten hold of it. Oh shit. Damage control time.

"Okay," Floyd said gruffly, finding his voice, "get in and let's talk." And before the man had finished closing the passenger door he had the BMW in reverse, leaping down the drive to speed into the darkness on the narrow winding highway, into the mountains, away from the distant glow of light that was the village of Soquel.

Rudy Tang couldn't believe his luck. He hadn't even had to bluff his way through knowing what it was all about; just the mention of that package and the fucking dweeb had rolled over like an old dog wanting his stomach scratched. *'How much do you want?'* he'd said, before Rudy could even give him the speech he'd made up about Chipper leaving him in hot water and the stake he needed to clear out and drop the whole thing. He'd got as far as Chipper's name and the guy had almost missed a curve in the road, falling over himself to offer Rudy money. It was about time his luck was changing.

He wouldn't be able to get it until morning; Rudy knew that. Even a guy like Cory Floyd didn't walk around with that kind of cash in his pocket. And he wanted to see the package. That was okay too. It was stashed under the seat in the van, which Rudy had parked off a driveway in some brush a couple of houses down from where he'd waited for Floyd.

While they drove back in silence toward Soquel and the van, Rudy was working on how the switch would take place the next morning. It should be a place in plain sight; open but not obvious. The parking lot of the shopping center down Mt. Hermon Road from Pan Global might work. Mid-morning, when there would be plenty of cars around so they wouldn't be noticed. He could pack the van tonight, explain to Camellia that they were moving, pick up the cash and then her and that stupid cat, and they were gone. He knew she wouldn't leave without the cat. It would be a pain in the butt, but so what? He smiled to himself at the thought of his little sister and how she would look in some decent clothes when he could buy them for her.

Rudy told Floyd to slow down as they approached the dirt driveway where he had left the van. The house it belonged to was out of sight behind a crest in the road and a bank of firs. Floyd cut his lights after he pulled in and came to a stop a few feet from the van. Rudy jumped out, walked to the passenger door and opened it. He was not going to get too close to Floyd—he might make a grab for the package—just let him see what it was and lock the van again. Then set up the meet. Rudy was smiling, bending over to reach under the seat in the darkness, when a cascade of brilliant lights exploded before his eyes for a fraction of a second, then receded into impenetrable black.

FORTY-FOUR

Megan Sullivan Stepped from the shower, cursing mildly under her breath as she stood dripping on the bath mat. She reached for the towel she had neglected to pull from the rack before she got in. It was the second time in three days she had forgotten to place it close enough to dry off while she was still standing in the old claw foot tub. Her exasperation peaked when she heard the sharp ring of the telephone in her bedroom. Wrapping the towel around her wet hair, she slipped on the pale green chenille bathrobe and, barefoot, stalked into the hall, leaving wet footprints on the hardwood floor.

"This had better be good," she barked into the phone, deciding that anyone calling her at 7:15 in the morning deserved whatever they got. She heard a deep laugh, slightly muffled by the toweling over her ear.

"And good morning to you, Sunshine," the voice continued as she adjusted the handset against her damp ear.

"TJ?"

"Guilty. Sorry it's so early, but I wanted to catch you before you went to work. Thought I might be able to convince you to play hooky today."

"That won't be too difficult the way this morning's starting out. What am I going to have the 24-hour flu over?"

"How about a nice boat ride?"

"Are you crazy? I wouldn't be lying if I did that; I'd be heaving my guts up. It's why I was never my father's son."

"Well, then, just a nice walk around your marina. Maybe look in at the office, talk to your partner, Mr. Cortez, about the balance sheet."

"You really think Sunny's cooking the books?"

"No. Not really. But he's cooking something, and I'd just like to find out what it is and whether Chipper might have known about it."

"It doesn't sound like a lot of fun, but I guess anything's better than going to work," Megan said, toweling her hair dry with one hand.

"Well, I can sweeten the pot a little. Lunch in Monterey?"

"That's better. I can be ready in thirty minutes; forty-five if you want me to look presentable."

"Take an hour. I'll pick you up at 8:30."

An early riser by nature, Professor Dean Deutch had finished his Spartan breakfast of whole wheat toast and half a fresh Bosc pear—he would have the other half with cottage cheese and rye crisp for lunch—and was well into a telnet session with the supercomputer facility at the University of Texas at Austin when he saw Cory Floyd's florid face at his salon door. Deutch motioned for him to enter, suppressing his surprise at the unannounced visit. It was unlike Floyd. Though reasonably intelligent and with a decided flair for the business end of a commercial enterprise, Cory lacked imagination in the professor's view, and was therefore highly predictable most of the time.

"Come in my dear boy, sit down. Lovely morning, isn't it? What's that you have there? Did our missing parcel finally show itself?"

Floyd took a seat across the small table from the professor, setting the package he'd been carrying in front of him, but refraining from loosening his grip on it. The paper wrapping was wrinkled; it had obviously been opened and carelessly rewrapped. And was it his imagination, or were the young CEO's hands shaking slightly? He was very definitely disturbed about something.

"May I fix you some coffee? Or tea, perhaps? No? Well, then, shall I have a look, or did you want to explain something to me first?"

"It's not a question anymore," Floyd said enigmatically.

"Not a question? What's not a question, dear boy?"

"Whether Chipper Sullivan had your discovery or not. He did."

Professor Deutch turned to his keyboard and spoke soothingly as he did so.

"Let me just finish off here, will you? Then we'll have a nice little talk about what you've found out. You have come across something, I take it. We'll look at it together and see what's to be done about it. All right? Sure you won't have a nice cup of tea? It'll do you a world of good."

Sunny Cortez raised his eyes from the spring line he had been adjusting on the *Laurel II*. The TollyCraft's owner, a maladroit but enthusiastic fisherman, never quite got it right. But he paid Sunny handsomely to pilot the boat whenever he wanted to take out a group of friends so he could entertain them without the worry of handling the boat himself, at which he was barely adequate without the distraction of guests. Beyond the bow anchor he had glimpsed a flash of flaming hair and when he stood, he saw the unmistakable stride of Megan Sullivan as she approached the office. TJ Billings was in her wake, his slight limp and thick graying hair equally unmistakable.

Sunny took his time with the line, then walked the length of the boat, checking for any other small details the owner might have neglected. He was a good customer and Sunny made it a practice to take care of good customers, though he cared more about the boats themselves and watched over them whether their owners paid him extra or not. When he was satisfied that the *Laurel II* was secured, he started for the office to see what had occasioned Meg's visit, in the company of the private detective her father had hired from the grave.

The office was warm and comfortable and the two of them, when he came in, were seated companionably in the wicker chairs, talking together as if they were old friends. Meg was smiling boldly, her hand just removed from TJ's shoulder, as if they had been sharing some confidence. She looked up and met his eyes with a frank gaze.

"Sunny. We were just talking about where to have lunch in Monterey. You lived there. What do you recommend as a former native? Not the touristy stuff."

Sunny grinned and fell in with the atmosphere.

"I lived and worked on the wharf. It's all touristy there. You want something downtown?"

"I don't know. You tell me. You couldn't have spent all your time on the wharf, for God's sake."

"Well, there are lots of little holes in the wall, and then there're the upscale places; the ones they tout in the tour magazines."

TJ made a face.

"Spare me the tour magazines, okay?"

"Right. Try Estralita, off Highway 1, just past the exit to Ft. Ord as you come into town—what used to be Ft. Ord. It's in a strip mall. Good Mexican, if you like that."

TJ remembered the pink facade at the entrance to Moss Landing.

"What about that place in town? 'The Whole Enchilada', just off the highway?"

Sunny grimaced.

"*Margaritaville*. Big Margarita glasses—mostly salt and ice. Estralita has good food and Mexican beer. No blenders. Besides, you said Monterey. If you want closer, there are a couple of places in Castroville."

"I was promised Monterey," Meg said. "If I want artichokes, I'll get them at Safeway."

Sunny shrugged and went behind the counter.

"It's a little early for lunch. Unless you're going to take the *Emmy T.* to Monterey."

Meg snorted.

"Actually, we came to go over the books. Mr. Marlowe here has an insatiable curiosity. I told him you'd be happy to cooperate, especially if I came along."

"Always at your service," Sunny said, holding the counter gate open. "I've been trying to get everything together for the accountant anyway. You'll need a financial statement if you're really going to try and sell this place."

"You have any better ideas about what I should do with it?" Meg asked.

TJ watched the younger man's expression, searching for any change from the open frankness he'd been displaying to Meg Sullivan.

"If you're not in a big hurry for the money, you could turn it over to me," he said with a smile that appeared perfectly genuine.

And so were the accounts genuine, as far as TJ could tell. They were maintained on the elderly computer, which Sunny Cortez handled competently, if not expertly. Payments for the berth rents; a substantial income from launching fees dating back to the previous salmon season; fishing party fees which Cortez explained accrued fifty percent to him rather than his normal thirty because he piloted the vessels himself. Everything in order.

Meg had watched over Cortez's shoulder at first, then, apparently bored, began roaming around the office, looking in desk drawers and finally the filing cabinets. When she came to the one that was locked, a frown creased her brow.

"What's in here, Sunny? The maps to the buried treasure?"

Cortez turned in his seat.

"I don't know. That was Harley's; he always kept it locked and I don't have the key. Don't you?"

She shook her head, still frowning.

"He wasn't one for locking things up. How hard would it be to open this?"

"Not very," said TJ quietly. "Want me to try?"

With the legal owner's assent he withdrew his pocketknife and began what he had nearly done the day before. The drawer yielded within a few minutes and he stood back so Meg could inspect the contents. She said nothing, but the color drained from her face until she looked almost ill. TJ thought for a moment she was going to faint, though she was the last person he would have pegged for the tendency. He moved a step closer, to be ready to catch her if she did. He could just see the top of what looked to be some sort of ledger or bound book in the first drawer as she began to rummage through it.

"What's in there?" Sunny echoed her own question from his seat at the computer desk.

"Pictures," she said in a whisper they could barely hear. "Of me when I was a kid. And my mother. I thought the old bastard had burned these years ago."

FORTY-FIVE

Lisbee HAD SLEPT late.   Hester was growling protests and pacing the kitchen floor at her feet waiting to be fed when she finally roused herself, and by the time she reached the office of Anadarko Grace, TJ had already gone and Uncle Beau was in a rare ill humor.

He sat morosely at his desk, staring at some notes, and Smiley, lying on the carpet near the office door with one eye cocked, was apparently giving him a wide berth. Considering herself to be at least as intelligent as a hound dog, Lisbee merely gave him a peck on the cheek, asked if he would like more coffee, and when he declined with a grunt, proceeded into her own office to boot up the computer system. She went through her email, which she usually did at home but had left today for the office because of the late hour, and quickly composed replies to several clients' queries, putting them off as of a lesser priority than her more immediate concern, which was to call Pan Global and see if Rudy Tang had been at work yesterday.

Cory Floyd was unavailable according to his secretary, but she transferred Lisbee to the department where Rudy worked and an anonymous, rather nasal female voice reported that yes, he had been in yesterday but had yet to show up today. He hadn't called in sick or anything, and if he didn't within an hour or so his ass was really going to be in trouble because their supervisor didn't have the sense of humor of a seagull and looked for ways to make things unpleasant for his charges. Lisbee thanked her and hung up.

Taking her cooling cup of coffee, Lisbee decided to beard the lion in his den. They needed to decide what to do about filing an official missing person report with the Sheriff's Department. The problem was not filing the report, it was that the girl, Camellia, as his closest relative, would be the one who had to file it. Given her vulnerable circumstances, and the possibility of interference from the social services regarding her welfare, Lisbee wanted Uncle Beau's advice. And Miss Sims's as well. When she entered his office and sat on the velvet cushioned wooden bench, Uncle Beau was rocked back in his chair, gazing at the vaulted ceiling of the old church, his fingers steepled on his chest.

"Anybody home up there?" she asked.

He turned to look at her and she felt a rush of relief when his lined face relaxed into a smile.

"Well, it's hard to say yet. But it sometimes helps to pass along where you think some divine intervention wouldn't come amiss, just in case somebody happens to be listening."

"Can't hurt," Lisbee said. "Have you talked to Miss Sims yet this morning?"

"Just before you got here. The girl's pretty upset. To be expected, I suppose. Her brother was at work yesterday, was he?"

Lisbee nodded.

"No word from him yet this morning though." She frowned into her coffee cup. "What does Miss Sims think about making an official report that Rudy's missing?"

"She doesn't think Camellia's in any state to do it herself. And she doesn't want to upset her any further with the questions she'd have to answer. Apparently she's never been told, or never acknowledged anyway, that the Sullivan boy is dead. Now with her brother gone missing and all, she's afraid it might be too much for Camellia to handle all at once."

"Why don't you handle it yourself? You're already on the books to look into her welfare for Miss Sims—her brother's whereabouts come under that heading, don't they?"

"I guess you could say that. Your friend the deputy's looking out for any official sign of him, isn't he? Accidents and such?"

Lisbee nodded again.

"He'll let me know if he hears anything."

"Well, then, I suppose I'd better get started. I'll drop by and talk to Miss Sims; get the key to their house so I can take a look and see if there's any sign that he planned to be gone a spell. Maybe I will have just one more cup of coffee and take it along with me."

"I'll get it," Lisbee said, rising from her seat as the phone began to ring. Beau lifted the handset.

"Anadarko Grace. Why, yes she is. Just one moment, please." He pressed the hold button and motioned to her. "Go on and take this; I'll get my coffee."

Lisbee returned to her office and punched the flashing button.

"Elizabeth Billings."

"Elizabeth, yes. How are you my dear? It's Dean Deutch here."

"Good morning, Professor. I'm just fine. And you?"

"Well, I'm not sure, to tell you the truth."

"Is something wrong?"

There was a momentary silence on the line.

"Rather ridiculous, really, but I seem to find myself in a circumstance that requires your professional services. I'm afraid I can't explain on the telephone. Could you possibly come down here? I know you're busy and it's probably inconvenient, but . . . ."

The note of urgency in Professor Deutch's voice was chilling. He'd never sound like that unless it was something grave. Lisbee looked at her watch.

"I'll be there in thirty minutes," she said.

FORTY-SIX

THE FACE BEHIND the glass was insubstantial, ghostly—almost like a reflection. It might have been a trick of the light, but when he slid back the salon door and she saw the pallor on his thin cheeks, Lisbee had the impression she could see through his skin to the naked skull. He was shaken and that frightened her. He had always been in total control of himself and his surroundings. Professor Deutch motioned her to a seat at the small table. With an effort, he found his voice.

"Thank you for coming so promptly. There's coffee; I'll just get you some." He started for the steps to the galley, not with his usual sprightly gait but moving like a tired old man. Lisbee began to protest.

"That's okay, I really don't need any . . . ."

"Please. It will allow me to collect my thoughts."

When he returned and was seated across from her, his large skeletal hands folded in front of him on the table, he was silent for so long she thought he had drifted off somewhere, forgotten she was there. With an effort, she controlled an impulse to say something soothing, though she hadn't any idea what that might be. Finally he began to speak.

"Forgive me, my dear, for being a foolish old man. It's just that it's so difficult to know where to begin. I have always been of the opinion that scientific discoveries, regardless of their eventual implementation by mankind, are inherently good.

How could anyone in my profession believe that knowledge is otherwise? Some theologians disagree, of course, but surely ignorance has cost the dearest price throughout history?"

He paused, but Lisbee guessed, correctly, that his questions were rhetorical.

"My faith in this precept is unshaken, but I'm afraid I have a newer and deeper appreciation of just how monumental an impact may result from the reactions of a few misguided individuals."

Haltingly at first, and then more rigorously as his enthusiasm overtook his misgivings, the professor revealed to Lisbee his discovery which rendered current encryption technology obsolete; his *little hole in the dike.* Though not strictly speaking a mathematician herself, Lisbee thought she grasped the theory he was explaining, and marveled at its simple genius. She became nearly as caught up in the mechanics of it as the Professor was, and it was only after he paused once more that the realization of what the consequences of its misuse could be dawned on her.

"Dear lord," she said softly.

"Indeed. You see the potential if by some chance it reaches the wrong hands. And that, I'm afraid, is exactly what has happened."

"Who?"

"The Sullivan boy. Before he died. At least the possibility exists; however, that is not why I solicited your help. I must explain a bit further—regarding my official capacity as consultant to Pan Global."

Lisbee listened in silence as the professor outlined his researches for the encryption company; his experiments with each new version of the software they produced and his revelation to Cory Floyd of the potential disaster they and everyone else who depended on the current technology faced if his discovery were independently duplicated, or if it were made available to unscrupulous individuals.

"Cory was concerned, of course, regarding my unforgivable lapse which might have allowed Chipper Sullivan to, ah, borrow the pertinent files from my machine. They are quite small, a few hundred kilobytes, and will therefore fit on the most humble medium. Easily hidden. I searched, of course, after the poor boy died. But to no avail."

"You searched the *Emmy T*? For a floppy?"

The professor bowed his head.

"I regret to say I did exactly that. And without the owner's permission. I'm not proud of my actions, but you must understand it was of paramount importance to discover if he really had obtained an illicit copy of it. You see, the timing was crucial. Pan Global, that is Cory Floyd, had been contacted by the government by then, and negotiations were underway for the most secret of agreements. Mr. Lowry, of the Electronic Data Integrity Service, was ready to place the nation's most valuable information in the hands of a commercial partner using the current, supposedly uncrackable, encryption technology."

Deutch went on to explain Lowry's plan to cut costs by employing the most sophisticated, but commercially developed, encryption software to allow the replacement and expansion of the government's existing classified computer networks with the millions of miles of unclassified lines making up the Internet. Lisbee sat speechless as he unwound the tale of his daily forays into the supercomputer labs across the world, examining the current research for any sign of an independent effort that might duplicate his own discovery. When he fell silent, she gazed into the untouched cup of coffee sitting before her on the table, now cold, a metallic skin resembling an oil slick covering its surface.

"If it helps at all, it wasn't in his room either," she said at last. "I checked through all the disks TJ got from his mother. There was nothing there."

The professor let loose an elaborate sigh.

"I'm grateful for that, of course. But right now my greatest concern is Cory Floyd himself. He was here to see me this morning. Very unlike himself." He told her of the package, its disappearance and potentially damaging cover letter.

"Cory was . . . how shall I put it? Beside himself? Out of control? Perhaps that is too strong. In any event, he had recovered the package, but seemed convinced that it had been compromised; that there was no longer a question of the Sullivan boy's not having obtained the files. Nor of his complicity in an attempt to extract the greatest price for their return."

"Complicity?"

"With his friend, Rudy Tang."

Lisbee stared at the professor.

"Rudy didn't come home last night."

"Oh, dear. I was afraid of something like this."

"Did Cory say he'd actually seen Rudy? Since work yesterday, I mean?"

"No. No, he didn't actually say anything that could be useful. It was all rather vague and, well, almost paranoid. I was greatly concerned about him. He's been under a good deal of strain since I told him of my discovery, especially lately, after his meetings with Mr. Lowry. So much depends on maintaining the secrecy, you see."

"Yes, I do see; and I'll bet Rudy Tang did, too."

FORTY-SEVEN

THE OLD MAN with the white hair reminded her of Santa Claus even though he didn't have a beard. His eyes were Santa Claus eyes she decided, kind of twinkly. And he was kind because Pineapple went right up to him and started purring, without even circling him first. That was a sure sign. That's what he'd done when Miss Sims came to visit and it was the first time Camellia had seen him take to someone right away. This was the second time.

He had come to Miss Sims's house to visit, and to talk to her about the key to their house. He was going to look for Rudy, and when he found him be sure he came home. She wondered if she should ask him to look out for Chipper too, while he was at it. If he was good at finding people, maybe he could get Chipper to come back from wherever he'd gone. He'd been gone a lot longer than Rudy had, though Camellia didn't know how many days, or even weeks, it had been. It suddenly struck her that that's probably where Rudy was; he'd gone to find Chipper and bring him back. She'd better tell the Santa man in case he didn't think of it.

"I bet Rudy's gone to find Chipper. Will you bring them both home?" she said. The old man smiled at her and reached out to stroke Pineapple's fur.

"Well, if that's the case, I'll sure see what I can do."

Camellia smiled back at him. She felt better already.

"Beau, it's for you." Aurelia Sims bent her coifed gray head through the doorway to the kitchen and motioned with a delicate hand. He rose from the sofa to join her and she handed him the telephone.

"Are you on your way to Rudy Tang's house?" Lisbee's voice was low and uncharacteristically grave.

"That's right."

"I'll meet you there in about half an hour."

"Is something wrong?"

"Probably. I can't talk now. I'll tell you when I get there," she said shortly and hung up.

Beau decided to walk the mile and a half from Aurelia Sims's house to the Tang cottage. Smiley had been waiting in his car in deference to the visiting feline and could use the exercise. The day was fall crisp with a watery sun low on the southern horizon, even at its zenith, and there were walkers and joggers and bicyclers in great profusion, though it was a weekday. To keep himself from slipping back into the gray mood that had engulfed him that morning, Beau began to puzzle on an inconsequential question that had occurred to him many times before in his outings with the brindle hound. Where in the world did they come from? All these people with apparently unlimited leisure to indulge in their favorite form of exercise? A few were of an age that could mean they were retired from long careers in the workforce, but most were much younger than that; fit, tanned, capable people who in his day would have been hard at work in the middle of the week. Some of the women might be housewives or homemakers, but not many any more. It took two incomes for most families to get by, especially out here in California where nothing came cheap.

His reflections had brought him no closer to an answer to this recurring enigma by the time he reached the small fenced yard, and he let himself through the gate and fitted the key to the front door, casting his thoughts back to the more immediate problems at hand. Lisbee had found something—or it had found her. And from the sound of her voice, Beau was not hopeful that it was something good.

When she arrived some ten minutes later, he had finished a cursory inspection of the premises which revealed nothing that might suggest Rudy Tang had not expected to come home the previous evening as he always did. Without preamble, she gave him an abbreviated version of the story Professor Deutch had told her. There was no word on Rudy from Justin Highstreet, and Cory Floyd was not in his office; she had checked on her way here, using the cell phone in her car. Lisbee stood in the middle of the tiny living room, arms folded, waiting for his reaction.

"Well, hell," was all he said before walking to the door of the small bedroom which held the computer equipment that hosted the Bulletin Board System run by Rudy Tang since the demise of his friend and cohort, Chipper Sullivan. He stood in the doorway, gazing at the motley collection of hardware—wires and cables snaking around and under pieces of cheap furniture; a Formica table that was probably a refugee from the tiny kitchen; some bare one-by-twelve's supported by gray, crumbling cinderblocks; and even a few laminated TV trays against the plasterboard walls, with manuals and floppy disks stacked haphazardly on them. He had purposely neglected to inspect this room, knowing Lisbee would be much better able to tell what had gone on in here and what, if anything, might indicate a hurried retreat.

"You'll want to check all this for that hijacked computer program, or whatever it is," he said finally, and she nodded.

"I sure won't be much help to you there. I'm going to look around outside; maybe see if there's anything in that little shed of a garage. Call me if you find anything." And he started for the back door into the yard with Smiley close on his heels.

The server had, as Mick Deering had prophesied, crashed. Lisbee's first task was to reboot the system, and when she had done so she observed that at first a trickle, and then a deluge of calls were being picked up by the stack of aging modems tucked into the brick and board shelves. She paid little attention to the activity that was now humming through the server; that was a matter for the authorities, if indeed it consisted primarily of traffic in black market goods. There could also be, and probably was, a large contingent of legitimate subscribers just glad their BBS was back in operation.

She began shuffling through the floppy disks. Most were unlabeled, and those that *had* labels couldn't be trusted. She would have to examine each one. After thirty minutes, she had discarded two-thirds of the nearly obsolete media into a neat stack beneath her feet as she sat in the straight-backed kitchen chair at the Formica-topped table. The old 386, which served as Rudy's CPU for mundane work while the much faster NT server with its Pentium processor was handling the incoming calls, was obliging, if slow. By the time she had satisfied herself that none of the floppies held anything but digital junk, the server was still perking along, doing the job for which it had been programmed without a whimper. She wondered idly what had caused it to crash, but rejected the thought as irrelevant. You never knew with the damned things. A phase of the moon could do it.

The files on the server were next. Rudy Tang had installed no passwords; why should he? It was his own house—who would have access to the machine but himself?—and Chipper Sullivan, of course, before he died. There was a neatness and logic in the file structure that smacked of the more computer-literate Sullivan boy; nothing of the haphazardness of the disks she had examined. But there were no personal files. Only the directories that contained the code and images for the website that Mick Deering had designed and constructed for Chipper.

Lisbee scanned the files, but found nothing untoward. Strictly Hyper Text Markup Language—HTML—tags, the programming code used to create web documents, with calls to a directory of graphics. The style of the web pages was sophisticated, as she would have expected from Mick, but there was nothing that could be hidden there. It was all in clear—quotations from Poe and other plain text that anyone could read and understand. She opened the graphics directory and examined the imagery files. All were either JPEG or GIF—two file types indicating the algorithms used to compress the pixel data. Mostly JPEG compression, which was standard for the Web; it offered an excellent rendition of digital photographs and required a minimum amount of storage and download time. GIFs took less space, but the quality was not as good. The only GIF image was an animation—the black raven, composed of several separate images linked for display in a specific sequence to give the impression of flight—like a movie or the works of a Disney artist, giving life to inanimate cartoon characters. Lisbee opened the animated GIF with a program that let her view each frame individually.

They paraded before her, each image clear and concise, one part of a whole that would replicate life and energy. It was a relatively simple technology which she understood well. Yet there was something that held her; made her think that perhaps here was something she should not overlook.

She walked into the living room and picked up the phone. After three rings she heard the voice of Professor Deutch.

"Yes?"

"It's Lisbee," she said, forgetting that her old teacher did not know her by that diminutive. "Elizabeth. I'm at Rudy Tang's house and I've been going through his system. There's nothing like you've been looking for, but there are these graphics files. Imagery that Chipper Sullivan supplied for their web page. It's probably nothing, I don't really know why I called. It's just that . . . ."

There was a silence on the other end of the line.

"My God," the professor said at last.

"What is it?"

"I'd not even thought of it. It's so . . . old-fashioned. Invisible ink and that sort of thing. But then, why not?"

Lisbee gave vent to her building frustration.

"What in the hell are you talking about?"

"Steganography, of course," the professor said and chuckled.

FORTY-EIGHT

"Literally, *COVERED WRITING*, from the Greek. It's been in existence in one form or another for eons; invisible inks, as I said, messages hidden in shoe heels, that sort of thing. Steganographic software is relatively new, of course. But it allows one to hide messages in graphic or sound files. The only restrictions are that the data must be relatively small, or else a graphic file, for example, could become skewed and the image appear distorted."

Lisbee realized that she had been listening to this tutorial with her mouth agape. She closed it forcibly and heard her teeth click.

"Elizabeth? Are you there?"

"I'm still here. Professor, are you trying to tell me that your files have been sitting on this web page all this time hidden in an image that anyone on the Internet could copy?"

"I won't know that for sure until I've examined the graphics, of course, but if they are anywhere I suspect this is where Chipper would have hidden them. It would be very like him. I told you he was clever."

"Don't you think I'd better disable the site, until you know for sure?"

"Yes, that would be wise, I think. But do give me time to copy the images to work with here. Is there a counter on the page to tell us how many people have visited it?"

"I don't know, but I can spill the *admin* data and see how many hits it's had and who they were. I can't believe there were all that many for a homegrown memorial to Edgar Allen Poe. And I don't remember seeing any tags in the HTML files that requested the site be included by any of the major search engines. It hasn't been up long enough for their webcrawlers to have found it on their own. I'll print out the access list and bring it by this evening so we can go over it."

"Good, good. Well then, we shall do what we can. I'll start copying the images now and you'll be able to watch my access on the server; when I've finished, go right ahead and bring down the site." The professor paused for a moment.

"Oh, and Elizabeth?"

"Yes?"

"Thank you, my dear. You were always one of my best students."

The house was empty when Cory Floyd let himself in the front door. The girls would be at school and his wife, Sharyn, must have gone shopping, or more likely to her Mother's. They were very close, Sharyn and her mother. Sometimes he thought that she'd never actually left home, but rather paid frequent visits to him and their daughters when her mother could spare her. They were rarely without benefit of his mother-in-law's advice on everything from raising the children to what kind of car Sharyn should be driving, although this wisdom was imparted second hand, through his wife. Madeline Connor prided herself on not interfering, and in fact rarely graced their home with her presence more than once or twice a year, usually during the holidays. Cory Floyd was often irritated by what he considered to be his wife's immaturity, but at the moment he was relieved that she wasn't home. The last thing he needed was her mooning around right now when there were important decisions to be made.

The Fedex package was waiting on the step and he hurried into his study with it. He pulled the zip tab and dumped its contents unceremoniously on his desk. There was no covering letter from Lowry, only the Memorandum of Agreement in duplicate, and three sets of intimidating looking forms to be filled out by the Pan Global employees he would choose to work on the demo for the next six months. *If* there was going to be a demo. If there would even *be* a Pan Global six months from now.

Damage control. He had to act—had to put the brakes on the menacing downward spiral that was engulfing him and his company. All the opportunities were there; the means to bring Pan Global up and over the top; but only if the old professor's discovery of how to crack existing encryption techniques never went any further. Deutch insisted that the chances of anyone else coming up with it independently were minuscule and Cory believed that; it was an acceptable risk. But Chipper Sullivan had been the leak. He had copied the information and hidden it somewhere, knowing what it would be worth to the right people. He'd let his friend Rudy Tang in on it, or at least part of it, but Sullivan was dead and wouldn't be passing it on to anyone else now. And neither would Rudy Tang.

Cory's thoughts jumped involuntarily back to the darkness. The old van and the figure leaning into the passenger side, long black hair streaming down his back. The horrible sound of metal against flesh and bone, deafening in the silence. He pushed the images hurriedly away.

The hidden files had to be found. And destroyed. When that was done, and only then, could he start looking forward again. Cory gathered the MOA and security questionnaires off his desk and stuffed them haphazardly back into the Fedex envelope. He was searching his pockets for the key to the two-drawer file behind his desk when he noticed the slow blinking of the light on his answering machine. The voice that issued from the tape when he pressed the play button was guarded, but barely concealed a note of elation.

"Cory, my dear boy, good news. The object has been found. No details here, of course, but it's unlikely it would have been discovered by anyone, although there is that possibility. I'll have a list of possible interceptions by this evening, and I'm sure it will take very little time to eliminate all of them. Very tricky; very clever it was, I must say. Just wanted to let you know—set your mind at ease, if you know what I mean. Your concern was not lost on me. Still, I'm sure everything is all right. I'll be in touch with you tomorrow."

FORTY-NINE

Lunch in Monterey was not a success. The little Mexican restaurant Sunny Cortez had recommended did have excellent food, but Meg Sullivan remained mostly silent, moodily picking at the *flautas* she had ordered and finally sending her cold plate back barely disturbed. TJ was aware of the emotional shock the contents of Harley's file cabinet had given her; in fact had suggested that they postpone the lunch. He had offered to take her and the family photographs back home so she could go through them, but she just shook her head and closed the file drawer with a marked slam.

"I've seen them before. Let's go eat," she had said brusquely.

TJ paid the bill and drove Meg home to the old schoolhouse, where she murmured a subdued "Thanks," before disappearing through the front door. He then drove on to Anadarko Grace, thinking it would probably take her some time to come to grips with this new version of the father she had so neatly categorized for so many years. The office was empty; the answering machine blinking solemnly in the quiet gloom. He checked the messages, thinking there might be something from Uncle Beau or Lisbee, or even some news of the Tang boy, but they were all inconsequential. An invitation to lunch the following week from one of his daughter's clients; a wrong number; and a syrupy request from a local fraternal organization to volunteer for a fund raising campaign they were initiating in support of the candidate they were backing for an empty seat on the City Council. TJ erased all but the one for Lisbee.

Although he was used to blind alleys, having followed a thousand miles of them throughout his career, TJ found himself particularly frustrated at the morning's lack of progress. He tried to talk himself out of it by admitting that he'd never really had any solid reason to suppose Sunny Cortez had been skimming profits from Bel Harbor, but that didn't help. On further introspection he realized that it wasn't the books—they were just one possibility. It was Sunny himself. TJ was convinced he was hiding something. It was just a matter of finding out what that something was. And whether it had any bearing on the death of Chipper Sullivan; or, a little farther out in left field, the disappearance of Rudy Tang. Admittedly, he could see no connection between Cortez and Tang, except the indirect one of their mutual relationships with the Sullivan kid, but that might be enough.

And there was another thing. Hanging back just outside his conscious reach was a small bell ringing, sometimes so faint he could barely hear it, but never quite going silent. It involved Cortez; that was its only certainty. A chance remark, barely noticed at the time but tucked away for later consideration? The more TJ nagged at it, the farther it slipped away. Better to let go of it—it would surface on its own eventually.

With Estralita's *chile rellenos* sitting heavily in his midsection, vaguely threatening to instigate one of his rare bouts of indigestion, TJ leaned back in the chair behind his desk and put his loafer-shod feet up on one corner, legs crossed at the ankles. From a bottom drawer he extracted the manila envelope that contained the information Harley Sullivan had left for him and spread its contents across the desk. He'd been over it all a dozen times, not that that was any guarantee he hadn't missed something. Idly shuffling through the papers, TJ finally selected the autopsy report and began reading.

'. . . well nourished Caucasian male, aged approximately twenty-three, . . . T-shaped scar on the left palm at the base of the thumb, two centimeters in length . . .' Some childhood injury, TJ thought. Playing ball? Or maybe fishing with his grandfather. An errant fishhook? The stomach contents, primarily rum, pineapple juice, and the downers that had combined to kill him, also contained traces of what had turned out to be his last meal, consumed some six hours before his death—sausage and mushroom pizza. His stomach rumbling under a loosened belt, TJ considered grimly that even without the drugs, that combination would probably have been enough to do him in. There'd been a few minor bruises, conjectured to have resulted from his fall to the forward cabin deck after losing consciousness. Nothing. It all came back to nothing. And then the bell began ringing again—loud.

Stuffing the papers back into the envelope, TJ reached for the phone and started dialing.

"It's TJ Billings. Listen, if you've got the time, I'd like to take the *Emmy T* out for a couple of hours this afternoon . . . four o'clock sounds good. I'll be there."

Monterey Bay was a smoothly undulating blue-green, barely beginning to reflect the hazy gold of the sun as it slipped toward the horizon.   The trawler rolled gently through the moderate swells; a very different boat from the one that had dipped and climbed the walls of water threatening to engulf it the last time he'd been out. Under the watchful eye of his tutor, TJ had performed all the checks, let loose the lines, and guided the *Emmy T* away from the dock and through the marker buoys at the channel mouth without help, and was now heading almost due west into an empty sea.

"What are the chances of running into a tanker or cruise ship or something?" he asked from his place at the helm seat, not taking his eyes from the view through the vast windows in front of him. Sunny Cortez, seated nonchalantly at the table behind him, smiled.

"Very slight until you get out to the ship channel."

"How far is that?"

"About fifteen miles."

TJ nodded, still not taking his eyes from the solitary horizon.

"What about fishing boats? It looks pretty empty out there."

"They're mostly in by now."

They continued to cruise at a steady seven knots in silence, as the sun slid further down, painting the water pink and gold. TJ began to relax, turning occasionally to see Cortez gazing at the sea, his face smooth and expressionless. When the thing had finally surfaced, the bell in his head clanging like a fire drill, he had been so certain. The fishing boat; the one that had signaled with flashing lights the time before. It was the *Emmy T* the message was for, not another fishing boat. She was the only one in a position to have seen the flashing on that bright sunny day. Any legitimate message for a member of the fleet could have—would have—been transmitted by radio.

He was less certain now. In the vastness surrounding them it seemed quite possible it had been a fluke; his imagination trying to come up with a lead. There could have been another boat behind them he hadn't seen. But it was all he had. Might as well make a fool of himself and follow it through. Sure as hell wouldn't be the first time. He glanced once more at the calm face of Sunny Cortez, then turned back to watch the swells, which seemed to be gaining strength as they moved west.

"So when did you start dealing drugs, Sunny? On the docks at Monterey, or after you went to work for Harley?"

FIFTY

"IT WAS THE animation he chose, of course. The files were dissected and one part was embedded in each frame; any distortion in a single image would be virtually impossible to detect because of the speed at which they were viewed, although the data were tiny, really, and there was no noticeable distortion in any of the images that I could see. Still, better safe and all that. He really was a remarkable boy—such a waste." Professor Dean Deutch was looking more like himself; the color was back in his thin face and his voice was animated. The Brown Betty teapot had been replaced by a svelte crystal decanter of extraordinarily good sherry, and from the pale pink glow on his prominent cheekbones, Lisbee deduced that the full glass on the table before him was probably not his first. She smiled and took another sip of her own.

"This is good," she said.

"It is, isn't it? I don't usually imbibe, but on such an occasion I thought a celebratory aperitif was in order. Is that the list of visitors to the website?"

Lisbee nodded and began thumbing through the thin sheaf of pages she had extracted from her notebook.

"There were more than I expected, but I've eliminated most of them—the ones from English Departments at several universities, for example. They were mostly single hits; none of them came back once they'd checked out the references."

"Did the page find its way to the search engine's archives, then?

"No. I checked them all. I suspect some local students found the thing and passed the link on to their friends who are interested in Poe. One trip would be enough for anybody if they weren't looking for something else; there are lots of better sources for doing research than what Chipper had on his site."

"Were there any visits you did find suspicious?"

Lisbee sat back against the cushions on the settee and swallowed the last of her sherry. The professor quickly grasped the decanter and refilled her glass.

"Only one. Several accesses almost on a daily basis for about two months. Then they stopped completely seven weeks ago. I looked up the domain name and it's assigned to Pan Global. My guess is it was Chipper himself, checking it out from work. Or possibly Rudy Tang, although I don't think he has the background to be involved in the technical end beyond keeping the BBS up and running. The fact that they stopped completely after Chipper died is fairly conclusive, don't you think?"

"Significant, surely. Nothing from mathematics or computer science departments then? Nor competitors of Pan Global? Government sites?"

Lisbee shook her head. Professor Deutch steepled his skeletal fingers under his chin and gazed into the distance beyond her. A full minute of intense concentration passed before he rose swiftly from his seat, jarring the table with the sudden movement.

"Well then; there you are," he said as he disappeared into the galley, calling over his shoulder, "I'll just be a moment." Presently his tuneless whistling could be heard in accompaniment to the rattling of dishes and cutlery.

While he was gone, Lisbee looked through the salon window at the empty berth next to the *Prime Number*, the fading light glistening on the gently undulating water. TJ was still out there somewhere in the *Emmy T.* It would have worried her, his taking the trawler out with darkness approaching, but after the minor shock of seeing his Jaguar in the parking lot, she had noticed that the marina office was closed and locked. Cortez was undoubtedly with him, and the young proprietor of Bel Harbor was an experienced seaman. That mollified her concern somewhat, but she was still marginally anxious, scanning the horizon for a sign of the returning vessel, when the sedate burring of her cell phone caused her to start, nearly upsetting the glass of sherry at her fingertips.

"Elizabeth Billings." Her voice sounded scratchy in her ears as she answered.

"It's Justin. They just found Rudy Tang." His tone was not one to inspire confidence.

"Is he . . . ?"

"Not quite, but it doesn't look good. The ambulance just left."

"Where was he?"

"His van went off the road, about seven miles out of Soquel. Couldn't see it from the highway—some hikers found it an hour ago."

"An accident?"

"Could be. They're going over it now. His head was so bloody it's hard to tell if he got it all on impact or not. We'll know better when they clean him up, or if he regains consciousness and can talk."

"If?"

"He was barely alive when we got here. Probably happened late last night. The paramedics weren't real optimistic; shock and exposure in addition to the head wounds. He probably won't make it."

"Shit." Lisbee's voice was barely audible.

"Say again?"

"I said 'thanks'—for letting me know. Will you keep me posted?"

"Sure. Where are you?"

"At Bel Harbor. With Professor Deutch. I'll be leaving soon and I'll call Uncle Beau. I don't know if they'll want to bring his sister to the hospital or not under the circumstances. Justin?"

"Yeah?"

"When will you be off?"

"I don't know. It could be late."

"I'll be up."

"Good," he said and broke the connection.

The professor was standing at the table, a plate of delicately arranged shrimp and lime wedges in his hand, when she ended the conversation. His face was drawn again, the pallor returned, making his cheekbones jut out beneath a delta of blue veins.

"Oh dear," he said quietly, setting the plate on the table and sinking onto the padded sofa. Lisbee looked gravely at the old man as the *Prime Number* shifted gently in her berth, rolling ever so slightly from the weight of being boarded. The salon door opened and a man, broad in the shoulders, filled the empty space.

"Hello, Cory," Elizabeth said.

FIFTY-ONE

WHEN TJ TURNED back to look at Sunny Cortez his expression hadn't changed; he was still gazing into the deepening purple distance. Finally he spoke.

"You've got it all wrong, man. Why are you trying to set me up? I've never done anything to you."

"I'm not trying to set you up. I just want some answers, and the ones I'm getting from you lack a little of hitting the mark. I want to know why you're hedging and what it is you're not telling, that's all."

Sunny shook his head.

"I don't know what you're talking about."

"Well, let me give you an example. That boat that flashed a signal at us the other day. It wasn't for some other fishing boat, it was for this one. I'm no seaman, but I'm not a fool either. Any legitimate message would have come over the marine radio . . . so, if it was illegitimate, what might it be? Out here off shore, some kind of smuggling comes to mind, and what's the dearest cargo to a smuggler's heart? Drugs."

"You've been seeing too many movies. Do you know how difficult it would be to come alongside another boat in that kind of sea?"

"That could have been the message—*'It's too rough, try again tomorrow'* or, *'I'm empty today, catch me next week.'* At least you're not denying the signal was for the *Emmy T.*"

Sunny got up and walked steadily toward the refrigerator, ignoring the slight roll of the cabin floor.

"Mind if I have a beer?"

"Not if you get me one, too."

He opened a can and handed it to TJ, then returned to his seat with his own.

"Even if it was for this boat, I don't own it. Why put me in the noose?"

"Because you had access to it most any time you wanted until Harley died and left it to me. And because you were able to come up with enough money to buy in for a third of Bel Harbor. I have a little trouble believing you saved it up from your job on the docks and working for Harley for a couple of years."

The sky was darkening as the last slice of the sun dipped below the water line. Stars began to appear above the bowl of rainbow colors that were fading rapidly. TJ thought it was probably time to turn around and go back; there were breaker switches that turned on the *Emmy T''*s running lights and those should be on by now, too, he supposed. But he didn't want to lose the momentum of the conversation he had going with Sunny Cortez. He decided he'd better speed up the pace a little.

"So the way I see it, the kid, Chipper, probably found out what you were doing with his grandpa's boat. Or maybe you were his dealer going in. After you'd made your bid for a partnership in the marina, Chipper saw a way to get some extra money to help him along in his computer business. 'Pay up or Harley finds out what you're doing and you're out on the docks again, if not in jail.' Something like that. Now let's say you didn't have quite enough after the buy-in to pay the greedy little bastard's blackmail too. The easiest thing in that case would be to see that he got a little more than he was used to in the next batch of dope you sold him.

"Besides, you probably weren't too red hot on the idea of him being your partner when Harley died anyway. Meg Sullivan would be a lot easier to deal with."

When TJ turned back to see what effect this little fairy tale had had on him, Sunny Cortez was staring blankly at his beer can. A sudden swell shifted the trawler and TJ grabbed for the wheel to steady himself. Cortez looked up.

"You've got it all wrong, man," he said again. Then, "You'd better turn her around and head back. The running lights are the third switch down on the left."

FIFTY-TWO

CORY FLOYD'S EYES widened beneath his heavy dark brows.

"What's she doing here?"

Lisbee glanced at Professor Deutch. His agitation was palpable in the small enclosure of the *Prime Number's* salon. His hands fluttered before him, and for a moment she imagined he would pick up a shrimp from the plate he had prepared and offer it to Floyd as a distraction, like throwing a piece of raw meat to a vicious guard dog. Instead, he began to speak; his voice only slightly higher in tone than normal.

"Ah, Cory, glad you're here. I would have been to see you tomorrow, but this is much cozier. Come and join us, won't you? We're having a small celebration. Elizabeth has been a tremendous help, and we've solved our little problem. Nothing to worry about, I assure you. We'll tell you all about it." He motioned frantically for Floyd to have a seat, but he remained standing by the doorway.

"How much have you told her?" he finally said, still speaking over Lisbee's head as if she weren't there, though the topic under discussion was her very presence. Irritated beyond the first spark of fear his arrival had caused her, she glared at him.

"Oh for God's sake sit down, Cory. Stop standing there like some goon from a B movie. Professor Deutch asked for my help because I was able to search Rudy Tang's BBS and I found where Chipper had hidden the copy of the algorithm he stole. It's safe; no one else found it." Floyd finally looked at her. At the mention of Rudy's name his face had tightened, but by the time she finished speaking it was relaxing into a slow smile. Her chill of fear returned, sending gooseflesh down her arms. She had an irresistible urge to look away, or even better, run, but she knew that would be a mistake. With an effort she managed to hold his gaze.

"Well, that's great," he said in an overly hearty voice. "You're the best; I've always said that. It's why I hired you as a consultant in the first place. I'd be interested to know how you did it."

Lisbee watched as Floyd moved silently to the helm seat, never taking his eyes from her. His thickly muscled chest seemed to swell under his thin jacket, and she noticed his fists were clenched, the large knuckles white with tension. She began relating the story of finding the website and the resultant discovery of the files hidden in the images of the raven, relieved to hear her own voice sounding steady and firm. Then she detailed their analysis of the list of visitors to the website and how they had eliminated them all as a potential threat. Throughout her story, Cory Floyd retained the glazed half-smile, occasionally nodding his head and interjecting a brief laudatory comment; "Good." "Right; great." When she had finished, his eyes stayed on her, the smile still in place.

"Well," he said at length, "I still have a question or two—okay?" Lisbee said nothing and the Professor broke in.

"Certainly, certainly my boy, but first let me get you a glass of something. Sherry? Something stronger?" His voice trailed off as Floyd continued regarding Lisbee, ignoring him completely.

"Like, for instance, why were you there at all? At Tang's house, I mean. And how did you know what to look for? Or to look for anything for that matter?"

"Uncle Beau asked me to go through his computer system; he's investigating Rudy's disappearance for his sister. She's a client."

"His disappearance?"

"He's been missing since last night. I thought you knew."

Floyd finally turned and gathered the professor back into the fold, glaring at him.

"Knew he was missing? Why would I? What's this old fart been telling you, anyway?"

Professor Deutch shrank back into the settee cushions and Lisbee thought for a moment he might faint. With more bravado than she felt, she turned on Floyd.

"Don't be an ignorant ass, Cory. Use your head. I've got sources you've never even imagined; I have to in this job. The word that's out is that Rudy's being set up for the burglary at Pan Global. If he wanted to disappear in a hurry he'd need some cash, and the only thing he's got worth trading is whatever Chipper told him about your little problem. You're the first one he'd hit on his way out of town. Isn't that what happened?"

Floyd's face was suddenly flushed with indecision. It was all Lisbee needed to convince her that he had seen Rudy

Tang; seen and talked to him, and maybe given him a push to shut him up. She could read the questions he was asking himself—should he admit meeting Rudy or deny the whole thing? What could or couldn't be proved against him? With more wisdom than she thought he possessed, he decided on sticking as close to the truth as he could get without incriminating himself.

"I saw him briefly, and he did ask for money, but I didn't give him any. I didn't get the impression he really knew what it was he was trying to sell. The one thing he convinced me of was that the Sullivan kid had stolen the files and hidden them somewhere. And we already knew that, or suspected it." The greasy smile returned. "So now that you've found them, that's that. Damage controlled. The only people in the world who know about your discovery are here in this room," he finished, turning back to the professor.

"Well, then, that's fine, isn't it?" Professor Deutch started to rise from his seat. "Can I get you that drink now? You agree a celebration is in order?"

Floyd moved from the helm seat so quickly Lisbee could not suppress a rasping indrawn breath of surprise. He pushed the professor roughly back onto the settee with his left hand, and in a smooth, arcing motion grasped a brass paperweight in the shape of a pelican from the shelf behind him with his right. Raising it high in the air, he brought it down on the back of the old man's skull with a sickening thud. The professor slumped against the cushions, a slowly widening thread of dark red blood seeping down his neck to disappear under his shirt collar. After Cory Floyd rose from the helm seat, his actions seemed to occur in slow motion while Lisbee sat paralyzed, unable to do anything but observe. She had a fleeting, irrational thought that he looked like a ballet dancer; crisp, pure, athletic movements full of strength and grace. A homicidal, bloody Baryshnikov. Feeling a bubble of hysterical laughter rising in her throat, she moved one hand to her mouth, trying to contain it. Through the salon window, across the empty slip beside them, the blackening sky was blossoming with pinpoints of light. She imagined in that last second that two of the stars were bigger than the others, and colored instead of white. Red and green, like they belonged on a Christmas tree.

FIFTY-THREE

TJ GRASPED THE spokes of the wheel and started turning, hand over hand, until the *Emmy T* began her slow arc, the needle of the compass remaining fixed while the direction indicator appeared to spin beneath it. The barely discernible horizon slid past until the lights of Monterey, and then the tall, lighted stacks of the Moss Landing power plant were visible in the distance. He switched on the breaker for the running lights and tried to relax in the helm seat, a mild depression washing over him. More to himself than the silent young man in the cabin behind him, he said, "Well, I probably do have it all wrong, but I sure would appreciate the hell out of somebody straightening me out and getting this monkey off my back."

"It was the kid," came the almost ethereal reply from the gloom. TJ continued looking straight ahead, not wishing to make any move that might interrupt what Sunny Cortez was saying or was about to say. Without actually seeing him, TJ felt Cortez rise and move to the refrigerator for another beer. After setting a fresh can in front of TJ at the helm, he took his own and returned to the settee.

"He wasn't dealing, exactly; not in any big way. A few goodies for his friends, maybe, but that was it. He didn't need the money—he took all he wanted from Harley, with or without him knowing. After I took over the books I saw what he was doing but he didn't care about that. He knew I wouldn't tell the old man. Harley wouldn't have believed me if I did, and I didn't want to hurt him anyway. He was a good man.

"That signal was a mistake; there's always some asshole who never gets the word. Chipper used to take the *Emmy T* whenever he wanted—he was a good sailor, I'll say that for him, and Harley was proud of him, liked to see him handling her on his own. Some of it was my fault, I guess. I told him one time, just shooting the shit, about some of the guys in the fishing fleet at Monterey. How they'd store up a little backlog from whoever was dealing at the best price and when things dried up, they had a way to supplement their income.

"It was Chipper's idea to use the boat. Get the high sign from whoever was ready to make a deal. Dumb, really, but he liked the adventure; smuggling, pirates of the Spanish Main, all that shit. He was still a kid. Never grew up. Never will, now.

"He wasn't bad really, just didn't think about anyone else. Harley or Meg. Full of his own importance, like a lot of them. I think Harley knew, or suspected at least. But he couldn't admit it, even to himself, because he loved his grandson more than anything."

TJ considered the story, watching the lights grow closer. It made sense. Harley could have done that in his grief and bitterness over the boy's death—convinced himself it was murder, maybe by some of his contacts, a deal gone bad. He'd apparently been turning a blind eye to Chipper's failings for a long time, unlike the kid's mother, who saw things through a harsher but clearer lens.

"I appreciate you telling me this, Sunny, and you don't have to answer, but there's still one thing that's bothering me. Where did you get the money to buy into Bel Harbor?"

Sunny laughed, breaking the tension that had enveloped the cabin of the *Emmy T.*

"I didn't. Oh, I had a little saved up, and I put that in the kitty, but the price I paid to Harley was in the form of a promise."

"A promise. What kind of promise, if you don't mind my asking?"

"A promise to look after someone he cared about when he was gone."

"Chipper?"

"No. His daughter. Meg."

The *Emmy T* passed through the flashing red and green buoys at the harbor entrance and TJ pulled back the throttle, slowing her to a whispering crawl. As he approached the docks of Bel Harbor, the whine of the stern thrusters sounded on the damp air like giant insects. Next to the empty berth that was their destination, the *Prime Number* blazed with lights, and TJ could see tiny figures through the curtainless windows. Though he had never struck him as a man who would, it looked like the Professor was having a party. When they drew closer, it appeared the old Chris Craft was actually rolling in her berth, much more than would result from the gentle flow of the water in the harbor. TJ motioned to Sunny Cortez to look through the window.

"What the hell's going on there?" he said, but almost before the words were out of his mouth, a slim shadow emerged from the cabin and was immediately jerked back.

Simultaneously, a piercing shriek of outrage splintered the night.

FIFTY-FOUR

Hᴇ ᴡᴀs sᴛᴀʀᴛɪɴɢ toward her now, and still she couldn't move. The smile had been replaced by a frown wrinkling his broad forehead beneath the curling black hair. He was saying something in a low voice, the words floating in the air between them.

"I really hate to do this, Elizabeth. I hope you realize that . . ."

She could see the bloody brass pelican in his right hand as if it were under a microscope; strands of gray hair stuck to the brownish smear on its square base. Her heart was hammering against her ribs, threatening to explode in her chest, but still her hands remained paralyzed there on the table in front of her. Small hands; slim fingered. What the hell could she do with them if they did work? He was too big, too strong. She needed some sort of weapon, but there was none. A painful cramp gripped her right thigh and without taking time to think she extended her leg under the table. Then retracted it and kicked with all her strength, landing a solid blow squarely on Cory Floyd's shin.

With a grunt of shock and pain, he dropped the brass paperweight. She was moving now, scuttling past his sweating body, toward the side cabin door. He momentarily lost his balance and fell backward as the boat rocked with her movement. Grasping the latch, she tugged frantically and the door finally began to slide open, the cold night air assaulting her, making her shiver but clearing her head. She was through the door, one foot on the clammy deck, when something seized her hair and jerked her back. She screamed and turned into him, arms flailing. One sharp elbow made contact, sending a searing jolt of fire through her shoulder. He fell back again, and she scrambled for the door.

On the deck now, slipping in the dampness. Climbing, grasping the railing, with nowhere to go. She had to get off on the dock, but the boarding steps were behind her. And so was Cory Floyd. She could hear him, his breath coming in ragged gasping sounds.

The *Emmy T* was floating toward the dock, her big diesel engine idling like a purring cat. It was time to make the turn, move the tiny joystick that controlled the stern thrusters so she would slip neatly into her berth. In front of him the slim shadow that was Lisbee reappeared and behind her another, much broader form. TJ watched as she grabbed the rails and slipped to one knee on the forward deck of the *Prime Number*. He was on her in an instant; they were struggling in the reflected light from the windows.

Behind him he could hear Sunny Cortez shouting at him to make the fucking turn. It was too far to jump with or without a bum ankle, and there was no time to dock the big trawler and still get to her before, before . . . . He grasped the red-handled throttle and pushed forward. The trawler shuddered and then began gaining speed. Cortez was at the helm now, pushing him aside and pulling back on the throttle, but not before the bow of the thirteen-ton *Emmy T* struck the *Prime Number'*s stern with a jarring crack.

Lisbee couldn't breathe. She was down on the clammy teak, some kind of brass fitting gouging painfully into her side. Cory Floyd, on one knee, leaned his weight into her chest, reaching for her throat. With the heels of both hands she was pushing with all her strength against his chin, bending his head back, but it wasn't working. She was running out of air.

Her head was swimming and she could see the black edges of unconsciousness closing in an ever narrowing circle when a bomb exploded and the world turned upside down. Floyd was thrown up and away from her and she felt herself lifted from the deck and flung against the railing. She grasped one metal strut with both hands and looked up in time to see him pitch over the bow, like a gymnast doing a dismount from the parallel bars, and land head first on the dock below. She waited for what seemed like hours, but he didn't get up. An engine was running somewhere, and someone was shouting or cursing, she couldn't tell which. Clinging to the thin rail, she heard the pounding of feet and knew Floyd was back after her again, but she didn't know how he was doing it because she could see him still lying there on the dock, not moving. And then she figured it out. It had all been a bad dream—TJ was here now, stroking her hair and telling her everything was all right. He would be pulling up the covers and saying *'go back to sleep; we'll talk about it in the morning'* any minute now, and that was just fine with her.

If there was anything she wanted, it was a good night's sleep.

FIFTY-FIVE

"IT WAS VERY nice of Deputy . . . Highstreet, is it? To offer to keep me apprised of Rudy's condition. There'll have to be surgery, he said, to relieve the pressure, but at least the poor boy is still alive."

Aurelia Sims, in a soft blue wool dress of severely simple cut, her black calf pumps shining dully in the glow of the lamp at her side, offered Beau a plate of cookies to go with the coffee she had just poured into the delicate china cup. When he declined, she placed the plate on the coffee table in front of him, next to the carafe.

"I haven't decided how to tell Camellia yet. It's so difficult."

"Might be best if you wait until we know what the outcome's going to be. No sense getting her hopes up too high."

Miss Sims nodded and changed the subject.

"I don't know if you're familiar with the techniques of tutoring, such as I've been doing for the last several years. They are many and varied, of course, but I've found it helpful in my own experience to make use of a tape recorder for documenting the lessons. It helps me assess the progress a student is making, and is often of value to them as well. Especially in learning a language.

"If I'm going to be truthful, which I nearly always try to be, I must admit also that it's been an invaluable aid to my memory, which is getting a bit rusty at my age. This is merely to let you understand that it's something I'm used to using. And that is why, although it is causing me some qualms now, I decided to record my conversations with Camellia. Because there might be something important in what she had to say, I didn't want to trust it to my memory."

Beau regarded the elegant old lady, noting the concern, even hesitation, in her manner.

"And was there? Something important?"

"Oh yes, there was. I'm going to play it for you now, and then I'm going to see that it's destroyed. You'll understand why when you hear it. It's a first hand account of the young Sullivan boy's death."

The girl's lilting, childish voice floated into the room through the small recorder's speakers:

It was a long ride. In the dark, with lights coming whizzing at us, then vanishing like ghosts. I would have been frightened except for Chipper. He was warm there next to me and he had his arm around me, smoothing my hair. I leaned my head against his flannel shirt because it was soft, and when I closed my eyes wishing the ghostlights would go away, they did.

Chipper put the knit cap on my head and helped me tuck my hair underneath it when the car finally stopped. He smiled at me and kissed the tip of my nose, like it was a small joke, just between the two of us. We walked together and the gravel crunched under our feet; then we went through a gate and onto the rough boards that creaked and swayed along with the boats.

I liked the boats, even in the dark. They looked like mountains, big and white as if it had just snowed on them. The square windows were covered with colored canvas, like sunglasses shading their eyes. Chipper's boat wore dark blue glasses that matched the stripe along its sides. A light glowed dim around the edges of the canvas, but there was no one there. It was left on, he said, to keep the boat company when he was gone. I liked that too, and wished I had a light to keep me company when he was away from me. But I didn't tell him that.

We climbed the steps and went inside, and it wasn't a boat anymore—it was our house. The living room and kitchen upstairs and two bedrooms downstairs. It was awfully cold at first, but he turned on the electric heater and soon it was warm, with the growl from the heater sounding like Pineapple purring. I wished I could have Pineapple in our house; that would have made everything perfect. He would like the boat-house, but not riding in the car to get to it.

Chipper got glasses from the ceiling where they hung upside down by their stems. I had never seen glasses hanging upside down like that before. It made me laugh. I'd seen something like it on television, but it was in a cave and the things upside down on the ceiling were bats. When I called them 'bat glasses' it made him *laugh.*

There was ice in the freezer, just like at home, and pineapple juice in the refrigerator below it. And the maple syrup, but in a strange bottle, not like the one I use on the waffles Rudy lets me make in the toaster. It was sweet like mine, but different. And there weren't any waffles to put it on—he just poured it right into the glass with the juice. I tried that once at home, but it didn't taste the same as it did in the boat-house.

I thought Chipper must have a headache when he took some aspirin from a little plastic bag in his pocket and swallowed them with the pineapple juice. I asked him if he did, and why the aspirin wasn't in a bottle. He smiled and rested his hand on my leg and said the bottle was too big to carry around. He said to drink my juice and we'd go take a nap and then his headache would go away.

I drank all the juice in my glass and it was strange how cold juice could make me feel so warm inside. And sleepy, my eyelids barely able to stay open. I was glad he wanted to take a nap because I wasn't sure I could stay awake much longer.

I always have a nightgown to sleep in at home, but Chipper said I didn't need one at the boat-house because he was there to keep me warm. When he started helping me undress, I nearly told him I could do that by myself—I'd been doing it alone for a long time now. I didn't, though.

He was smiling and making a soft noise in his throat, sitting on the bed beside me, and his hands felt warm and tickled a bit, so that I giggled.

When he pulled the covers up under my chin and sat on the other side of the bed, I watched him take off his shirt and jeans. The little bit of light from upstairs was like a sliver of the moon because the door was only half open, and I could see the naked skin of his back, silvery-white. He was so big—much bigger than Rudy. I was afraid I would get squashed under him, but he told me it was okay, his weight pressing on me but not enough to push the breath out of me. He ran his hands down my sides until I shivered and pushed against him, trying to get closer. And then there was the rocking. It felt so good, rocking together, back and forth, up and down, like on a swing only close together and so warm. His breath was heavy against my neck and finally he groaned and shuddered and then the rocking stopped.

And I was so happy, until I felt the wetness between my legs, felt it sliding from my body onto the sheets and I started to cry, thinking I had wet the bed, because I hadn't done that for such a long time and it would probably make him mad. But when he asked me why I was crying and I told him, he said it was okay.

"It was me, not you," he said. "And who gives a shit, anyway?" We both laughed then and he kissed me and said he was going up to take some more aspirin with the pineapple juice that was left. But I fell asleep before he came back. It seemed like I slept a long time, but when I woke up it was still dark and Chipper said it was time to go home. That was the first time we went to our boat-house. The last time was after I had the flu and Rudy took me to the doctor, but I was feeling better by then. That was when Chipper decided he'd have to go away. Only he didn't tell me where he was going . . . or that he'd be gone so long. I wish he would have told me, because I got scared that last time.

When I opened my eyes it was still dark. I thought for a minute I was in my own bed at home, and I reached for Pineapple, but he wasn't there. Then I remembered we were on the boat-house. But the bed was empty anyway. Chipper wasn't there either. I thought at first he'd just gone up for more aspirin for his headache—he always seemed to get headaches when we had the pineapple juice. I told him once maybe it was the juice that was causing them, but he just laughed. I pushed back the covers and sat on the edge of the bed, feeling the carpet thick on my bare feet. I found my long sweater and put it on and went upstairs.

The living room was empty, too, and when I tried to look in the other bedroom at the front of the boat-house I couldn't get the door open. It was stuck. I stepped outside and looked around, but there wasn't anyone; just the dark boats, and I started to get frightened. I didn't know why Chipper had gone away and left me alone, and I wanted Rudy.

But Rudy had gone out. He was going to be late, he said. That's why Chipper had said we'd have time to go to the boat-house. I looked at my watch, this one that Rudy gave me, I never take it off. It was three o'clock. And still dark. Rudy would be home by now and he'd be worried and mad that I didn't tell him where we were going.

So I called him from the phone on the boathouse and he was mad, but it sounded more like he was mad at Chipper, though I don't know why. I told him Chipper must have had to go away somewhere and he said he'd come and get me. It took a long time before he got there and when he did he looked really mad until he tried to open the bedroom door that was stuck, and then he was very quiet but he wasn't mad anymore.

I asked him if he knew where Chipper might have gone, but he just shook his head and said 'Let's go home,' and his voice sounded funny, kind of hoarse like he was getting a cold.

I think Rudy must know where Chipper went, but he still doesn't like it when I ask him about when he's going to come back.

"They were lovers," Beau said quietly.

"Yes. And I think I know now why Rudy stopped Camellia from seeing me. I believe she is going to have a child. He knew it, and was sure I would guess as time went on."

"Children having children. Dear Lord help us."

Aurelia Sims removed the tape cassette from the recorder, and began pulling the thin tape from its housing. When she had gathered it all into a spider's web, she dislodged it from the spool and threw it into the fireplace, where it sizzled and disappeared almost immediately.

"I wanted you to hear this, Beau, because I trust you to be an honorable man and I believe it will allow you to set your nephew's mind at rest about the Sullivan boy's death. It seems obvious to me there was no foul play involved. A mistake, perhaps, by a selfish and misguided boy, but nothing more."

Beau nodded.

"I'll tell TJ. And I hope he'll let it go at that."

FIFTY-SIX

THE WEEK BEFORE Christmas, not unusually, was bright and clear with temperatures approaching seventy-five degrees by mid-afternoon. Normally bracketed by storms and heavy rain, these few days of holiday respite were taken in stride when they occurred, and last minute shoppers in shorts and tee shirts littered the mall landscapes, as if they had been wearing the summer staples under their jackets and slickers all the time.

Lisbee, dressed more conservatively in jeans though wearing the requisite tee in brilliant green to mark the season, strode through the living room, past her father's six foot noble fir which sported decorations she recalled from early childhood, and into the kitchen, where she dropped a large shopping bag unceremoniously into a vacant chair at the table. TJ, a tablet of yellow legal paper, red and green pens, and several folded documents spread before him, looked up and smiled. Uncle Beau stood at the sink, the regular rhythm of knife on chopping block sounding as he worked. Without turning around, Beau acknowledged her presence.

"Sage or thyme, Elizabeth?"

"Thyme. And don't forget the bacon. I ran out of paper so I came to finish up here. It's worth your life getting into the stores to buy some more."

"In the den. On your father's desk. That's why he's in here, bothering me while I'm trying to concentrate on the stuffing."

TJ shook his head slowly and pointed toward the refrigerator.

"If you can get past the sensitive gourmet, there's beer."

Lisbee rummaged through the holiday provisions and extracted two cans, giving Beau a swift hug as she reached around him for a glass for herself and returned to the table.

"What's all that?" she said, indicating the papers at TJ's elbow.

"Boat stuff. Insurance, repairs."

"Are they finished? Is it out of the yard?" Her father nodded.

"Super. When are we going out? It'd be criminal to waste this weather."

When he didn't answer, Lisbee looked at Uncle Beau, who was studiously attending peeled onions.

"TJ?"

"I don't know. I'm thinking about selling it. Got an offer from a guy while it was in the yard."

"You're kidding. Why sell it? I thought you liked it."

"I do, but . . . ."

Beau finally rinsed his hands and turned, leaning against the counter.

"Your father has some notion that he hasn't really earned it according to the instructions in Harley's will."

"They were very specific," TJ said. "He didn't just say *'find out what happened.'* We already knew that, or were pretty damn sure that the boy did it to himself. Harley wanted me to find a killer, to prove him right. And I didn't do it."

Lisbee looked at her father thoughtfully.

"Maybe you did and you just haven't realized it yet."

"Mick Deering told me the word on the 'Net was that Chipper died of overconfidence. I, we all, took that to mean he OD'd thinking he could get away with it. But what if it meant something else? That he thought he was untouchable, maybe. Out of reach of even the most compelling motive. Put aside monetary gain and the fact Cory Floyd didn't know he had stolen the data yet—who had the best motive to kill him?"

"Rudy Tang," TJ said. "Because of what he did to Camellia. Rudy could have scored some dope with his BBS connections without any trouble, something a lot stronger than Chipper was used to, and he wouldn't have questioned it coming from Rudy. But he didn't know that she was pregnant until after Chipper died. The timing's all off."

"Maybe not," Beau said. He reached into the bulging refrigerator for a beer and joined his nephew and grandniece at the table.

"You didn't hear the recording Miss Sims made of the girl's story, and it's been destroyed now. But there was something on it I neglected to mention; didn't think it was important at the time. About that last night she spent with Chipper on the boat. Camellia seems to have a sort of fixation about time. Like that watch her brother gave her—she never takes it off. She doesn't relate things to dates on a calendar, but she has her own way of tagging them to other events she can remember. She said the last night she spent on the boat with the boy was after she had the flu. After Rudy had taken her to see a doctor."

TJ leaned his chair back on its two hind legs.

"So he did know. Or it's a good bet he did."

"Mick could probably find out if Rudy did some business with the pill pushers, but that's as far as it goes," Lisbee said. "We could never prove he gave the stuff to Chipper. Rudy's still in a coma and Justin says it's even odds whether he'll come out of it or not. And even if he did, he'd be a fool to admit it, or maybe he wouldn't even remember it at all. There is such a thing as legitimate amnesia after a blow on the head."

TJ mused over the last inch of beer in his glass.

"He's all that poor little girl has left in the world if he does recover. I don't think Harley would have wanted that. Besides, his instructions didn't mention a thing about proving—only finding."

FIFTY-SEVEN

The SUN WAS shining brightly on the morning of January 17th when Lisbee stepped aboard the *Prime Number* to be greeted by Professor Dean Deutch, brandishing his Brown Betty teapot.

"So good of you to come, Elizabeth. I can't tell you how satisfying it is to be back home—to have a home to come back to for that matter. Please, sit down and have some tea."

"TJ said his insurance covered all your repairs."

"It did indeed, and young Mr. Cortez saw to everything while I was in the hospital. All as good as new, I'm happy to say, including my incredibly hard head. And all thanks to your most extraordinary father, and to you, too, my dear, of course."

Lisbee smiled and took her place at the table in front of the steaming mug of tea.

"I didn't do anything. I was in the same soup as you were. It was TJ's show and I'm not sure he's ever going to lose that silly grin he's been wearing for the last two months. I hate it when he's smug."

"Surely not. A man of his perception? You're very lucky to have him."

"I know, but don't you ever tell him I said so."

The professor grinned a conspiratorial grin and disappeared into the galley, returning with a heaping plate of croissants and a tub of butter.

"I'm afraid I must confess to getting you here under false pretenses," he said after seating himself beside her.

"You don't need a consultant after all?"

"Well, naturally, I can always use the assistance of one as talented as yourself. And I do have an astonishing backlog accruing from the time I spent recuperating. But I really wanted to know, if you're at liberty to tell me, of course, what the outcome of all this has been. I understand young Rudy Tang is still in the hospital?"

"A convalescent facility, actually. He's undergoing physical therapy. His surgery left him partially paralyzed on the right side initially, but they're making pretty good progress from what I hear. It's still going to be a long time before he's able to manage on his own, though."

Professor Deutch shook his head.

"There was no doubt that poor Cory Floyd was responsible?"

"None at all. In addition to Rudy's account of what happened, Cory's fingerprints were found all over the van from loading Rudy into the driver's seat and giving it a push off the highway. He would have faced three counts of attempted murder if he'd survived."

"And our little story might well have come out after all. The man did not have what I would call a strong constitution. I gathered the authorities were not especially happy with our version of Cory's being distraught at what he thought was a conspiracy to steal his company's latest software. Did you get that feeling?"

"Sure. But there's nothing they can do about it."

"No. I suppose there isn't."

"Although I have to say it's put something of a crimp in my love life."

At the Bel Harbor Marina office, Beau Billings tied Smiley's leash to a handy post beside the door and followed TJ inside, trying to ignore the hound's most accomplished look of long-suffering rejection. Sunny Cortez was seated behind the counter at the computer. He looked up and grinned when he saw who his visitors were.

"If you're about to pull out your goddamned checkbook and pay your berth rent, don't do it. I just got this sucker to balance and I'm not going to do it over again."

"Never saw a man of business so reluctant to take in money, did you Uncle Beau?"

"Never did."

Sunny rose and went to the rack of coffee mugs on the wall by the filing cabinets. He pulled two off their pegs, both emblazoned with the legend *"Emmy T"* in gold, with *"TJ"* under it on one and *"Beau"* on the other.

"Coffee?"

"Sure. I didn't come for anything but socializing anyway. You'll have to beg me for the rent from now on."

Beau and TJ took the wicker chairs and Sunny leaned against the counter, one foot cocked on the coffee table, his elbows resting on the countertop.

"Been a while since I've seen you," he said. "Weather keeping you away?"

"It was 'til today. Looks good enough to take her out and dust her off. And I also wanted to find out how you're doing on that promise you sold Harley."

Sunny's eyes crinkled and a slow smile spread across his face.

"Meg? Hard to say sometimes. She's a strong-willed woman."

"I know."

"At least she's decided not to sell Bel Harbor."

"That's a start. She ever take all those old pictures Harley kept in the file?"

"Yeah. Just before Christmas."

Beau leaned back in his chair and rested a foot in an unaccustomed but impeccable boat shoe on the table next to Sunny's.

"It's always been a mystery to me how Christmastime causes most folks to become downright sentimental about family and such."

"Yeah, maybe, but I don't think it's had much effect on her attitude about becoming a grandmother," Sunny said. "That Miss Sims has been to see her a couple of times, but all she says is she wishes the old bat would leave her alone."

"Well, there's still lots of time. Miss Sims has a pretty strong will of her own from what I've observed."

TJ rose and, taking the empty mug from Beau, went through the door to the small kitchen and washed their cups, carefully replacing them on their pegs.

"What's it like out there?" he asked Sunny as he opened the office door to the unrepressed delight of Smiley, who was straining at his leash.

"Four to five, swells to seven. Not a problem."

Lisbee and Professor Deutch stood on the deck of the *Prime Number* as Beau, Smiley, and TJ approached the *Emmy T.* The professor waved and TJ returned a salute.

"Going out with us?" he said to Lisbee.

"Might as well. I've just been hired and fired in less than thirty minutes. I think that may be a new record for me."

"Can't I offer you something before . . ." the professor began, when a muted ringing sounded from inside the salon. "Oh, drat. Excuse me a moment, won't you?"

In the salon, he picked up the phone.

"Dean Deutch here."

"Professor Deutch? You don't know me; my name is Lowry. I work for the government. It's come to my attention that you may be in a position to do a very great service for your country . . . ."